Scars on the Soul

Among other works by Françoise Sagan

Fiction

BONJOUR TRISTESSE
A CERTAIN SMILE
THOSE WITHOUT SHADOWS
AIMEZ-VOUS BRAHMS
THE WONDERFUL CLOUDS
LA CHAMADE

Nonfiction

TOZIQUE (with drawings by Bernard Buffet)

Drama

CHATEAU EN SUEDE

A NOVEL BY

Françoise Sagan

Scars on the Soul

Translated from the French
by JOANNA KILMARTIN

McGRAW-HILL BOOK COMPANY
New York   St. Louis   San Francisco
Düsseldorf   Mexico

3456789BPBP7987654

Library of Congress Cataloging in Publication Data
— — — — — — — — —
    Scars on the soul.

    Translation of Des bleus a l'âme.
    I. Title.
PZ4.Q9Sc [PQ2633.U74]   843'.9'14   73-19755
ISBN 0-07-054415-8

To Charlotte Aillaud

"I have said that the soul is not more than the body,
And I have said that the body is not more than the soul,
And nothing, not God, is greater to one than one's self is,
And whoever walks a furlong without sympathy walks
to his own funeral drest in his shroud, . . ."
Walt Whitman
Song of Myself

Scars on the Soul

arch 1971

$\mathcal{M}$ I should like to have written: "Sebastian went up the stairs four at a time, puffing and blowing a little." I should have enjoyed resurrecting those characters of ten years ago, Sebastian and his sister Eleanor—characters in a play, of course, but a lighthearted play, one of mine—depicting them flat broke but still gay, cynical and fastidious, trying in vain to "recoup" in a Paris depressed by its own mediocrity. Unfortunately, the mediocrity of Paris, or my own, has got the better of my crazier whims, and today I'm painfully trying to remember how and when "it" began. "It" being the revulsion, the boredom, the distaste I now feel for a way of life that until now, and for very good reasons, had always attracted me. More, I think it was in 1969 and I don't think, alas, that the events of 1968, the elation and the letdown, had much to do with it. Or age either. I'm thirty-five, my teeth are good, and if I feel attracted to someone, on the whole it still works. Except that I'm no longer interested. I'd like to be in love and even to suffer and even to tremble at the sound of the telephone. Or to play the same record ten times running and wake in the mornings with that feeling of natural euphoria I used to take for granted. "They took away my taste for water, now they've taken away my taste for love." That's from a Jacques Brel record, I think. Anyway, I can't seem to function any longer and I even doubt whether I'll show this to my publisher. It isn't literature, it isn't a true confession, it's someone tapping away at her typewriter because she's afraid of herself and the typewriter and the mornings and the evenings and everything else. And of other people. Fear isn't very nice; in fact, it's rather shameful, and I've never felt it before. That's all. But that "all" terrifies me.

I'm not alone in my plight. In this spring of 1971 in Paris, everyone I see or hear seems unsettled, frightened. Perhaps death is prowling around us and we sense it and are tormenting ourselves about nothing. For after all, that's not the problem. Death—I'm not talking about illness—death, to me, is velvet-clad, gloved, black, and in any case irremediable, absolute. And I yearn for the absolute as I did at fifteen. But the sad thing is that I've experienced enough of life's pleasures to know that, for me, this notion of the absolute can only be a step backwards, a confession of weakness—that I force myself to look upon as purely temporary. Out of pride, no doubt, and once again, out of fear. My death is the least of evils.

No, it's the perpetual, the ubiquitous violence, the misunderstandings, the anger, so often justified, the loneliness, the sense of rushing headlong towards disaster. It's the young who refuse to accept—having had it flung in their faces so often—that they'll lose their youth one day, and the "mature" people who for the past three years have fought tooth and nail against growing older and are now floundering. And the women who want equality with men, and the good arguments and the good faith of some and the grotesque obtuseness of others, human just the same and subject to the same god, the only god, whom they try to deny: Time. But who reads Proust?

And the new jargon, and the difficulty of communicating, and the milk of human kindness, springing up from time to time. Rarely though. And occasionally a face to admire. And life, mad life. I've always thought of it as a savage she-wolf, crazily maternal. Bloody mama, Jocasta, Leah, all rolled into one, and always, of course, in the end, Medea. Flinging us down here, on a planet which it now seems—oh, final affront—is not even unique; and when I say "affront" I mean "affront," since ours, after all, was supposed to be the only life, the only thought, the only music, the only history. And what if there were others? What if our mother, that lying adulteress, had had other children, elsewhere? When man, Apollo man, rockets into space, it isn't in order to find his brother, I'm quite sure of that. It's to confirm that he hasn't any brothers, that the miserable three score years and ten which she has given him are his and his alone. One has only to look at the Martians of popular imagination. Why are they always small and ugly? Because we're jealous. Then again: "There's no grass on the moon, is there?" No, "grass belongs to us." And the whole of this good earth of ours, so chauvinistic, so terror-stricken, relaxes and at once starts cheerfully tearing itself apart, snatching the grass from its mouth or soaking it in blood, in the same equally senseless impulse.

And all those cretins who concern themselves with "the people," who talk about "the people" with such pathetic awkwardness in their left-wing garb and exhaust us in the end because of the trouble we have to take, those of us who detest the Right, to protect them, to prevent some raging (or, for that matter, docile) lunatic from really reducing that wretched garb to unwearable rags. The people. Unaware that the very word is insulting, that there's a man plus a man plus a woman plus a child plus a man, etc., that each individual is wholly distinct in everything, even in his deepest aspirations, and that as a rule, for lack of means, this individual will be able neither to hear nor to see nor to read them. Sartre, when he climbed onto his tub, awkwardly, honestly, perhaps understood. And Diogenes, from the interior of his tub, speaking to all and sundry. It's people such as they, who are compassionate and have the intelligence of their compassion, that are held up to ridicule. But what do they care? In our day it's a noble thing, ridicule, *being* ridiculed, for a keen mind. Noble and disquieting—because noble. Neither Stendhal nor Balzac would have borne it. (In their work, of course.) For me, the only prophet in this respect was Dostoevsky.

Here I've been talking about life instead of about the debonair and desperate Swedish aristocrat, Sebastian van Milhem. But who knows? He may re-emerge and I'll talk about his affairs. It's my job, after all; I write, I enjoy writing, and I make a very good living out of it. It seems to me that life, in its female-animal aspect, carries some of its offspring around by the scruff of the neck like a wise and gentle mother cat (which assures you a reasonably comfortable existence). And some by the small of the back, in which precarious position, seeking a fall as a blessed release, many of our contemporaries find themselves. Or by one paw, and never mind the lovesick, the hopelessly trapped, the seriously ill, and a few of the poets. Never mind them. But that's absurd. I shall always mind about poetry; it's the one thing I've always loved and never known how to write.

And yet I would readily conjure up even the smell of grass and scatter a basketful of dried and scented grasses through the pages of this cynical novel. Now that I'm reduced to this: naming things. For the smell of grass, when I stretch myself out in it, bury my face in it, is something I now feel obliged to name to myself: this is the smell of grass, Madame. As for the sea, the crazy sea, I have to introduce my body to it, too: this is your best friend, the sea. My body acknowledges it, but doesn't rush to greet it. I'm a long-suffering mother at a watering place, dragging along a fractious child: her own body. "Say good morning to Madame Dupont, who was so kind to you when she was taking the cure here last year (or ten years ago)." And the fractious child recoils. Recoils, sometimes, at the very suggestion of love and its enchantments. As my eyes recoil, horrified, from those magazine advertisements in glorious technicolor, in which limpid seas lap against red rocks and miles upon miles of impeccable beaches are displayed, all for 1300 Frs. return. "Oh, let them go," sighs my fascist body, "let them all go, let them get their suntans and have their fun in those places that were so often the center and the love of my life, my special territory. Let them keep them, for that matter. Long live the Club Méditerranée. Down with the sea of that name! Let her, poor fool, frolic with her young executives, her not-so-young executives, her campers! Personally, I shall sing her praises no more, I shall put her out of my mind; and if I should happen to be passing at some suitable moment, in April, say, I'll dip a toe or a chilly, listless hand. She and I, who once upon a time. . . ." How sad! That's what growing old must be: no longer recognizing one's nearest and dearest. And what shall I say of all those other bodies that have accompanied mine, side by side, over the past fifteen years, to which I would return from time to time to sleep or to unwind, and which I now shun as though I were suddenly imprisoned once more in what Éluard called "that thin, proud body, wild bird body, creature of my childhood."

Sebastian ran up the stairs four at a time, puffing and blowing a little. He was beginning to find the sixth floor a bit high for him. It wasn't his weight that bothered him, but ten thousand cigarettes in the past few years and an equal number of drinks, the very variety of which made him laugh. In fact, he might almost have distinguished the past few years one from another by his favorite drinks rather than his women. There had been Negroni year, which corresponded to Hedda's year, and Dry Martini year which, though longer, coincided with Mariella Della. And Rum year, in Brazil, with Anne-Marie. My God, what fun he'd had! Not that, all things considered, he was a heavy drinker or even a womanizer, though he delighted in the combination of a woman and a drink. In any case, his sister Eleanor was the sole mistress of his existence, his sister, and in her case without alcohol or with every sort of alcohol. Life without her, drink without her, were like lukewarm water.

Not a bad thing, all said and done, to have one's life circumscribed to that extent by someone who—whatever she might say—was as much his slave as he was hers. From time to time she would become restive, marry, disappear, and then, after a few chaotic months, a few embroilments about which she would only tell him much later—but with what hilarious giggles—she would come back to him. Rich or poor, exhausted or bursting with health, melancholy or gay, the wild, the incomparable, the beautiful Eleanor, his sister, would always come back to him.

On this occasion, they had just arrived together from a long stay in Scandinavia with one of Eleanor's husbands, and their circumstances looked bad. It was only by a miraculous chance that an old friend of Sebastian's had lent them this two-room flat in the Rue de Fleurus. And they could hardly have had much money either in the bank or in their pockets. Eleanor would willingly have handed over her two or three splendid pieces of jewelry, since possessions meant nothing to her, but to what purpose? In any case, jewelry was an asset to a woman.

Sebastian rang their bell and she opened the door at once, in her dressing gown.

"Oh, you poor boy," she said, helping him to a rickety chair. "Oh, you poor boy, puffing up the stairs at your age. I could hear you coming up and was afraid you mightn't make it."

He put his hand on his heart, feigning exhaustion.

"I'm getting old," he said.

"What about me?" She laughed. "At the bottom of those stairs I'm Isadora Duncan, I positively float. By the time I reach the top, I'm more like Fats Domino. Did you find someone?"

"Someone" being that providential person who, because of their charm, their wit, their luck, would act as temporary provider for brother and sister. This person had so far never failed to materialize and was usually discovered by Sebastian, Eleanor, as in this case, being too lazy to go out.

"Not a soul," said Sebastian. "Arturo is in the Argentine, the Villavers are on holiday; and, believe it or not, Nicholas is working."

A look of doubt and slight horror appeared in Eleanor's eyes. (Work had never been a strong point with the van Milhems.)

"What a town," she said. "Mind you, there's one good thing: it doesn't matter what I wear. The big couturiers are out; a curtain, trousers, a bit of my jewelry on smart occasions, anything goes. You've only got to look around you in the streets. As long as I don't forget I'm thirty-nine, I'm safe. In any case, I shan't be the only one."

"Just as well," Sebastian said, "but I always knew you'd have nothing to worry about."

It was true: with her immensely long legs, her lean, muscular body, her well-defined features, high cheekbones, clear, almond-shaped eyes, Eleanor was still superb to look at. As for him, underlying his habitual, quizzical expression, he had the same bone structure as his sister. No, they'd get by all right. He stretched out his legs.

"The tiresome thing is, apparently there's a shortage of men around the place. I'm going to have to do my bit, sooner than you, probably."

"It serves you right," she said. "But how do you know?"

"Nicholas told me. It seems that lots of men, fed up with their wives, have taken to making love to one another, and the town's overrun by baying women in search of prey. And *they've* no sooner quieted down, than the students take over. Ah, parasitism is no longer what it was."

"No obscenities. Look how beautiful Paris is."

He leaned on the window sill beside her. A pink light suffused the wall opposite and glinted off the surrounding rooftops. A smell of fresh earth rose from the Luxembourg Gardens, overpowering the petrol fumes. He laughed.

"If you're going to wear a curtain, I suppose I can let my hair grow?"

"Hurry up, then. It'll soon start falling out."

He gave her a brotherly kick on the ankle. He no longer had a care in the world.

Perhaps I should turn the story of my two cuckoos into a play after all. So far, this hardly resembles the beginning of a novel. Perhaps I ought to have—what's the word? —"placed" my characters, described the setting. The setting, especially, is pretty minimal. But settings bore me, except by a few writers who take such meticulous, delectable pleasure in them that I find myself smiling in sympathy. Now there, admittedly, rereading what I've written, it doesn't amount to much: six floors, a rickety chair, rooftops (that makes sense on the sixth floor). In fact, the modest and precarious circumstances of my protagonists seem to me amply described by those six flights of stairs. I've always loathed stairs: I get out of breath going up and vertigo coming down. (I once gave someone up because he lived on the fifth floor. He never knew why.) If by attributing my personal dislikes to the van Milhems, I'm leaving them in an empty apartment, so be it. They're gay and carefree, and that's the best of décors. Especially as I'm going to have to find someone to feed them, and someone who isn't ludicrously conventional, at that. Where, I don't know: the rich are always wailing about having no money, the poor haven't any but say so more quietly, and then there's income tax, etc. It'll have to be a foreigner. That's what we've come to in France in 1971. For the sake of verisimilitude, I'm going to be compelled to have my delightful van Milhems supported by a foreigner. Preferably domiciled in Switzerland. It's very wounding for my national pride. Moreover, I can't put Eleanor to work in Marie-Martine or a ready-to-wear shop. That would be like launching Sebastian into banking or the Stock Exchange. It would be the death of them both. Contrary to general belief, idleness is as powerful a drug as work. Prevent a hard worker from doing his job, and he'll go into a decline, become depressed, lose weight, and so on. But your truly lazy man, after a few weeks' work, will also fall into a state of "deprivation." He'll go into a decline, become depressed, lose weight, and the rest. I've no intention of killing Sebastion and Eleanor with work. I've often been taken to task because my little circle is idle and blasé and this and that; but that's no reason to sacrifice my two languid Swedes on the altar of criticism. I'll think about it later on, with different characters, in another book (God and my publisher permitting). Some day I'll write about pay envelopes, car installment payments, television, and normal people. If there are any left. Considering what we inflict on them. I know people who have cars like little metal boxes and secretly enjoy sitting in traffic jams in the middle of this dear old familiar pollution. They're happy to take an hour or an hour and a half between their homes and their offices. Because, for one whole hour, they're *alone* in their little boxes. They're safe from company, from conversation, from "aggression," as the psychiatrists would say. But just try getting a man or a woman who goes out to work to admit it: the car as refuge, igloo, womb, etc. No, in my view, what men spend their Sundays polishing with a special cloth isn't an instrument of aggression, it's their privacy, their one luxury.

Beware of gaiety. I distrust that insidious euphoria which, after a difficult beginning, grips a writer at the end of two or three chapters and has him muttering to himself:

"Hurray, machinery's getting going again!" or "Hurray, we're off!" Innocent mechanic's phrases, true, but occasionally followed by: "Hurray, I won't have to commit suicide after all." (A more poetic observation, but sometimes true.) That's how the creator goes off the rails, distinguishing himself, by this abrupt change of key, from his classmates, the rest of humanity. Such euphoria is dangerous, because you believe you've "laid the foundations" (these constant references to manual jobs), and in these circumstances, the worst terror behind you, what's wrong with a bit of a breather? Especially if Deauville, deserted and bathed in the slanting yellow sunlight of March, is on your doorstep. I could understand, the other day, looking at those black, solitary buildings against the bright sky, at the decorously abandoned sea (we've never had a very passionate relationship, the Channel and I, for reasons of temperature), I could understand why all the young film directors drag their cameras and their heroes there in winter. I thought to myself then that I couldn't bear another film sequence of a man and a woman running along a beach, any more than I could bear yet another shot of two people (or a dozen), regardless of their sex, naked in bed with the sheet pulled back. Here and now, I should warn anyone who wants titillation that there won't be a trace of it in this novel. At the most: "Eleanor didn't come home that night." But it's true, isn't it! What's become of night's wild delights, the whispered words in the dark, the "secrecy," the profound secrecy of physical love? Where is the violence, the beauty, the dignity of pleasure? You see a woman with her eyes closed twisting her head from left to right on a pillow, and the silhouette of some poor fellow's muscled back jerking rhythmically, and you wait placidly in your cinema seat for them to get it over. You begin to envy people who can be shocked by this; at least they're being entertained. What a bore it is, this mass, this tonnage of human flesh, tanned or pallid, standing, sitting, or lying, which is shoved under our noses these days! The body and its pleasures have become consumer goods, like everything else. Poor things, thinking they've overcome stupid prejudices when in fact they've ruined a splendid mythology. There are moments when I'm on the point of writing, "But I digress," an old-fashioned courtesy to the reader, but pointless in this case, since my purpose is to digress. Nevertheless, this blow-by-blow account of eroticism has irritated me. I'm returning to my van Milhems, "who frequently indulge in that sort of thing, but never talk about it."

*T*he restaurant was excellent. Eleanor had ordered nine oysters, which writhed visibly under the impact of the lemon juice, a grilled sole, and a bottle of very dry Pouilly Fuissé. Sebastian, who was hungrier, had tucked away an *oeuf en gelée* and a *steak au poivre* (the real thing), washed down with Beaujolais. There was no *vin de Bouzy*, a fact which they momentarily deplored. Contrary to her predictions, Eleanor wasn't dressed in a curtain. Waving some magic wand which she alone seemed to possess, she had run into an old girl friend of the kind every woman dreams of, plain, devoted, and efficient, who had taken her off to a ready-to-wear shop run by a man she knew, where one could order things on credit. Fascinated by Eleanor, this man had there and then designed several dresses for her, waving aside her offer, admittedly sheer braggadocio, to give him a check. And lo and behold, it was a sumptuously dressed Eleanor who was now guzzling Sebastian's (and therefore her own) last remaining nine thousand old francs on the terrace of a *brasserie* in the Rue Marboeuf.

"After this lunch, according to my calculations, we'll have about three thousand francs left," Sebastian said, screwing up his eyes against the sun. "You're sure you don't want anything else? In that case, we've got enough for a taxi."

"It doesn't make sense," Eleanor said. "If I'd eaten one of those pastries, a taxi would have been a virtual necessity to get me home. Life is badly arranged."

They smiled at one another. In the harsh spring sunlight, tiny wrinkles were clearly visible on both their faces. *Dear Eleanor*, thought Sebastian, *dear Eleanor, I'll get you out of this somehow*. Sudden emotion brought a lump to his throat and made him speechless.

"Your steak was too peppery," said Eleanor absently, "you've got tears in your eyes."

She had lowered her eyes. Was she telling herself that they were nothing but a pair of good-for-nothings in a town which suddenly seemed alien, bustling, indifferent to the charms and the lures of the van Milhems? True, men were looking at her, but to see and be seen they should have been at Maxim's or the Plaza-Athénée. And his suit was hardly smart enough for that. He finished his wine at a gulp.

"Tonight," Eleanor said thoughtfully, "we'll buy a can of ravioli. I adore ravioli. Then, if it wouldn't bore you, and if you know how to work your friend's radio, we'll listen to the Champs-Élysées concert. It's being broadcast live. We'll open the window, it'll be marvelous."

"What are they playing?"

"Mahler, Schubert, Strauss. I looked this morning. What a delicious lunch, Sebastian."

She stretched out her long arms, her slim hands in front of her in a gesture of contentment. A man behind her noticed the gesture and Sebastian, amused, saw him grow pale with desire. He had in fact been staring at Eleanor from the moment she entered the room, with a bright, unblinking gaze that finally embarrassed Sebastian, sitting facing him. He wore a shabby suit and a frightful tie and had a brief case beside him. Doubtless some local bank clerk with a mild obsession about women. But the innocence of his stare suggested something more. A touch of madness, perhaps. Moreover, when they got up to leave, he got up too, as though he had been sharing their table, and, at his first sight of Eleanor's face, gave her a furtive childlike look that took her aback.

"His eyes never once left the back of your neck," Sebastian said, seeing his sister's look of surprise. "Shall we walk a bit, or go straight home?"

"I'm dying to finish my book," she said.

She would lose herself in books, sometimes for a whole day, and the devoted girl friend had discovered a lending library in the neighborhood, whose owner was quickly charmed into assuaging Eleanor's insatiable literary hunger. She read anything and everything, stretched out on the sofa or on her bed, sometimes for hours on end, while Sebastian wandered in and out, chatted to the locals in the bar around the corner or the keepers in the Luxembourg Gardens, and trained himself to plod methodically up the six flights of stairs. Tonight, after the ravioli and Mahler, this idyllic existence must come to an end. A thought that filled him with quiet despair.

Still no solution for the van Milhems. Impossible to find easy money in Paris just now, even for them. The intrusion of the fixated clerk, which I hadn't foreseen, intrigues me. What am I to do with him? Eleanor has a horror of crackpots, if I remember rightly. Anyway, I'd like to point out to my faithful readers that it's the first time in eighteen years of novel writing that I've offered them a menu. A real menu. Oysters, fish, etc. And wine. Even an approximate price. I can see I shall end up by writing interminable novels stuffed with detail. Just watch me describe a house, the exterior, the interior, the color of the curtains, the style of the furniture, the grandfather's features, the granddaughter's dress, the smell of the attic, the ritual at mealtimes, the place settings, the glasses, the tablecloths and, to round it all off, something like: "There now arrived, on a bed of bay leaves, surrounded by blood-red tomatoes and pimentos, a dead carp, whose gray skin, flaking off here and there, further accentuated its dazzling whiteness." Perhaps that's where happiness lies, for a writer. No more light music—on with the brass band! While I'm on the subject of light music, a second warning to the unfortunate—and I hope faithful—reader: just as there will be no smut in this book, neither will there be the least trace of autobiography, not a single amusing anecdote about Saint-Tropez vintage '54, nothing about my way of life, my friends, and so forth. For two reasons. The more important, in my view, being that it's nobody's business but mine. And secondly, once I embark on facts, my imagination—truly the mad boarder*—will lead me astray, distorting my account in favor of anything that appeals to my sense of the ridiculous. By avoiding the particular, I shan't be in danger of lying. The worst I shall do is get my quotations wrong. Amen. But in all good faith.

It would be comic, however, if this good faith (mine), so often the despair of journalists—and how I sympathize with them (Dali's interviews fill me with glee)—it would be amusing if this good faith, this placid, bovine creature I've been dragging around with me since the day I was born, (I'm speaking, of course, about general topics), were

---

* *La folle du logis* (Malebranche).

suddenly to have become, with all the *muletas* waved in front of its muzzle—Israel, Russia, Poland, the New Novel, Youth, the Middle East, Communism, Solzhenitsyn, the Americans, Vietnam, etc.—if this poor beast, incapable of munching and assimilating the fodder necessary to its growth and its understanding of a world in which, after all, I drag out an existence like everyone else, were to have become the maddened bull which goads me into writing this eccentric book in fits and starts. A reckless bull, "at once broken-hearted and stony-hearted" (to paraphrase Chamfort).* Not that I wish to rip apart my *picadors*— the men who claim to have all the answers and in fact have nothing of the kind, poor things, but go on blowing their trumpets nonetheless. They're my friends, of course. My enemies have been crying wolf, or Jew, or nigger, or what have you ever since I can remember. The *picadors* I mean are those who still pay lip service to the dove democracy, that freedom which is so precious to them—and to me, for that matter—but which I, for one, am beginning to suspect would prefer to leave its feathers in their overenthusiastic hands and fly away naked into the blue, rather than perch anywhere in the world at present. Even if, on her return, homesick for our loving words, she is nearly shot to pieces by those who imitate our voices. When I say "our," I mean only those poor fools who don't regard themselves as a matter of course as judges or as experts. There aren't many left, I'm afraid. Let's get back to our Swedes, let's smother them in silk, gold, and mazurkas. The unrhythmical "jerks" (first on one foot, then on the other) of our political leaders and thinkers exasperate me. Let's forget them.

* *En vivant et en voyant les hommes, il faut que le coeur se brise ou se bronze.* Chamfort. Tr.

*T*he concert had been very enjoyable, even though Eleanor had let the ravioli burn and Sebastian had been left with slight hunger pangs which he tried to appease with cigarettes. The window was still open to the night air and Eleanor still sitting on the floor, half turned away from him, so that he could see only her profile, so familiar and so remote, calmly turned towards the night. *The only woman I've ever wanted to ask: what are you thinking about?* he reflected. And also the only one who would never have told him.

The telephone rang, making them jump. No one knew they were there, on their island in the Latin Quarter, and Sebastian hesitated a moment before answering it. Then he picked up the receiver gingerly; he sensed that life was about to call them to order, in the nick of time for their finances, maybe, but too soon for their peace of mind. *Why shouldn't they just kill themselves here and now, he thought, after forty years of good and loyal service in the cause of living?* He knew that Eleanor, though not remotely suicidal, would have joined him.

"Hello?" said a voice, male but high-pitched. "Is that you, Robert?"

"Robert Bessy is away," Sebastian said politely. "He should be back any day now."

"In that case, who're you?" asked the voice.

People's manners certainly haven't improved, thought Sebastian. He made an effort to control himself.

"He was kind enough to lend me his flat while he was away."

"Then you must be Sebastian. How marvelous! Robert's always talking about you. Listen, I wanted to ask him to the opening of a new club tonight—very smart, very amusing. The Jedelmans . . . Do you know the Jedelmans? Would it amuse you to come along?"

Sebastian looked inquiringly at Eleanor. The voice was reverberating as if through a loud-speaker.

"I'm afraid I don't know your name," Sebastian said cautiously.

"Gilbert. Gilbert Benoit. Are you game, then? Here's the address. . . ."

"I'm staying here with my sister," Sebastian cut in. "I should think we could be ready in half an hour, but we wouldn't dream of going by ourselves, without knowing Monsieur and Madame . . . ?"

"Jedelman," babbled the voice. "But it's a club, and. . . ."

"Jedelman, good. Can you pick us up at the Rue de Fleurus in half an hour or would you prefer us to meet you later on?"

Eleanor, bright-eyed, was watching him. He was playing his cards damn well, for they had literally not enough money for a taxi, a bottle of Chianti having slipped in alongside the can of ravioli at the grocer's, as though of its own accord.

"I'll be waiting down below," said the voice. "Of course. It hadn't occurred to me. . . ."

"By the way," Sebastian said, "my name is Sebastian van Milhem and my sister's is Eleanor van Milhem. I mention this because of the introductions you'll have to make. See you shortly."

He hung up and burst out laughing. Eleanor was grinning up at him.

"Who on earth are the Jedelmans?"

"God knows. The rich love to go slumming these days. They all want their own club. What are you going to wear?"

"My sea-green dress, I think. Make yourself beautiful, brother dear, you may find yourself having to do your bit in more ways than one."

He looked at her.

"Well, if the photographs in my room and Gilbert's voice are anything to go by, it looks as though your kind friend, our host, is as queer as could be."

"Fool that I am!" exclaimed Sebastian, aghast. "You're right, I'd completely forgotten. What a prospect!"

Two hours later, they were sitting at a large, noisy table, Sebastian's knee being sought from time to time by that of the rich Mme. Jedelman, who was no longer in the first flush of youth. But still, she was massaged, showered, lacquered, manicured, and Sebastian thought philosophically that he had seen worse. Eleanor, on the other hand, seemed somewhat exasperated with her neighbor. After the minor sensation caused by their arrival (where had they sprung from, and who were they, these two blond strangers, so tall and so aloof, a brother and sister into the bargain?), Gilbert, delighted with his "catch," had escorted them to the table of honor. M. Jedelman, apparently weary of his wife's caprices, had had to be taken home, dead drunk, at eleven o'clock. Two film stars, a singer, a famous woman gossip-columnist, and an unknown man made up Mme. Jedelman's table, around which the photographers fluttered like moths. Gilbert did his best to answer questions about the van Milhems, but as he knew nothing whatsoever about them except the fact that Robert had been Sebastian's lifelong and unconditional admirer, he took refuge in an air of mystification, if not insinuation, which irritated everybody.

"No, monsieur," said Eleanor's voice suddenly, and Sebastian pricked up his ears. "No, I haven't seen all those films."

"But that's incredible. You mean to say you've never heard of *Bonnie and Clyde?*"

The indignant cinema buff appealed to the rest of the table.

"She claims. . . ."

"Madame," interrupted Eleanor silkily, "Madame claims."

"Madame claims," the poor man continued with a laugh, "that she's never heard of *Bonnie and Clyde.*"

"As I've already told you, monsieur, I've been living in Sweden for ten years in a snowbound castle. My husband didn't possess a private cinema for showing films "at home," as you put it. And we never went near Stockholm. That's all there is to it."

There was a sudden silence; Eleanor's voice, without having been raised, had become distinctly sharp.

"You're getting cross, my sweet," said Sebastian.

"It's so exhausting to repeat the same thing over and over again and to listen to the same thing over and over again."

"I apologize, I apologize over and over again," said the cinema buff sarcastically, "but to whom, then, do we owe this return from the frozen north?"

"The castle has been sold and my ex-husband is in

prison," Eleanor said calmly. "For double murder. We created our own cinema. Sebastian, I'm tired."

Sebastian was already on his feet beside her, smiling. They thanked Mme. Jedelman, a formality so rare that it only added to her stupefaction, and went out leaving a stunned silence in their wake. On the staircase to the street, Sebastian was laughing so much he could hardly get up the steps. Someone ran after them: it was the singer. He had a nice round open face.

"Can I give you a lift?" he asked.

Eleanor acquiesced, and, without so much as a glance at him, climbed into an enormous American car and gave him their address. Then Sebastian's helpless laughter communicated itself first to her, then to the singer, until they gave in to the latter's pleas to go on somewhere else to have a drink on it. He drove them home at dawn, blind drunk.

"Drive carefully," said Eleanor amiably.

"Of course. What a marvelous evening. And what a joke, what a great joke."

"It wasn't a joke," Sebastian said gently. "Good night."

July 1971

It really is a glorious summer, this summer of 1971. It's fine and sunny; haymaking has begun. On my way here the other day, I stopped not far from Lieuray. Beneath a row of poplars. I lay down in the hay; the myriad tiny dark green leaves on the trees twisted and turned in the sunlight; I was rediscovering something. The car was parked on the side of the road like a big patient beast of burden. I had all the time in the world; I had run out of time. It wasn't at all disagreeable.

Since, fundamentally, the only idol, the only God I acknowledge is Time, it follows that I cannot experience real pleasure or pain except in relation to Time. I knew that this poplar would outlast me, that this hay, on the contrary, would wither and die before me; I knew I was expected at home and also that I could just as easily spend another hour beneath this tree. I knew that any haste on my part would be as stupid as any delay. And for the rest of my life. I knew everything. Including the fact that such knowledge meant nothing. Nothing but a privileged moment. The only authentic moments, in my view. When I say "authentic," I mean "instructive," which is just as silly. I shall never know enough. Never enough to be absolutely happy, never enough to have an abstract passion that will satisfy me body and soul, never enough for "anything." But such moments of happiness, of integration with life, if one recalls them clearly, form in the end a sort of blanket, a sort of comforting patchwork quilt with which to cover up the naked, rawboned, shivering body of our solitude.

Now it's out, the key word: solitude. That little mechanical hare that is let loose on the racetrack and pursued by the frenzied, panting greyhounds of our passions, our friendships, the little hare which they never catch but which perforce they always believe to be attainable. Right up to the moment when the door of the trap is slammed in their faces. The little door in front of which they end up screeching to a halt or bashing their heads against, like Pluto. The number of Plutos there are among human beings. . . .

But it's now two months since I gave a thought either to Sebastian or to Eleanor. How have they managed to eat, my poor van Milhems, what have they been living on in my absence? I feel a twinge of remorse (not too serious) in my role as guardian. I must try and remember the name of those rich people they landed up with . . . ah, yes, the Jedelmans. And I must decide whether or not in my absence Sebastian has done the necessary with that lady, not without a certain amount of grumbling, such as, "I'm not a little gigolo any longer. After all, I'm getting on." Here we are, nearly in August. They can't still be in the Rue de Fleurus, nor on the Côte d'Azur—that's finished. Deauville, perhaps? At all events, it would be amusing to witness the seduction scene between Mme. Jedelman and Sebastian. Let's think up a *décor:* Louis XV, genuine but "ritzy," one of those late afternoons, mild, tender, and blue, such as only Paris in summer can provide; let's have a mustard-colored sofa and a few pieces of Knoll furniture, for "contrast." And let's have, with Sebastian, who needs it to give him courage, a large whisky and water. No, a neat whisky.

"Oh God," Sebastian said under his breath, just as he had the night before, but aloud, in front of his sister. His thoughts veered from agonizing doubt as to his sexual capacities to equally agonizing certainty as to Mme. Jedelman's intentions. *Oh God, how can I get out of this? She's going to fling herself at me, she's going to drag me down into a maelstrom.* Like every child of the North, Sebastian had a superstitious horror of maelstroms.

He was stretching his long and, alas, trouser-covered legs in the Jedelman's sumptuous drawing room (by Boulle-Lalenne) in the Avenue Montaigne. Mme. Jedelman was lying languorously on a sofa. The blond Swede had made a strong impression on her, and she had invited him round—Sebastian said "summoned"—the very next day. There could be no question of refusal, since they were completely broke. Eleanor, compassionate and ironical, had escorted him as far as the landing like someone seeing an elder brother off to the front. And now there she was, that woman—"la Jedelman," as she was savagely referred to in Paris. There she lay, primped, pumiced, powdered, old, admirable. No, to be fair, not old—simply no longer young. And it showed: in her neck, her armpits, her knees, her thighs, in all those cruel areas which are as revealing in a woman of a certain age as a Michelin map, every detail only too clearly marked—in short, past it.

Nora Jedelman watched with curiosity as he paced up and down. He wasn't, it was abundantly clear, what she was accustomed to: a young gigolo. No, he had a distinction of bearing, beautiful hands, a straightforward expression that intrigued her. She wondered, with a curiosity that almost equalled his, what had brought him there, first into her drawing room, later, she hoped, into her bed. However, as he appeared to be asking himself the same question, she decided to put an end to the uncertainty even if it meant taking active measures. She rose lightly from her sofa, in a deliberately relaxed feline movement, which reminded her sharply that she was due for a visit to her osteopath next day, and glided towards Sebastian. He heard her approaching and stood frozen to the spot in front of the window, trying to call to mind some woman who had excited him, or some really effective piece of erotica. Too late. Already she was pressed against him, draped arms enfolded him, she was clasping him by the neck and the most expensive teeth New York can provide clashed with his.

To his immense surprise, he performed tolerably well, and she insisted on giving him a beautiful pair of cuff links. These he went out and sold at once: Eleanor, his lyrebird, his sister, his accomplice, the love of his life, would be royally entertained that evening.

January 1972

It's now almost six months since I abandoned this novel, my pertinent reflections, and my impertinent Swedes. Adverse circumstances, a crazy existence, idleness . . . And then, last October, an autumn so lovely, so richly colored, so heartbreaking in its splendor that from sheer happiness I wondered how I could survive it. Alone in Normandy, exhausted but carefree, watching with amazement the rapid healing of a long laceration near my heart, watching it turn into a pink, smooth, barely perceptible scar which I would doubtless touch, later on, with an incredulous finger—the finger of memory—as though to convince myself of my own vulnerability. And meanwhile, rediscovering the scent of grass and earth, immersing myself in it, singing *La Traviata* with reckless abandon (you might say) at the wheel of my car, as I drove into Deauville. And in the autumnal town, deserted, blazing hot, I gazed at the empty sea, the frenzied gulls skimming the breakwaters, the white sun, and here and there against the light, occasional figures who might have come straight out of Visconti's *Death in Venice*. There I was, alone, finally alone, letting my hands hang down like dead birds on either side of my deck chair. Restored to solitude, to the dreams of adolescence, to everything we should never have left but which "other people,"* —hell, heaven—are forever forcing us to abandon. But now other people were powerless to come between me and this triumphal autumn.

Yes, but what could my Swedes have been doing all summer? I worried about them during August in the Place de l'Atelier in Montmartre, where we were putting on a play. Local housewives, hair in curlers, bag in hand, did their daily shopping, dogs trotted happily by, transvestites sauntered in the harsh sunlight, traces of make-up still showing. Sitting on the terrace of my favorite café, I would send the van Milhems off on a cruise with the Jedelmans, or on a provincial tour with the young singer; I thought up a variety of adventures for them which I didn't write down, which I knew I would forget, for instance during the next rehearsal. Deliberately irresponsible, I didn't so much as scribble a word of it on a scrap of paper. From time to time, someone would give me a dog or a child to look after, while the owner, armed with a shopping cart, ran the gauntlet of the local supermarket. I would bandy words with a happy-go-lucky local layabout. I was happy. Later there would be the darkened auditorium, the spotlights, and the actors' problems, but for the moment the summer was gentle, Parisian, and serenely blue. I couldn't help myself. Here ends this chapter

* "*L'enfer, c'est les autres,*" *Huis-clos,* Jean-Paul Sartre (Tr.).

of excuses and alibis. Now I am back in Normandy. It's wet and cold; I shan't leave here until this book is finished, unless it's at gun-point. I have spoken. Amen.

"Do put that record on again," Eleanor said.

Sebastian put out a hand and nudged the arm of the record player at his feet. He didn't need to ask which record. Having gone through a classical period, Eleanor now had a craze for a Charles Trenet record and played nothing else:

> "On a dying branch
> The last bird of summer
> is swaying. . . ."

They were sitting in a swing seat on the terrace of the Jedelman villa at Cap d'Ail. After an awkward moment or two, Sebastian had developed a certain affection for Nora Jedelman. He called her "Lady Bird," much to her annoyance. Henry Jedelman he nicknamed "Mr. President" and, whenever he had had a bit too much to drink, would do a political assassination turn in the worst possible taste. Eleanor, having insinuated herself into the couple's affections, was once more buried in her beloved books, this time by the sea. Browned, amiable, and placid, she had watched the summer days pass as in a dream as she turned over the pages of her novels. Several of their host's smart friends had made advances to her, in vain. On the other hand, Sebastian suspected her of nocturnal assignations with the Jedelmans' gardener, an undeniably handsome young man. But he never mentioned the subject. Much as they teased one another in private about their "romances," it was understood that their short-lived, clandestine passions should remain secret. He was well aware that it was their inviolable respect for each other's sensuality (combined with a consistent irony towards each other's emotional entanglements) that had enabled them to live together so long. By the same token, they abhorred the exhibitionism that seemed to be the rule nowadays, in this part of the world especially. They took refuge in high-necked shirts. After swimming in 1900-style bathing suits, they had scarcely dried themselves before making a dash for their clothes. They were considered bizarre and exotic, the more so since both had remarkably good figures. They thought themselves merely decent. To them, pleasure in the human body was something simple, tender, and natural, like a taste for water or a love of horses, dogs, and fire, and had nothing to do with licentiousness or aesthetics. Witness Sebastian, who took Nora Jedelman in his arms night after night without the slightest qualm, inured as he was by now to her perfume, her skin, and her somewhat querulous manner of seeking caresses. Filled with the immense tenderness of familiarity, his docile body obeyed. In any case, for them, Nordics born and bred, the sun wasn't the imperious and often sadistic god it appeared to be for others. And this, without their knowing it, increased their prestige: to turn one's back on the sun and sun-worship so unaffectedly in our time and in such a place was tantamount to turning one's back on money.

Most of the Jedelmans' friends were Americans, very rich but not yet very refined despite their constant coming and going between the United States and Europe. More often than not, it must be said, they were dependent on one another's society, most Paris salons remaining obstinately closed to them. They were sought after for charity functions and their generosity sometimes earned them an invitation to luncheon, but only at the Plaza-Athénée. Consequently, they were more than puzzled by the presence of the van Milhems, so evidently aristocratic, and by the liaison, no less evident, between Sebastian and Nora Jedelman. There was nothing of the gigolo about him (she'd had a good few of those!), and yet he and his sister were clearly living off their hosts. An old admirer of Nora's, rejected for drunkenness, ventured a remark on the subject and received a swift punch on the nose from Sebastian which put an end to the discussion. In short, they were not like other people; they were dangerous, and therefore attractive. Women far more beautiful than Nora and equally rich circled around Sebastian that summer. In vain. Well-preserved American men found themselves up against Eleanor's total indifference. Indeed, had poor Nora's tastes not been so well known and so conventional, they would have been suspected of the worst perversions.

"Tonight your faithful heart is here.
But tomorrow the swallows will be gone from the beach...."

Trenet was singing, the sea was turning gray. Nora appeared, wearing a mauve silk tunic which made Eleanor blink slightly.

"It's cocktail time," she said. "My God, that record ... It's pretty but so sad. Especially now."

"Turn it off," Eleanor said to Sebastian.

She smiled sweetly at Nora, who returned her smile with a tinge of doubt. There was a great deal she would have liked to know about Eleanor, and it was no good interrogating Sebastian, who instantly shut up like a clam. All she knew was that wherever Eleanor was, Sebastian was bound to be. And if this was reassuring in one sense, it was a trifle vexing in another. She had even pushed Dave Burby, a magnificent catch and a charming fellow, into Eleanor's arms. Without success. And who was this Hugo who was in prison in Sweden? And whence had she herself acquired this mysterious and courteous lover who accepted her presents with absent-minded politeness and who, at the age of forty, had fits of uncontrollable laughter and the inexplicable moods of a youth? She was growing fond of him, in spite of her profound cynicism—she had always known how to buy and what she was buying. That was what worried her. What did he intend to do in Paris? Where did he intend to live with his dreamy sister? Was he counting on her or on luck? He never spoke to her about going back, and yet they were all due to leave in three days' time.

Mario the gardener was coming up the path with an armful of gaudy dahlias which he held out to Nora with a smile. Eleanor gazed at him tenderly. When she had opened her bedroom window on their first morning there, she had seen that slim, bronzed back, the deft movements of those long arms as he pruned a tree, the brown neck. When he turned around, he had smiled at her politely at first, then stopped smiling. Whereupon *she* had smiled at him before closing her window. When the household was sleeping or on those evenings when everyone went to Monte Carlo or Cannes, she would go and meet him at the bottom of the garden. There was the tool shed, which smelt of fresh mint and pine needles, there were the local village hops where he would take her dancing, there was Mario's delighted laugh, Mario's fresh mouth, Mario's glowing body, a body which had no need of massage. He was unspoiled, tender, and carefree, and she could relax in his company, away from that over-furnished house, those loudmouthed people, the clinking of dollars. Sebastian had taken the responsibility for their holiday, after all. Sebastian, the ideal brother.

"Give those dahlias to Madame van Milhem," said Nora. "Aren't they beautiful? That mauve. . . ."

Mario turned towards Eleanor and handed her the bouquet. His shirt fell open and she saw, on his neck, the purple mark left by her own teeth two nights before, the same color as the open blooms. She touched his hand accidentally and he smiled at her. And Sebastian, amazed, saw the reflection of a thousand memories and regrets mingle with the setting sun in his sister's pale eyes.

Yes, I know: I've relapsed into my old frivolous ways. That famous little Saganesque world where real problems don't exist. Well, it's true. The reason is that I too am getting fed up, in spite of my infinite patience. After having stated and believed (which I still do) that a capable woman should be paid as much as a capable man; after having stated that women should be free to choose whether or not to have a baby, and that abortion should be legalized, since otherwise it's a mere nuisance for women with means and a sinister butchery for the rest; after having sworn by all I hold sacred that I myself had had an abortion, and having read in a weekly magazine that the whole thing could be summed up in the slogan, "Women, your womb is yours and yours alone" (how sad, for one thing, but above all what a phrase!); after having signed a multitude of petitions; after having listened to the woes of bankers, grocers, taxi drivers, all apparently on the brink of ruin, and having myself been literally stripped of all I possess by a tax collector turned raving lunatic (one should've been wary of Giscard d'Estaing from the outset: I never trusted those polo-necks of his. Where are they now, by the way?); after having nearly smashed fifteen television sets from sheer nausea and nearly fallen out of my theater seat from boredom during ten "popular" shows; after having witnessed the apathy of some, the impotent rage of others, the good will, bad faith, and chaos which prevail in this smug Louis-Philippard régime; after having seen old-age pensioners shivering with cold, standing in line for their blue "benefit" cards; after having listened to extremist speeches, moderate speeches, stupid speeches, intelligent speeches; after having found myself—in spite of my dashing sports car—back among the have-nots; after all that, dear reader, I'm going to escape this instant to an imaginary dream-world "where money doesn't count." That's that. It's my right, after all, just as it's the right of every citizen not to buy my complete works. This age often exasperates me, I confess. I'm not a glutton for work, and conscientiousness isn't my strong point. But now, thanks to literature, I'm going to enjoy myself with my friends the van Milhems. I have spoken. Amen.

*W*ithout being in the least sadistic, Nora Jedelman enjoyed making her power felt. So she
waited until they were in her Cadillac between
Orly and Paris before asking Sebastian and Eleanor where
she could drop them.

"Eight, Rue Madame," Sebastian said airily. "If it's not
out of your way."

She felt snubbed. She was hoping to hear either "at the
Crillon," meaning he was cornered, or "wherever you suggest," meaning he trusted her. She had held her tongue for
ten whole days, all to no purpose. She was at a loss.

"Do you have friends there?"

"We don't live only with friends," said Sebastian with an
easy, friendly laugh. "Someone we know has found us a
two-room flat. Very attractive, I gather, and the rent's
reasonable."

*You'll only have to sell your Cartier watch or your
cigarette case*, thought Nora crossly. In fact, she had de-

cided in her own mind to put Eleanor in the spare room for the time being, while Sebastian could have the study next to her own room. She had visualized herself as a cross between a Lady Bountiful and a fairy godmother come to the rescue. This unexpected initiative deprived her not only of her role but of Sebastian's familiar, lazy presence. Now she would be returning to her immense flat alone—her husband was still in New York—except for her chihuahuas. Panic gripped her.

"It's ridiculous," she said, "I could easily have put you up."

"You've put up with us quite enough," said Eleanor calmly, "all this summer. We don't want to impose."

She's making fun of Nora, thought Sebastian, amused. *I must say it's justified, for once. What's the idea of leaving people in the air like that? When I think what I've gone through to raise money in three days, selling all those cuff links and expressing money orders to poor old Robert. Especially when I loathe haggling and lining up at post offices. It's lucky that Robert knows this part of Paris so well. I hope it'll be liveable in. Oh well, for three months. . .* He had had to pay three months' rent in advance.

The car stopped in front of an old apartment building. Nora seemed momentarily shattered.

"We'll telephone you very soon," Eleanor said politely.

They were both standing on the pavement, holding their suitcases, not even knowing how to get in, but slim, blond, and unconcerned. *Payable but not buyable*, thought Nora despairingly. And in any event, together. Not alone. She braced herself, gave them a wave, and fell back in her seat. The Cadillac drove off. Brother and sister smiled at one another.

"I'm glad about one thing," said Eleanor, "it's on the ground floor. Where's the concierge?"

The flat was gloomy in the extreme, giving onto an

exiguous garden, no more than a strip of grass. A bare room separated two bedrooms, minuscule and silent. There was a red divan and a bottle of whisky on the only table, with a note from Robert, the faithful Robert, welcoming them.

"What do you think of it?" asked the concierge. "It's a bit dark in summer, but in winter. . . ."

"It's fine," said Eleanor, stretching out on the divan. "Thanks a lot. Where did I put my book?"

And, to the astonishment of the concierge, she rummaged in a large handbag and went back to the thriller she had started on the airplane. The suitcases lay in a jumble on the floor and Sebastian prowled like a cat through the three rooms.

"It's perfect," he said at last. "Perfect. By the way, Madame" (addressing the concierge), "I can't help admiring your make-up."

"Quite right," said Eleanor, looking up. "I noticed it too. It's most unusual and attractive."

The concierge backed out, all smiles. It was true, she took a lot of trouble with her appearance; this M. van Milhem had something. His sister too, come to that. Out of the top drawer, you could tell from their manner (and their luggage). A little vague, perhaps. They wouldn't stay long, she supposed, and already, obscurely, she was missing them.

"I must telephone Nora," said Sebastian. "She hasn't got our number, after all, and it was unkind to abandon her alone in that Cadillac, like a suitcase."

"Ah, but a Vuitton suitcase," said Eleanor, still engrossed in her novel. It was plain to see that she had found the perfect refuge in that worn, shapeless, and rather grubby divan.

She had placed her cigarettes and matches within reach, and taken off her shoes. Her thriller, even if it was a bit too sordid and full of detectives who were a bit too squeamish, certainly wasn't boring. Sebastian, meanwhile, paced up and down. Now that the novelty had worn off, the flat appeared ludicrously small, squalid, and quite incompatible with the sort of lives they led. Sebastian was beginning to show symptoms of what the Germans call *Katzenjammer*. For once, his sister's air of nonchalant calm filled him with a sort of nervous irritability, something that rarely happened to him, a condition which owed more to inaction (he didn't know what to do with himself from one moment to the next) than to the uncertainty of their general situation. He had no inclination to unpack, search for coathangers, put things away. Nor did he have any desire to go to some café or other, although as a rule cafés were his favorite haunts. The fact was that he didn't want to be left alone —for he suddenly felt very much alone in the face of Eleanor's exaggerated impassivity as she read her detective story. He felt she ought to "do something" (the words were in quotes in his head) and realized belatedly that this "something" had been done for the past two or three months—thanks to the physical attraction he exercised over her and thanks to her money—by Nora Jedelman. He felt adolescent, sulky, ignored, and considered that Eleanor— who hadn't put herself out by one iota all summer—might at the very least show some awareness of it. In short, he felt like Chéri without Lea, and a forty-year-old Chéri at that; his demoralization was complete.

"Why a Vuitton?" he asked aggressively.

"They're the most solid," replied Eleanor, still without looking at him. And at the thought of the undoubted solidity, comfort, and organization of the Jedelmans, Sebastian felt a nostalgia that was literally physical.

Sebastian van Milhem was, in a way, like old Karamazov. He found something to appeal to him in all women. And certain women he had even preferred for their physical defects rather than their qualities. As long as they never talked to him about such things, either gaily or sadly, he had never been repelled by overdeveloped hips, a scrawny neck, or a wrinkled hand. For him, love, dark love, had nothing to do with Miss France but a great deal to do with Gilles de Rais, Henry VIII, Baudelaire and his heavy mulatto mistress. He knew that many a man—often a man of genius—has been captivated by one of those large ill-favored women solely because of her exultant acceptance of her own body as of a friend, an animal dedicated as much to her pleasure as to the man's, a body, in a word, in love with love. And warm. It was all men wished for: to lose themselves, having aroused it, in someone else's pleasure, to be both master and servant, whipper and whipped.

Sebastian had always been susceptible to all this, and now that he had established a sexual relationship with this woman who was older than himself and less attractive as a woman than he as a man, he realized that her admiration for him had become something more than a physical stimulant. What he felt was a sort of pride, generous and unashamed, which he might have translated *à la Clovis:* "Bow your head, proud Sebastian, worship her who worships you —and content yourself with that, for it can sometimes suffice."*

"What do you mean, 'the most solid?'"

Eleanor turned towards him, put her novel down in her lap, and burst out laughing.

"Stop acting the gentleman, darling. I didn't mean Nora's money or even her body. I was thinking of her genuine affection for you. And I agree that you ought to telephone her, she's probably lonely and scared. If I were you, I'd be off to her like a shot, and tomorrow when you come back you'll

* *"Courbe la tête, fier Sicambre, adore ce que tu as brûlé, brûle ce que tu as adoré."* Baptism of King Clovis I at Reims in 496.

find a ravishing house, all fixed up by the elves and fairies —in other words, me."

They looked at one another warily, like a couple of Siamese cats suddenly hesitant or at cross purposes at the sight of a mouse. There was no sign either of contempt or pity between them, merely, for once, no complicity.

An hour later, in the taxi taking him to the Avenue Montaigne where a delighted Nora awaited him, Sebastian thought to himself that the reprobate, the gypsy, the Van Gogh of the partnership was no longer he but Eleanor, who, in some way, and he didn't know where or when, had thrown down her weapons.

February 1972

I swore that I wouldn't leave here (my country retreat) except at gun-point and with my finished manuscript under my arm. But alas, the fates are against me. There's an astral phenomenon hovering over the van Milhems and myself at present, as a result of which, having plunged several feet off the road, here I am in Paris, broken-boned and X-rayed. Nothing serious, I need hardly say. I really don't believe—and I trust my faithful readers are touching wood—I really don't believe the vehicle exists, however high-powered, horse-powered, or even horse-drawn, that could destroy me. Only my moral arguments and my good resolutions are destructible. Such as: "I'm off to the country, I'm going to work, I've had enough fun and games, it's time I wrote something worthwhile." Close quotes.

Now I come to think of it, there have been a lot of

quotation marks in my life, as well as a few exclamation marks (passion), question marks (nervous depression), suspension marks (indifference) and, having got that far along the road to the full stop that was due to be placed solemnly at the end of my manuscript (awaited with flattering impatience by my publisher), here I am held up by yet more punctuation marks—stitches—strapped, swaddled (at my age!) in elastic bandages that I could well have done without. Or could I? As long as my indifference (suspension marks) doesn't reassert itself and, taking advantage of this ideal alibi—my accident—I don't relapse into that happy state of non-being which consists of gazing out of the window, with a sort of mindless, motionless ferocity, at the trees in the Luxembourg Gardens. And which also consists nowadays of refusing systematically every reception, every first night, every place to which I'm invited *qua* Sagan, "La Sagan" as they say in Italy. Refusals that are not in the least calculated but simply a reflection of my tendency to giggle nervously at the mere thought of the image people still have of me. Not that this image hasn't had its uses, but I've nevertheless spent the best part of eighteen years hidden behind a screen of Ferraris, bottles of whisky, gossip, marriages, divorces, in short, what the public thinks of as the artist's life. However, I ought to be grateful for this delightful mask which, however rudimentary, does reflect undeniable tastes of mine: speed, the sea, midnight, brilliance, blackness, risk and thus self-discovery. For nothing will alter my conviction that only by pursuing the extremes in one's nature, with all its contradictions, appetites, aversions, rages, can one hope to understand a little —oh, I admit only a very little—of what life is about. At any rate, my life.

I might add, and here I put on a moral veil (it's a great pity that veils have disappeared, they were most becoming), I might add that if it came to the crunch, I would still be prepared to die for certain moral and aesthetic principles, but I have no wish to shout my beliefs from the rooftops. It only needs someone, some day, to attack them to my face for it to be quite clear what they are. Besides, it's a well-known fact that my signature at the bottom of a manifesto makes a rather frivolous impression. People have often reproached me for it in the very same breath as they ask for my signature, which I've never given except for serious reasons. I haven't often been taken seriously and it's understandable; but it should be realized that it was difficult in 1954 (my hour of glory) for me to choose between the two roles offered to me: scandalous writer or conventional young girl. I was, after all, neither. In fact, I would have found it easier to be a scandalous young girl or a conventional writer. I certainly wasn't going to choose between two equally false propositions for the sake of people whom in any case I didn't respect. My only option, and I'm deeply thankful for it, was to do what I wanted to do: have my fling. And a fine fling I've had, what's more, in between writing various novels and various plays. And that's my story in a nutshell. What else was I to do, after all? I've always been tempted to burn the candle at both ends, drink, play the fool. And what if I enjoy this absurd and frivolous game in our petty, sordid, and cruel age which nevertheless, by some extraordinary stroke of luck for which I am duly grateful, has also provided me with the means of escaping it. Ah, ah!

And what about you, dear readers, what are your lives like? Does your mother love you? And your father? Was he an example to you, or a nightmare? Whom did you love before life caught you in its trap? And has anyone yet told you what color your eyes really are, or your hair? And are you scared at night? And do you dream aloud? And if you're a man, are you a prey to those terrible fits of gloom that horrify insensitive women, those who don't understand —and are proud of it, to make matters worse—that every woman should hold a man beneath her wing, in the warm, whenever she can, and look after him? Do you realize that everyone, from your boss to your concierge, or that horrible traffic cop in the street, or, come to that, poor old Mao, who's responsible for an entire nation, do you realize that each and every one of them feels himself alone and is almost as afraid of life as he is of death—just like you, in fact? Such commonplaces are frightening only because they are always forgotten in so-called human relationships. People want to win, or simply to survive.

Just look at yourselves, little Frenchmen, well-fed, ill-mannered, showing off wherever you are—even to your partner in the act of love. Conformism and snobbery lurk under the bedclothes with the same arrogant complacency as in drawing rooms. No one, but no one, ever behaves "well" in bed unless they love or are loved—two conditions seldom fulfilled. And sometimes—horror of horrors!—it's as though no one loved anyone. As though the whole tense, incoherent, inevitable, almost cruel dialogue we have, or try to have, with one another had suddenly become a sort of iron curtain. Speaking as someone who is always trying vaguely but doggedly to understand and who has remained on good terms with life, it sometimes seems as though I can't go on any longer, as though my interlocutors can't go on any longer. And I want to shake the dust from my sandals and flee to India. (Though I doubt whether the hippy trail would be exactly suitable for a Maserati.) And yet the people I talk to and who talk to me are my friends, and we understand each other. But in the end I think of us as being like those soldiers clad in iron and steel on the strange vessels invented by Fellini in *Satyricon*, who are being carried towards the beach where Tiberius is to die. Except that those boats, as Fellini himself told me, were imaginary. They could never have floated, and the first warrior to lose his balance would have sunk without trace if Fellini hadn't kept an eye on them. But God is not Fellini, and one day we shall all find ourselves out of our depth without having understood very much. But with a little luck, we shall find a hand, iron-gloved or not, gripping our own.

*H*aving finished her thriller, which ended as badly as a thriller possibly can—the guilty killed, the innocent wounded, and the detectives more and more disillusioned— Eleanor examined with a sort of wry amusement the dark red walls, the Louis-Philippe table with the three knick-knacks perched on top of it, that were henceforth to be her constant companions. Sebastian had fled, a very rare occurrence. She could perfectly well understand him. For her, every action, every love affair, every relationship was a sort of compromise: you won, you lost, or, in Sebastian's case, you got the jitters. After taking a few vague and list-less steps around the empty flat, she ended up by finding a mirror and gazing at herself in it. Clearly she must renew her make-up, put on mascara and lipstick and thus, by artificial means, revivify the one reality she still felt certain of, her body. She no longer wanted anything. She was no longer afraid of anything. "As for living," to quote Villiers de l'Isle-Adam, "our servants will do that for us." There was something so absurd in the grimaces she made in blacking the lashes of those eyes that had really seen far too much, in renewing the shape of that mouth that had known far too many other mouths, something so preposterous in her combing and shaping that hair which had invariably been destined to be disarranged by other hands, impatient, virile hands which had never under any circumstances gone so far or, more precisely, so high as to reach the rachidian bulb deep in the nape of the neck which, we are told, is the center, the great reasoner, the chairman and managing director of all the sensations.

Eleanor had neither the strength nor the desire to unpack. Paris seemed to her as lustreless as a dimmed light bulb, and this almost unbearably gloomy flat, instead of making things worse, in fact accorded with a state of mind which she scarcely even needed to formulate: *"Well, there we are, at least summer's over and done with."* Having made herself up to look a stranger to herself, to her brother, to anyone, knowing that she was incapable of going out in the circumstances she had created for herself, knowing that she was incapable of doing anything, except perhaps reading another thriller—but this would have to be bought, and she was incapable of crossing the threshold—she lay down again on the decrepit sofa, fully made up and incidentally very beautiful, and waited. She waited first of all for her heart to calm down, for the crazy imbecile which had never beaten faster for anyone—and a part of her had often reproached it for that—was now beating like an overwound clock, too regular, too insistent, and so loud that her temples were throbbing. There was literally nothing she could do. She couldn't talk to the concierge, nice though she found her. She couldn't point out to Sebastian the absurdity of his behavior because she was, after all, the cause of it. She couldn't go and visit Hugo because the walls of Stockholm prison were too thick. She couldn't go back to Mario (shades of summer), who would certainly have forgotten her just as she had forgotten him. There had always been, in the background of her life, a kind of deathly sadness, a resigned loneliness against which she had fought for ten years, roughly between the ages of eighteen and twenty-eight; and now that it was completely ineradicable, she felt it welling up, more powerful, uglier, intensified in this dark and squalid flat where even her brother, her Castor, her Pollux, had abandoned her. She thought briefly of some white pills which she knew to be quick-acting, but dismissing this as a little too vulgar, a little too obvious to be exact, she took herself to bed in one of the two beds obligingly made up by the concierge. If, in her sleep, she embraced the pillow as though it were a child or a man, it was really because sleep overcame her natural impulses.

If there's a tiresome side to this delightful profession—vocation—need—mental suicide—compensation—it is that after eighteen years, which has been my stint, one has suffered, in the true sense of the word, every conceivable type of remark. For instance, I've always been blessed with jolly ladies or earnest young people who tell me how much they've enjoyed (a) *Bonjour Tristesse* and (b) of my plays, *Château en Suède*. However well-intentioned, this is mildly depressing for an author, because you have the impression of having produced two beautiful healthy children who have done well for themselves and, thereafter, a succession of little lame ducks which, poor things, have been less presentable. This category of readers is the most usual. Next, there are those who have "seen" one's books: "I enjoyed *Bonjour Tristesse* as much as everyone else, but actually my special weakness is for *Aimez-vous Brahms*. Goodness, wasn't Ingrid Bergman marvelous in that!" The third category is more subtle: "Technically, you know, that play was badly produced." (Here I blush with shame since I produced it myself.) "But I think of all your plays my favorite is *Bonheur, Impair et Passe*." The fourth category is more specialized still and thus even more unorthodox: "As a matter of fact, the only book of yours I've liked" (the implication being that the rest belonged in the wastepaper basket), "the only one that has something violent, obsessional about it, is *Les Merveilleux Nuages*." One's resulting behavior is altogether peculiar, a mixture of the mother hen ready to defend her chicks against unwarranted attacks and of resigned acquiescence—it all depends on the day and the looks of the speaker—which can lead you to fly at someone's throat thinking, *You poor fool, that's my best book!* Without in fact knowing which. Or alternatively, *How right you are, the whole thing's not worth the paper it's written on.*

This mixture of ingenuousness, offensiveness, and politeness with which people talk to you about your work is pretty staggering, when you come to think of it. Nevertheless, it's perfectly logical: you present them with two or three hundred pages of prose—in my case more like two hundred—for which they pay fifteen or twenty francs, or twenty-five for a seat in the theater, and they feel they have the right, if not the duty, to inform you of their reactions. I even wonder whether some of them don't believe they're doing you a favor. What they never think of adding to the price of the book is the sort of colossal VAT—mental, moral, psychological, morbid, unendurable—represented by the silence that sometimes reigns between someone who likes writing and the blank sheet of paper in front of him. Not to mention the countless dodges to avoid seeing the desk at which one should be sitting, and the countless dodges to avoid seeing the sun or the rain outside, both terrible temptations. I've always had the greatest admiration for those people—and there seem to be a great many—who write in cafés. I suspect that in a café I'd spend my time watching the faces of the other customers, chatting with the waiter, making eyes, or trying to, at some handsome Latin American. The least thing distracts me once I'm no longer alone. Let there be anything amusing, anything distressing, and it monopolizes my attention. I need to be locked in with a double lock by an inflexible hand—a hand that has to be mine, alas, and God knows my hands don't lack flexibility—before I can get down to work. Once or twice in my life I've tried to get other people to lock me in, kind souls who were concerned about me and had little faith in my will power; but then my defunct will power sprang up like a flea, and I was prepared to scale balconies, slide down drainpipes, scream the place down until I was let out. Screaming, of course, that literature was a matter of inspiration, that I refused to be a bureaucrat, that I wasn't being paid piece rates, that I was no longer a twelve-year-old, etc., etc.

It's a strange life, the writer's. He has to keep himself on a tight rein, to a well-regulated pace, his backbone rigid, when ideally he should be like a runaway horse, mane flying in the wind, leaping with the greatest of ease such ridiculous obstacles as grammar, syntax, or laziness, the latter being a gigantic fence. When I think that this profession is called a liberal profession, when I think that you don't even have a boss to rap you over the knuckles, that there's no one, literally no one, to correct our copy, and when I think that freedom, in the last analysis, is only what you can grab and that the only person you can grab it from in this case is yourself—burglar burgled, biter bit, that's our lot; we're our own worst tormentors—when I think of my miserable fate, which consists of doing what I want when I want and, what's more, being extremely well paid for it, I feel like bursting into tears. Anyway, I hope that my readers and my publishers will understand what I mean and will have enough imagination to feel sorry for me.

In that case, I can hear you saying, why write at all? In the first place, for ignoble reasons: because I'm an old campaigner and if I don't write for two or three years I feel like a half-wit. Alas! no sooner are my books published than a certain section of the critics treats me exactly as though I *were* a half-wit. By nature easily swayed, I stop writing, not without a feeling of considerable relief. Then, two years later, the echo of those beloved voices (the critics) having died away, my own judgment reasserts itself: "*My poor dear, you're nothing but a half-wit.*" You see what a delightful vicious circle it is, what fun it is to be a "successful writer" in Paris in 1972. Wait, I still haven't finished complaining! This life of honey and roses, of indulgence, gaiety, and folly—you must be able to endure it! You need a will of iron to resist the boredom, the obligations, the conventions, in short everything that goes to make up, on whatever social level, the rallying points for all and sundry. You need to be very well-balanced if you're to roam freely, wherever you like, without this becoming for you yourself no more than a delicious busman's holiday.

*S*ebastian lay on his back between the deliciously soft sheets (from Porthault's) of Nora Jedelman's bed. It was a warm night and the footsteps and voices of late passersby in the Avenue Montaigne could be heard through the open window. Everything had been comforting at first: Nora's welcome, for once almost shy, no doubt from relief; the infernal but endearing yaps of the chihuahuas; and, above all, the vast expanse of beige carpet recalling the sea he had just left, and as reassuring. Then a somewhat premature log fire, several whiskies, with ice this time, and finally, of course, someone who needed him, loved him, and told him so. But now he felt a deserter. The heavily beringed hand resting on his shoulder seemed to grow heavier and heavier, while the voice, slightly nasal even when whispering, became more and more penetrating.

"Poor Eleanor," the voice said, and the word "poor" immediately put Sebastian's back up. "You've left her all alone."

"My sister adores being alone," Sebastian replied. "As you should know."

"Your sister's odd," the voice said. "I used to wonder . . . you know, when I introduced her to that charming Dave Burby, she didn't so much as look at him. She was happier talking to the girl he brought with him, Candice."

"Really?" murmured Sebastian absently.

"I even wondered for a moment" (there was an embarrassed giggle in the darkness) "whether your sister mightn't prefer women."

Sebastian yawned and turned on his side.

"If that Candice girl had attracted her—and I must say I found her much more amusing than Burby—Eleanor wouldn't have hesitated for a moment," he said.

"My God," wailed Nora, whose Protestant sentiments were occasionally aroused, especially after making love.

"Don't worry," Sebastian went on, "Eleanor slept with the gardener all summer."

"My God," exclaimed Nora, whose snobbery was even more acute than her conventionality, "with Mario?"

"Yes, with Mario," said Sebastian. "As a matter of fact, apart from me he was the best-looking man around."

There was a moment's icy silence, highly agreeable to Sebastian, who was growing allergic to the sheets, the chihuahuas huddled beneath the dressing table, and this woman with her never-ending questions. The silence was less agreeable to Nora, who, like many people from a relatively modest background who have acquired a certain degree of wealth together with what they called in their horrible jargon a certain "status," considered a liaison with a servant the height of depravity. Although all such women have a tendency (indeed a conscious desire) to turn their lovers into valets, the opposite would seem to them un-thinkable. All things considered, she would have preferred Eleanor to have had a dubious liaison with the Candice girl, who was at least the daughter of a well-known Dallas textile manufacturer. There could obviously be no question of her condemning Eleanor's behavior to Sebastian's face; she was well aware that that would automatically result in his leaving her for good. But as mistress of the house, it was her duty to stigmatize such goings-on and make her dis-approval felt, tactfully of course, to Sebastian. Besides, the poor darling no doubt went through agonies because of his sister's penchant for servants. Like all slightly dimwitted people, she instantly confused an isolated incident with a long-standing vice. Consequently, she visualized Sebastian dragging his sister from hotel to hotel, avoiding good-look-ing barmen, dodging dubious waiters, in constant despair at Eleanor's lack of "breeding." The cynicism he affected was surely no more than a front he put on for his sister's sake. Gorged, overwhelmed with noble sentiments, her eyes al-most brimming with tears, she put her head on his shoulder and squeezed his hand eloquently. At this, Sebastian felt the laughter welling up inside him. He had said what he'd said without thinking, for a laugh, as usual, and also because it was true; but the last thing he expected his harmless tale to produce (God knows, they had heard worse, Eleanor and he) was such a virginal reaction. That of a Latin or Nordic woman would have been infinitely preferable, someone who said gaily, "But of course, Mario. What a fool I am, I'd never have thought it." Instead, all America lay there beside him, and even though the sheets were Porthault sheets, the *Mayflower* was sailing alongside, and with it Quakerism, money, what's done and what isn't done, the Bible, and far and away the most important, the comments of her girl friends. Between these soft European sheets, these famous sheets covered with pale-tinted flowers, European flowers, a fierce wind blew that came from the prairies, the American Constitution, the Far West, and the banks of Boston. He was delighted at the indignation he sensed in the small, plump, comfortable body beside him, the little body that owed its enjoyment far more to Bostonian dollars than to the precepts of the Bible. Suddenly, as he was choking back the first spasm of laughter, he thought of Eleanor in the sordid furnished flat where he had abandoned her, thought of her long and slender form, her hands lying open—she always slept with her hands open—thought of her rather too elongated eyelids closed over her gray eyes, gray like his own, thought of her utter lack of vulgarity or calculation; and, not for the first time, the realization that they were of the same blood and, if not twins, forever condemned to the same reflexes, the same scruples, stabbed him to the quick, frightening him. "*This time*," he told himself, now sitting on the bed, his eyes still shining with tears of laughter (at the mere thought of the *Mayflower*), "*I really will be degrading myself if I stay here*," and, still laughing, he got up and dressed, in spite of poor Nora's tearful questions and avowals of love. Unable to utter a word, unable even to explain that he had come with the best intentions in the world and that pity for her loneliness in this oversized flat had counted for as much as his own restlessness in his decision to come; unable, therefore, to reassure her, he went down the stairs four at a time, still roaring with laughter, and emerged into the cold early morning air of the Avenue Montaigne, where he began running in the direction of the Rue Madame—at least for the short time it took him to find a taxi. No sooner had he arrived than he woke Eleanor up by tripping over his suitcase in the hall, and she sat up in bed and murmured, "Oh, it's you," with an air of amiable surprise, as though she had been expecting someone else. Then he sat on her bed and told her everything and they laughed so much all night, with fifty cigarette stubs in each ashtray marked "Martini," and a bottle that they constantly passed back and forth— they laughed so much that at noon on the following day they were still asleep, exhausted, happy, together again.

What I find agreeable about this novel that I'm writing from day to day, and what I sincerely hope, is that this time no one, really no one, will come to me and say, "You know, it's a funny thing, but Sebastian is so like me," or "Eleanor is absolutely me." (I'm less worried about Nora Jedelman.) Nothing is more tedious than this process of identification that seems, alas, to be at the root of literary success, at any rate of mine. I've had the most monstrous women explain to me how much of themselves they recognized in Paule in *Aimez-vous Brahms*, or whatever; I've known strange people, utterly remote from my imagining, who, in their own, closely correspond to my heroes. But I can't believe that anyone is going to see his or her alter ego in one of these two crazy Swedes. Perhaps a few licentious spirits will tell me that they too know all about incest. But otherwise? It seems to me hard to identify oneself with characters like these.

Nevertheless, when the monstrous women in question murmured, "You know, that happened to me," I was sure that in a way it was true. It isn't common sense that is paramount in this world, it's wishful thinking. And the plain woman who imagines herself having to choose between a steady middle-aged man and an overeager lover isn't making it up: at some time or other she has had occasion to believe it, or at least the burning desire to do so; and in the last analysis our fantasy life bears a close resemblance to, in fact is almost indistinguishable from, the life we actually live. Inasmuch as the most precious ingredient—the gold, the salt, the very water—to be found in this repast, this strange repast which is known as conversation between two human beings, inasmuch as this ingredient is imagination, and is exceedingly rare, and is the only thing that people need, desire, and sometimes possess, but can never command; this thing called imagination, which is justly known as the mad boarder in the house of the mind, which alone can prevent a house from being built on safe, practical, and boring foundations—in short, to end my sentence, we would do well to realize that it is the only thing that counts. What I'm trying to say is that if we don't use a little imagination in our relations with our friends, we may find that they have killed themselves stupidly for the simple reason that, one night, we were lacking in imagination where they were concerned. By the same token, it may happen that we ourselves, alone and in utter despair for one reason or another, suddenly feel a glow of warmth and the will to live simply because some minor occurrence or other awoke the poor mad creature. It may happen, if one is engaged in so-called creative work, that one finds oneself chasing the mad boarder for nights on end, half bewitched, half terrified, like children chasing bats in country houses in summer. It may happen that one has the impression, on meeting a person, of being confronted with someone maimed, almost totally disfigured—regardless of his or her intrinsic beauty —simply and solely because the mad boarder has never been under their roof. It may happen that one falls in love with a frantic liar because, trapped between two lies and cornered (squeezed, to use an expression from bridge) in front of witnesses, he gets out of it with a third lie that puts him in an admirable light. God knows I've met plenty of mythomaniacs, as they are contemptuously called nowadays, in my life. I'm not speaking of defensive mythomania, which is always rather depressing; I'm speaking of the other sort, which is designed to please. I've been its happy victim for a very long time and have learned to detect it by purely physical signs, of which I ought to draw up a list for the readers of women's magazines, as follows: an air of calm, a rather monotonous voice, a way of looking you straight in the eye with more than usual gravity and, *pace* all those Provençal films, an absence of exaggerated gestures. Mythomaniacs hold a very special charm for me; more often than not they lie gratuitously; you could almost say that they lie as much to please you as to please themselves. There is the masochistic mythomaniac (rare, alas) who tells stories against himself, and that is the primary form of humor; then there is the paranoid mythomaniac (the most common, alas) who joyfully recounts his triumphs, his successes, his glorious moments. I cannot and would not for the world interrupt either—unless they were deadly bores. (There is also, tragically, the mythomaniac without imagination, the obessive mythomaniac, the kind who scatters all the night owls, as a scarecrow scatters birds, the moment he enters a night club or a bar.) I have two reasons for not wanting to interrupt them: first, because they're trying to change their lives by reconstructing them—and what else is literature, after all?—and second, because it's out of a desire to please that they seek to lead us through their hoops. If only sceptics would understand that some of the lies they are told, and especially some of the tall stories, are a kind of tribute to themselves: they're being credited with enough intelligence to grasp the basic premise, enough imagination to hope for a dénouement, enough childishness to suppose that there is one, and enough sensitivity not to say, "Stop talking such rubbish." People whose lives have been enriched by such farfetched, bizarre fabrications, and who complain about them, should realize that they have been nourished and refreshed thereby, and that through them, for once and for nothing, the imperious, loving, glowing hand of the mad boarder has been laid on their forehead.

Mme. Schiller, the concierge, had brought them some strong black coffee to wake them up and made a timely offer to unpack for them. She found it really rather shocking that this Mme. van Milhem's lovely outfits should still be lying crushed together at the bottom of a suitcase after twenty-four hours. And this natural sense of outrage in a woman who knew how to make the best of herself (as we have seen) and consequently had a respect for elegance, was beginning to be reinforced by the slightly anxious solicitude, the spontaneous devotion that the van Milhems always managed to arouse whenever they chanced to be traveling on their own. Already she had taken in hand the problems of heating, coal, electricity, and other public corporations, secretly delighted with these two belated children who had suddenly fallen into her arms (M. Schiller had never wanted children). In language that was flowery but effective, she held forth on the telephone while brother and sister nonchalantly munched their toast. The presence of Mme. Schiller in their life, and in the organization of it, seemed to them as natural—dreadful though it is to say—as that of Nora Jedelman. Indeed, they found her less obtrusive and, to Eleanor's eyes, far better made up.

"Poor old Nora," said Sebastian, "if she wants to ring up, she'll never get through. Our flat's a regular quartermaster-general's office."

"While she showered you with ravishing trinkets, you gave her a poisoned gift," Eleanor said. "That was unkind."

"What gift?" Sebastion asked.

"You gave her back the taste for love," said Eleanor, stretching her limbs and going into the bathroom (or what passed for one), only to re-emerge and tell Mme. Schiller that there was no hot water.

It so happened that Mme. Schiller's best friend was the wife of the plumber (an elusive fellow) and she reveled in the chance to show off about it.

"I've got about four thousand francs left," said Sebastian. "The rent's paid for three months, but we've got to feed and clothe ourselves."

"Oh, clothes," said Eleanor, "when one's as brown as we are. . . ."

"All the same, it's a bit inadequate as a substitute," said Sebastian. "No, I'll get a job."

Eleanor's outburst of laughter almost sabotaged the delicate negotiations between Mme. Schiller and the plumber's wife. Eleanor seldom laughed aloud, but when she did, it was with a low, irresistible, contagious laugh, what her brother called "a Garbo laugh." Sebastian was annoyed.

"When you've quite calmed down, I'll telephone Robert. Or else, if you'd prefer, we can buy three thousand francs' worth of whisky and polish it off here and now. With any luck it might be the death of us."

"I doubt it, with our constitutions," replied Eleanor. "Why don't you ask Mme. Schiller? She'll find you a job as a keeper in the Luxembourg Gardens."

"I'm sure she could, but that's against my principles.

Can you see me chasing after lovers and children, turning away dogs, and blowing my whistle like a madman at five o'clock? No thanks!"

"I wouldn't mind doing dressmaking by the day," said Eleanor suddenly. "I'd stay here, and I'd sew with one hand and read with the other."

"Unfortunately, you can't sew, and anyhow I think you need two hands," said Sebastian.

They sat there, blissfully absorbed. They loved solemnly exchanging ideas for impracticable and humble jobs, and had they been capable of doing them, no doubt such relatively independent occupations would have been morally more acceptable than being kept by others. (Morally in the sense of morale, not morality.)

"I've got the plumber," cried Mme. Schiller. "I caught him on the wing and he'll be with us this evening."

The "us" made them smile: they had managed to acquire a mother. Carried away by her enthusiasm, Sebastian picked up the telephone and dialed the Rue de Fleurus, where he got Robert Bessy (who was just about to go out but, naturally, would be around at once). Smiling, he turned back to Eleanor.

"Parisians seem to live by adverbs. They're always 'just' on the point of doing something but will 'naturally' be delighted to come around, and he'll 'certainly' set about 'actively' finding me a job, you'll see."

"I'm going to try and make myself presentable," said Eleanor, "plumber or no plumber. Robert may not be particularly susceptible to women, but I don't propose to meet him in my dressing gown."

All at once she felt in a good mood. Sebastian was again fancy-free, there was Mme. Schiller to look after them, and the flat had acquired a certain lived-in charm.

"Don't worry," she said on her way to the bathroom,

"you looked after the summer. Now I'm going to take over."

With a smirk on his face that indicated it was about time, Sebastian made himself comfortable on the red divan and leafed through M. Schiller's copy of the *Parisien Libéré*. He, too, felt as happy as could be.

Robert Bessy was a man of medium height, rather stout, dressed in a style too young for him, and he clearly had a passionate admiration for Sebastian. He kissed Eleanor's hand, apologized for not having found them somewhere better to live—they expostulated at this—and accepted the dregs of his own bottle in a toothbrush glass. He was about forty years old; public relations man for a fashion house here, a theater there, organizer of innumerable Parisian functions, he seemed to think it perfectly feasible, if a little alarming, to co-opt Sebastian as a partner. He tried to give him a general idea of what the job would entail.

"It's a profession in which you need above all to be sociable, quick-witted, tactful, charming—in other words, all your qualities, Sebastian."

Eleanor had become scarlet in the face in an effort to stifle her laughter. Sebastian was irritated.

"My sister's an idiot. I no longer know many people in Paris, and sometimes I'm a bit tactless; but as for charm and quick-wittedness, my dear sister, allow me to say that I can give you a point or two."

"Oh, quite, quite," said Eleanor, her laughter exploding.

"At first," continued Robert Bessy, a little disconcerted, "you'll be rather shocked by certain things. It's a world where the priorities are not quite what you're accustomed to. But you'll get used to it. All you'll need is a little patience."

"And quick wits," Eleanor interjected.

"It's all fixed, then," said Sebastian regally, as though he were doing his old schoolfriend a favor. "I'll start next week. That'll give me time to replenish my wardrobe, which leaves a good deal to be desired."

A tiny spark of panic appeared in Robert's eyes.

"You haven't asked me anything about money," he said. "It's very much a hand-to-mouth profession, you know."

"I trust you, I trust you," said Sebastian gaily. "You've never been stingy that I know of."

The spark of panic became a furnace.

"All the same, I think I should warn you. . . ."

"I never discuss money in front of a woman," said Sebastian curtly, whereupon Robert apologized, beating a retreat, and Eleanor understood the strange ascendancy that her deplorable brother had over him, and had kept for twenty years. A few cutting remarks, like that one, in the name of good taste. At school, Robert must constantly have made the comparison, just as he did today, between himself, the cocker spaniel eager to please, and Sebastian, the intelligent greyhound. For, just as the impressions of childhood or adolescence are registered and engraved on the memory far more deeply than those of middleage, so there are certain influences, certain attractions, mental or physical, which, if experienced at the tender, that's to say the awkward age, continue to exert their power thirty years later. Perhaps because what really attracts us in these unhappy years of our youth is the unattainable, and Sebastian, to his friend, had remained and always would remain, despite the passage of time, Sebastian the unattainable.

Having found them a roof and undertaken to provide them with a means of livelihood, Robert Bessy could hardly do less than invite them to lunch, which he duly did. It was a very gay lunch. Eleanor was in her best form and attracted looks from all sides in the luxurious restaurant to which Robert took them. Noticing this and, in spite of his unqualified devotion, having a fair idea how this pair of cuckoos had been living over the past fifteen years, Robert thought with relief that he might not have to go on paying Sebastian very long for pretending to work. Already he was thinking up a few well-planned dinner parties which might relieve him of his responsibility. At the same time he thought nostalgically that ten years earlier he would have been overjoyed at the prospect of working with Sebastian, even of watching him go through the motions, because of the spice it would have added to his life. Yes, ten years ago, at thirty, he would still have been prepared to take all kinds of risks, and share them with someone he admired. In the meantime, though, he had been successful, had acquired responsibilities, and had managed to carve out a niche for himself in this cruel and exclusive Parisian world. As he chewed his lobster, he wondered sadly whether the expression wasn't only too horribly apt and whether this niche, so carefully hollowed out, wasn't also his tomb.

A red February sun was setting behind black trees. From the window of her house in Normandy, the wretched scribbler watched the day drawing to its close. During the last forty-eight hours she had failed to write a single word. She ought to have been very unhappy about this. Trying to write without success was like making love without pleasure, drinking without getting drunk, traveling without ever arriving. It was being locked in limbo. True, the days went by imperceptibly, indistinguishably, and the weather, calm at last, was exquisitely mild, almost ecstatic in its stillness. All the same, she must live, work, return eventually to Paris, to "other people." She must pull herself together. Meanwhile, the sunlit mornings were beautiful, the earth was touched with frost, the dog played with a stick for hours on end, and the log fires crackled in accompaniment to the mammoth English novel, so rashly begun. Pull herself together . . . But she'd have to be unhappy first. It was only too true, though: the whole thing was becoming a painful chore. When she was eighteen, she had written a nice little French composition that had been published and had made her famous. She had refused to take it tragically, even seriously; in any case, writing was *a priori* a pleasure to her. And here she was, eighteen years later, obliged to take herself very seriously indeed if her situation, and that of her household, was not to become tragic. And yet she hadn't the slightest desire to write. Already, remorse for not having done "a day's work" was weighing on her conscience. Taxes, debts, all sorts of lugubrious topics came between her and her poetic reveries. One lets things happen to one, easygoing habits develop, one lets other people compose an Identikit picture of oneself, one lets everything go, time, money, love affairs, and one finds oneself in front of a typewriter as dumb as a worn-out accountant. And always, in counterpoint, that hint of inner laughter directed against oneself. That self-mockery. Oh yes, she readily admitted that she drove with bare feet—like everyone else, in fact, on the way back from the beach, because sand in your shoes is uncomfortable—oh yes, she readily admitted that whisky was one of her most faithful standbys—because life is not exactly kind to those half-flayed creatures known as human beings. Oh yes! But she wouldn't ever apologize for anything, as there didn't seem to her to be anyone worth apologizing to. At the most, in certain private and intimate circumstances, she might ask forgiveness in the dark, with true humility, of someone she had hurt. But to apologize for this amiable doll-like creature she was supposed to be, and perhaps in fact was, sometimes without realizing it, not on her life! One must cherish one's effigies, if one can tolerate them, perhaps more lovingly than one cherishes one's intrinsic self. That's the ABC of pride. And of humor.

———

"I, me, myself. . . ." Whistling with happiness, the Good Lady of Honfleur glanced out of the other window: the cows still grazed the short winter grass, the dog was playing with his stick like a lunatic, the trees were spread out against the sky, and all was still. No birds, no ideas. As a matter of fact, she was more likely to be awakened the following morning by the song of birds than by the bubbling over of her ideas. She slept like a log here, her damaged arm stretched out beside her, at an angle, like another person. Waking in the morning to find it numb—since the poor thing really was fractured—she felt like comforting it, even shaking it by the hand. Her determined indifference to physical pain and her no less determined benevolence towards herself sometimes worried our scribbler. Schizophrenia, like a bat (*calva sorices*), was flying low that year. That would be the last straw. For, after all, just as she had had her wounds stitched up without an anesthetic, with a sort of detachment that was totally unsimulated, so she couldn't settle down, for instance, to read, without making herself a little nest of pillows, cigarettes, Kleenex, a little nest that still never seemed to her quite perfect enough for her beloved self.

The Good Lady of Honfleur gave a deep sigh: a night bird, the first, the one that went "hulihuli-a," had burst into song. The sun had vanished and she needed a drink. She had done no work. "Another day wasted," she said aloud, but something inside her, as she looked at the already darkened lawn, murmured: "Another day saved." Life sometimes offers such breathing spaces, when one can look at oneself in the mirror with a slight smile, half condescending, half conspiratorial, without demanding anything more than to be alive and at ease with oneself, while the evening bird goes "hulihuli-a." But these breathing spaces are rare: the tigers in our different engines are quick to come to life and tear one another apart.

*T*he telephone hasn't rung for three minutes," said Sebastian. "It's delightful. Don't you think so, Mademoiselle?"

The secretary looked at him uncertainly. All Robert Bessy's colleagues put on a show of being busy, made telephone calls themselves if the instrument stopped ringing, and called her "honey" or "Elisa." This tall, quiet, nonchalant man was as unlike a public relations man as it was possible to be. She even found his courtesy disconcerting: he helped her on with her coat, got up to light her cigarettes, and seemed quite unaware of the breezy style that prevailed in the firm. He had only been there three days and already the office had changed. People had stopped shouting and running and muttered "sorry" whenever they bumped into one another in doorways. Whatever would M. Bessy say when he got back from New York? Moreover, the rare telephone calls that this M. van Milhem received were strange: some were from his sister, to whom he talked as though she were his mistress, and some from Mme. Jedelman, his mistress, with whom he adopted the tone of an elder brother.

"Monsieur van Milhem," she said timidly, "you won't forget Bruno Raffet at six o'clock, will you?"

"Bruno Raffet?"

She sighed. Bruno Raffet was the star, the white hope of the Bessy stable. He was twenty-five, excessively handsome, and not untalented, and the film magazines talked of no one else. She got up and fetched the Raffet file and put it down in front of Sebastian.

"Perhaps you'd better read this," she said. "He's pretty well-known and rather touchy."

Sebastian smiled, opened the file, and looked admiringly at the splendid animal that strutted through its pages.

"He must be attractive to women, wouldn't you say?" he inquired.

A deep sigh gave him his answer. He noted the regular features, the heavy-lidded eyes, the dazzling teeth, the silky, wolfish air that was visible even in these glossy photographs. A greedy wolf, at that. Unfortunately, he had seen none of his films.

"What am I supposed to talk to him about?" he asked.

She shrugged her shoulders.

"I don't know. It's Monsieur Bessy who, er . . . discovered him, and he often comes in to ask for, er . . . advice."

She was blushing slightly. Sebastian, remembering his friend Bessy's inclinations, thought that this wolf cub must lead him quite a dance.

"What advice do you think I ought to give him?" he asked gaily. "Aside from continuing to brush those beautiful teeth twice a day. . . ."

"I didn't know where to find him to put him off."

"It should be fun," said Sebastian.

And fun, in fact, is what it was. Because Eleanor, finding herself in the neighborhood, stopped in to collect him and they waited together for the young film star to arrive; because Eleanor was in a very good mood and went out of her way to be nice to poor Elisa, who was fascinated by her; and because Sebastian's "colleagues" came in, one after the other, to be introduced to her. Perched on Sebastian's desk, one of her long legs touching the ground, Eleanor accepted the homage of one and all. An atmosphere of well-bred refinement, of Versailles-like courtliness, began to reign in these gloss-painted offices where hitherto efficiency had been the byword and the only demonstration of respect a slap on the back. In the midst of all this the young wolf arrived and paused on the threshold, astonished and rather nonplussed, sniffing the air before entering. Sebastian noticed him and decided that he was a natural-born actor whose looks were not entirely synthetic. Bruno Raffet was indeed very handsome: he had a mat complexion that flushed as easily as a boy's, very blond hair—one was tempted to say a very blond pelt—and big, rather heavy hands that, curiously enough, one could imagine becoming delicate and slender by the time he was forty, for professional reasons. He had in addition a little blue mark in the white of his left eye that gave him a predatory look at times, as though, having burst a blood vessel in his eye by dint of constant wariness and watchfulness, this go-getting young man had turned into a veritable beast of prey. He asked politely for Robert Bessy and, visibly intrigued, shook hands with Sebastian. He faltered only when confronted with Eleanor. This woman wasn't one of those starlets who were always cluttering up Bessy's office, nor what is nowadays referred to as a society woman (in other words, a rich woman whose wealth is acceptable), nor a script-writer. Who could this be? As for her brother, this tall vague ninny so out of place in these surroundings that he suddenly wondered if dear Robert hadn't fallen for him—he didn't help to clarify matters.

In the days when he had gone hungry and thirsty, as hungry and thirsty for glory as for a sandwich, Bruno Raffet had had what are known as pederastic relations with Robert Bessy. But his notion of pederasty was exclusively bound up with the idea of comfort. When he awoke in a man's bed, he could be sure of finding an electric razor, a bathrobe that fitted him, a particular mode of expression, vigorous or extravagant, that was always the same. In a woman's, on the other hand, he awoke to a breakfast tray on his knees, a lace napkin tucked under his chin, an admiring housemaid, and he would depart no less content but a good deal less well-shaven. Sex, then, for Bruno Raffet, had so far been confined to its "Ideal Homes" aspect. Blessed, moreover, with a keen sexual appetite, and being himself easily satisfied, and having retained the ability to sleep like a child and wake up reasonably lively, he was the prototype of that breed, bisexual until the age of thirty, who can equally well beat someone up in a café for a perfectly justified remark or allow himself to be beaten for the pleasure of some elderly gentleman or pink-haired lady. Uncertain product of uncertain times, he had but one certitude: that the money he pocketed was indispensable, undeserved and, in any case, his for the taking. Consequently, when he came up against the wall of indifference that lay behind Eleanor's eyes, Eleanor's demeanor, he was no less taken aback than Christopher Columbus on first coming across the simple savages of North America. He was still young enough, or vulnerable enough, to be puzzled by it; and Sebastian, seeing this, knew that he would suffer. Nothing could be more disastrous for a young wolf than to come across M. Seguin's affectionate but inaccessible she-goat*—but a M. Seguin 1972 vintage of course. He knew in advance that even if he succeeded in biting Eleanor she wouldn't bleat in protest, and that the morsel of her flesh that he carried away would leave a special and no doubt irreplaceable taste in his mouth. All this was determined between them from the moment he was introduced to her, but only Sebastian was fully aware of it. He might have been no more than yet another young animal to Eleanor, but what she noticed first of all, and what committed her to this affair, was the minute blue mark and the white speck in his eye. Because of this she ascribed to him the affectionate and clumsy character of a dog she had had as a child. Eleanor much preferred dogs to wolves these days, not because of her age but as a result of various experiences. It was on the basis of this double misapprehension, animal-sentimental and intellectual, that their love affair was launched. To complete the bestiary, Sebastian, perched behind his desk like an enormous owl, seemed implicitly to have appointed himself guardian of their nights and days.

How square I am—not one of my heroes takes drugs! But when you come to think of it, it's an absolute farce that in our day and age, when all the great taboos have been overcome, when sex—and its adjuncts—is a source of taxable income, when fraud, theft, and dishonesty have virtually become drawing-room jokes, people should be rapped over the knuckles for this one thing: drugs. They will tell you, of course, that alcohol or tobacco are as bad, if not worse. Personally, I'm on the side of the authorities for once, because if one is at all familiar with that world, one realizes that only one in a hundred thousand recovers

* *La chèvre de M. Seguin,* from *Lettres de mon Moulin* by Alphonse Daudet.

from drug addiction, and at what a price, after what damage! The popular image we have of it clearly demonstrates this—and popular images, in their naïveté, are nearly always closer to the truth than abstract arguments. There is a world of difference between the cheerful drunkard in a bar, fat, reeling, and repulsive, true, but his face "lit up" as they say—another popular image—and the gaunt young man alone in a room, his hands trembling as he plunges the syringe into a bulging vein, the difference being the absence of "other people": the dipsomaniac gets pickled openly and the drug addict hides himself away. However that may be, it's not my intention either to eulogize alcohol or to attack drugs in the name of morality; I'm interested only in whether they make people happier or sadder. And besides, the nub of the matter lies not in this differentiation but in the cruel and undeniable fact that nowadays human beings, whether intelligent or stupid, sensitive or insensitive, lively or boring, are generally the victim of one of these dictators: alcohol, drugs, or the chemist (tranquillizers). As though life were nothing but a long, greasy road, down which one slides at terrifying speed towards a dark, unknown tunnel while desperately trying to establish footholds which one after another give way, whether their names are whisky, librium, or heroin (and realizing that the last-named needs renewing more often than the rest and is less reliable). Absence of religion, pollution, lack of ideals or lack of time, relations between men and women, false security, et cetera, et cetera—the litany of whys and wherefores that is chanted to us makes perfectly agreeable hearing and is almost reassuring in its monotony. But in the last analysis, why do you, I, me, myself, we, they—like some terrifying declension—whether we're twenty or fifty, whether we're rich or poor (and don't start telling me about the peasants: the sale of tranquillizers has multiplied tenfold over the past two years in the provinces, and in the most quiet rural districts at that), why do we always find ourselves, at any given moment, with our hand stretched out, not towards our fellow creatures, but toward a phial, a tube, or a bottle? It isn't the ever-increasing sum of human anguish that disturbs me: I imagine that it has always existed and that even the most beautiful, gifted, and erudite Greeks must occasionally, by the shores of the world's most beautiful sea, during the greatest period in the history of their beautiful country, have flung themselves down on the sand, torn their hair, and bitten their nails in terror. No, what disturbs me is that today all they would require is an understanding doctor, a prescription, and one of the six thousand or eighteen thousand bottles of tranquillizers, to calm them down within ten minutes. What disturbs me above all is the idea that they wouldn't even go and roll in the sand: they'd have some Equanil in their peplums.

*E*leanor and the young man were dancing in a night club. . . .

Help! What have I said? Here I am back in Sagan-land and night clubs! It's an odd experience for me these days as I read the newspapers to see the extent to which an author, whether he's called Troyat or Jardin or what you will, has only to introduce his characters into a night club for the critics immediately to invoke my poor little name. As for the wretched author who has the temerity to extol the charms of a sports car, I wish him luck. The majority of the critics are appalling hypocrites. What could be more enjoyable than to drive in the sunshine in a beautiful open car, its engine growling at your feet like a caged tiger? What could be more enjoyable than to know that a whisky on the rocks awaits you at a villa on the other side of this golf course, among people as lively as yourself, and as free from material worries? What could be more natural, after all, than this search for and discovery of an agreeable spot, away from pressing problems? Yes, what hypocrites they are, these people! There's nothing disgraceful about money as long as one spends it, or throws it out of the window (preferably when there's someone passing underneath). In other words, as long as one turns it into something gaudy, baroque, absurd and, naturally, liquid. Money is only disgraceful because of the way it's earned and above all the way it's hoarded. I'd like to see those cheap demagogues saying the opposite to those who really know: people who travel second class would surely much prefer to arrive at the aforementioned villa with its ice cubes and its mimosa. Except that they're not invited, for reasons which may offend justice but which mean that they will never be able to accept our cheerful assurance that they are the righteous ones in the matter, and the blessed.

So, Eleanor was dancing in this night club with this blond young man with the golden future, a future of fame, fatigue, old age, and oblivion—one of those glorious destinies in which one recognizes one's face in newspapers one despises—at least at the outset—and which one bitterly resents later on when one no longer appears in them. Actors are a bit like that and so, often, are writers, painters, film directors, anyone who has been in the limelight.

So, Eleanor was dancing with Bruno, and their movements swept them across the dance floor, the music flowing over them, carrying them along with it; and Bruno's evident desire combined with Eleanor's apparent indifference directed their steps into patterns and rhythms that they would never have discovered otherwise, together. She enjoyed retreating as he advanced, she liked the feel of his thighs hard against her own and his slightly dazed expression that meant one thing only: "I want you." Behind all this—all of which she was accustomed to—she sensed the terrifying phrase, "I can't answer for anything." She smiled when he suggested a drink downstairs, away from the noise, away from Sebastian, who was deep in conversation with God knows who. The cloakroom girl was a friend of Bruno's, and on the way downstairs he gave her a familiar sign before taking Eleanor into the telephone booth, one hand on her shoulder and the other around her waist. He had had rather too much to drink, and he no longer knew quite who she was or what he wanted from her, especially after that dinner with people whose elegance, wit, and gaiety had been too much for him, people for whom life and the pleasures of living had been reduced to a fine art. He wanted to give this woman a shock, to leave his mark on her. But when he drew her towards him, it was she who, laughing gently, kissed his moist neck and put her hands to his belt at the same moment as he did. Eleanor's eyes glistened in the dark for an instant before she closed her elongated lids, and then they let themselves drift, engulfed in a world of discarded clothes, warm hands, gentle caresses, the whole accomplished with a kind of deft skill that was astonishing because devoid of cynicism, something he had never experienced before. Some time later he came to with his head on her shoulder, his eyes closed, or rather clenched with pleasure, marveling that her mouth could be so fresh. As for Eleanor, looking at this passionate young animal, she thought to herself that it was a long time since she had taken such a risk. (She was unaware of the connivance of the cloakroom girl, and she had always loathed scandal.) But the boy had had to be assuaged, and she knew that the only way to reassure someone lay in pleasure shared. People are so easy and relaxed after making love: a hand on an arm or a hip in the dark, the sleeping figure stretching, sighing, going back to sleep. No one should sleep alone. Live alone, perhaps, but not sleep alone. She knew that there was no danger in the raw experience of life, which could be hard, of course, and sometimes tedious—but at least kept one from dreaming, except where there is passion (and that in itself is a battle, often cruel but at least clear-cut, or at least governed by clear-cut rules). On the other hand, her tumultuous dreams and wild awakenings at dawn, her heart pounding, alarmed her much more. Those agonizing dawns described by Rimbaud, whom she had read thanks to Sebastian and whose work she knew better than that of any other poet. She wasn't afraid of dying, for to die is nothing in itself, no more than cutting a final wisdom tooth. It was the image of death that she was chary of. In her dreams and, what was worse, in the images she projected of them, Eleanor saw death as a relentless figure with a haughty profile, dressed in gray lace and a hat, and laughing politely at inanities like any well-mannered person at a dinner party that is dragging on and from which she will attempt to slip away civilly, but taking you with her in the process. Her absolute revulsion stemmed from this: she really thought of death as a monstrous old lady who comes to violate us, slowly in the case of illness, suddenly in the case of accident, but always bent on violation. For her there was no such thing as a heroic death. No one can die well or even at peace. One clings on to everything, one's agonies included, even people afflicted with "a long and painful illness" as the papers say. (Strange, the press will openly use the words "erection, bedpan, hepatitis, bladder," but never "cancer.") Such false prudishness is slightly nauseating. Oh yes, my mistake, one may talk about lung cancer: that's tobacco. Anyhow, for once it has to be acknowledged that Eleanor, the beauteous, aloof Eleanor, as unapproachable as the Princess of Aquitaine whose name she bore, had rediscovered in this young stranger, whose profession and whose photographs, whose likes and dislikes she had at first despised, something so violent, so desperate, so panic-stricken that she was profoundly touched by it. There are people like that, wounded without having received a single blow, and while they still hold all the cards—and here, I suppose, we must go back to Freud, to their little mummies who failed to give them enough affection, to their wicked daddies who slept with their little mummies, and to themselves, listening, wide-eyed in the dark, to the sounds from the conjugal bed; in short, to all the folklore, sometimes justified, more often boring, and in any case humiliating. If, by the age of fifteen, I hadn't recognized the fact that my parents' love for one another was also physical, I would have been not only a fool, but *a posteriori* an ungrateful one.

I'm beginning to mix everything up, Eleanor and myself, her life and mine, and this is only natural, such being my intention, as the faithful reader will discover should he reach the end of this weird lucubration. So I shall leave Eleanor, her knees trembling a little in the telephone booth, her arms around the neck of a young man she scarcely knows but whose impulsiveness appeals to her. Now that she knows his weight, his smell, his breath, she won't hesitate to go to bed with him. Eleanor has never had any time for progressive women—or what are known as progressive women. As far as she's concerned, men are clumsy, attractive, inconsistent, silly, or touching. She doesn't give a damn for Women's Lib. Equal work, equal pay, yes. Naturally enough, since in any case she doesn't work. The whole thing bores her. And then men sleep so nicely; they sleep like dogs (gun dogs) or like hedgehogs, half curled up, or like superb lions, sprawling and snoring; but always, if you're fond of them, with a nonchalant, proprietorial elbow in your stomach so that you can't sleep. And we poor women, our eyes open in the dark, we support this weight, so close, so dictatorial, without stirring a muscle. Ah, there, yes, when there's a leg lying on top of yours for hours and giving you pins and needles, there you feel, long live Women's Lib! Until a lonely hand, a naked hand as Aragon would say, stretches out towards you, childishly or tenderly, and grips yours. The ways of love are all the same, whether infantile, childish, sexual, tender, sadistic, erotic, or whispered. It's simply a question of understanding, of understanding oneself above all: in bed, in broad daylight, madly or not at all, in shadow, in sunlight, in despair or at table. Otherwise, it's no use. Any of it. And the little time we have left for living, while we're still alive, in other words capable of giving pleasure, and the little time we have left for thinking (or pretending to) in this vast, mindless cacophony that daily life has become, ineluctable, uncontrollable, and truly unacceptable to any civilized person, we must make absolutely certain that we share. There are even times when I long for, yes, long for the advent of that steel-gray airplane, the sudden roar of the engine, a little too loud, the stunned faces raised towards the sound, and the black package, hardly visible, that will drop from it. I've come to long for the explosion, the shattering of the heavens, of our eyes, our eardrums, and even the unimaginable furnace and the primitive, inevitable cry, grotesque in our age of technological progress: "Mother!" The only thing I'd be afraid of, should this horror befall us, would be finding myself alone in an empty house. To die, yes, but to die with my nose buried in someone's neck while the earth explodes or is ruined beyond repair. I believe I'd have a feeling of pride, of wild delight, of poetry—the last, unique opportunity to realize that within me there was a backbone, a defiance, a passion for others or for love or what you will, and that God was powerless against it.

I'm raving, I'm raving and talking nonsense, but so what! I'm feeling rather carried away, after two days in Paris in the company of sensible, practical people whose lives are so well organized that they're dying at top speed, and even, horror of horrors, aware of what's happening to them. No fun in life for them. All the poets were nocturnal creatures, alcoholic and unhinged. Truly, we should buy shares in Shell and washing machines in order to be respected and sure of living to a ripe old age. And comfortable in the withered bosom of our old age? No, thanks! Long live night clubs, and long live the merry or melancholy solitude of those who huddle together therein! Long live the false and true warmth of a false and true friendship struck up there! Long live the false tenderness of chance encounters and long live, finally, what everyone else does in slow motion but which we, the night-prowlers, do at a gallop, speeded up: the discovery of a new face, a wild affair, a romantic friendship, the brotherhood of alcohol on the brain replacing the brotherhood of blood on the wrist! We're not noble savages any longer. What of it? We're tired Europeans. And that is why, to get back to the point at last, Eleanor was momentarily dazzled, on the evening in question, by the excitement, and the desire to conceal his excitement, exhibited by that unpromising child who was now, at twenty-eight years of age, the number one hope of the French cinema, Bruno Raffet.

March 72

Out of the window of my train, between Deauville and Paris, I can see a placid goat sitting, literally sitting, all alone, beside a glinting stream. Further on, three men stripped to the waist, two of them alabaster white and the third bronzed and handsome, are burning the stubble (and their fire, eclipsed by the pale sun, only burns the brighter—a hemophiliac fire, as it were). Tut, tut, what a pretty piece of prose! I used to want my life to be one long, classical French essay: quotations from Proust throughout, from Chateaubriand in the holidays, Rimbaud at eighteen, Sartre at twenty-five, Scott Fitzgerald at thirty. I've left out a few, of course, too many indeed, and too deliberately. My life in fact is like a hurried, slap-dash essay of the kind written by the hopeless pupil who has never learned to quote, except from time to time, for her own pleasure, her own satisfaction, and her private enjoyment. Indeed, I live at such a rate that now I can no longer distinguish the months or the years, and the deliberate movements and the cigarette butts of those itinerant farm workers seem to me to represent the height of luxury. I too, on the whole, am living slowly at the moment. But I have the impression that they remember every instant, whereas for me these six months spent working in the country have become a waltzlike blur with glimpses of trees, first black, then dark green, then apple green, and of birds, at first shy and shivering under gray skies, then chattering and preening themselves against a sky reddened by the early spring sun. In case I am thought unduly sensitive to the seasons (cf. this book: "Ah, what an autumn, ah, what a spring"), it's only because there was no winter that year, 1971, over that frozen ice rink of time, between the two seasons.

Lying on her stomach in the unfamiliar bed, safe in the knowledge that her back was shapely, golden, and smooth to the touch, Eleanor examined one after another the weird objects that were strewn about the floor of the room. There were carved wooden heads, more or less African in origin (mostly less), there were a few pieces of pottery, there was what she detected as being a sense of taste—or more precisely a notion of taste—on the part of this tasteless young man. He had instinct, but not an iota of taste. He was one of those men who make a beeline for the people they need, or who need them, or who simply attract them, but who, faced with a work of art, stand there waving their arms, demanding dates, details, references that they would never dream of asking from any human being because they would already know (from instinct) his entire life history. Eleanor, who had been slightly put off by Bruno Raffet's rumored reputation for a certain degree of homosexual aestheticism—since nothing depressed her more in a very young man than collector's mania—found this total lack of discernment in what were clearly very expensive purchases a distinct recommendation in her new lover. She could tell that the bogus eccentricity of this flat, far from being dictated by the taste of some elderly protector, reflected the lack of taste of its owner, who had scattered everything indiscriminately for the admiration, whether malicious or merely ignorant, of all comers. It made her laugh, but her laugh was gentle, compassionate, and almost tender. He was sleeping at her side, his head hunched between his shoulders, as tense in sleep as he was during the day, and for a moment she pitied him from the bottom of her heart for being inevitably doomed to be a flesh-eater. One day, unless he fell victim to the panoply, the curtain-fire of alcoholism, drugs, and the rest, he would be one of those men-dogs trained to jump at the muzzles of Leicas and television cameras, one of those men-dogs who, like their female counterparts, will roll over onto their backs, waving their paws in the air, at the mere suggestion of a front-page photograph. Meanwhile, he was good to look at in the morning light, surrounded by his fetishes acquired from some ritzy junk shop, all the better-looking, indeed, for the fact that these old wood carvings were fake whereas his young skin was genuine, all the better-looking for the fact that the intellectual effort, so absurd and pretentious, that he had made to acquire some genuine carvings had failed. Within ten years he would either be an impoverished has-been or, quite possibly, a cultivated man. And all he could rely on, in order to pass from one stage to the next, if all went well (this latter stage being regarded as privileged), were his most gratuitous qualities—his skin, his dazzling eyes, his sexual potency—and his basest—his ambition, his lack of scruple, and his mercenariness. Eleanor, who, as we know, cared nothing for such things, since culture, elegance, and above all disinterestedness had been hers from the cradle, also knew that these attributes were the prerogative of a particular human breed—not noble in the heraldic sense of the term—but people of whatever social background who, to put it crudely, are always ready to empty their pockets; and she was seized with a curious tenderness for this over-endowed young stranger. Not for a second did it cross her mind that he might one day make her suffer. He had too many trump cards, she no longer had enough; he valued those he held too greatly, she no longer valued those she had left. In matters of love, it is worth remembering that the only indestructible *Panzer*, the only long-range gun, the only unavoidable mine and, horror of horrors, the only nuclear bomb we cannot hurl at the other person, the bomb that *ipso facto* horribly prolongs the battle, is indifference. She had behind her a stockpile of such weapons sufficient to lay waste the rich pastures of this young man's torso and those flanks of his sown with golden hairs like harvest corn; she had enough rusty artillery to aim straight at this heart beating in the dark next to her own. As for the bomb that she hoped she would never have to use, it was the simple little phrase, so overworked these days, her private sentimental Hiroshima, "You bore me." And the vanquished victor, in his deep childlike slumber, with his blond hair and his fists clenched before his face in an instinctive gesture of defence, perhaps against her, perhaps against a former life of which she knew nothing, filled her with a sort of gentle melancholy on her own account. It was time she went back to Sebastian, the ideal brother who was distant yet always within reach, ineffectual yet equal to anything, crazy and yet so wise, aloof and yet so considerate, insecure and yet so confident, this living paradox, the only man, not whom she had ever loved but who had ever intrigued her. She left the sleeper surrounded by his mute African heads, some of them terrifying in their ancient malevolence on the brand-new carpet, she left the handsome young man asleep, knowing that he might wake up at any moment; and, like a Cocteau heroine, she telephoned for a taxi in an urgent whisper, the sort of voice one uses to summon a priest or some undesirable ex-lover. Then, leaving her romantic stage whisper in the telephone receiver, she ran down the stairs whistling an old tune from Offenbach that had suddenly come into her head not because it fitted her mood but because it fitted the rhythm of her footsteps on the staircase. Like Sebastian two months earlier, she walked a little way in the blue, dazzling, Parisian dawn, reflecting, as he had reflected, that she had emerged unscathed, but forgetting that the very fact of her posing this question to herself meant that it was no longer true.

*T*hat same morning, a morning that had none of the wanness of dawn since the autumn was unusually resplendent, it was Sebastian's turn to wait. He had watched Eleanor allowing herself to be captured by, or more exactly capturing, the young man. He had laughed about it at first, then had begun to wonder; and finally, he had been hurt to the quick at being left on his own in the flat, like an orphan. Such a thing had never happened to him. Over the past six months, without realizing it, he had grown accustomed to being the one who went out; and to be the one who stayed at home, or rather waited up, was extremely painful to him, and somehow anomalous. To take his mind off it, he picked up a pencil and began listing all the different forms of absence that he could think of. (When things were going badly, or not too well, Sebastian had the healthy impulse to analyze the reasons and write them down.) His neat summary went as follows:

1. The absence of X when one doesn't love X, but X remains absent nonetheless (cf. Proust). Here, the imagination can begin to wander with unforeseeable consequences ranging from sudden passion to total indifference.

2. The absence of X when one loves X and knows one is loved in return, but X remains absent. Now here, the imagination runs wild: "Is he dead, in prison, lying hurt somewhere?" This is the authentic lover's nightmare.

3. The absence of X when one knows one loves X but one isn't sure of X's feelings. This time one is not so much terrified as horrified: "Where is he? Has he done it on purpose? Is he having a game with me? If so, what and why?"

Sebastian found this catalogue both relevant and soothing, and he lay down, fully dressed, on the nearest bed, because for some obscure reason he didn't want to be undressed when his sister returned. Perhaps he was always playing a part. He tried to ignore the howl of loneliness that welled up inside him as he thought what his daily life, in essence, amounted to: Nora Jedelman, whom he now visited only out of pity, a job in which he couldn't decently believe, and now the physical absence of his alter ego, Eleanor. Not that he disapproved of or even for a moment pictured to himself the pleasures from which Eleanor was just then extricating herself—he knew only too well that pleasure exists only in loving, at any rate the pleasure he regarded as valid, and he knew equally well that for the moment it was out of the question that she could be in love with this youngster—but he would have liked her to be there, he would have liked to be sharing a nightcap with her, to be having a chat with her, to be holding a post mortem on the evening, in short, not to be alone any more. The howl, or rather the throb of loneliness was no longer merely nagging: it was obsessive. Until it seemed that God himself should have blocked His ears, except that God's ears would have been blocked long ago if He had any. Between the cries of children and the cries of adults from bombing and from hunger, in this century or another, that miserable and sadistic old man would have had a severe cramp in his arms. I hate the idea of God, any God—I hope believers will forgive me—but then, why do they believe? Is He really necessary? Or at any rate, why did He have to make Himself necessary solely by way of compensation? And yet I swear I was once a Catholic, collecting holy pictures and even singing, in a convent in 1943, among other things, "Nearer, my God, to Thee" in the same breath as "We're with you, Marshal Pétain." Come to think of it, between the ages of four and six I was an exemplary child, healthy in mind and body, pious, guzzling my turnips along with the rest and chanting my prayers as enthusiastically as all the other children of my age. (Later on, it's true, I became less healthy and less pure, thanks to life and the dearth of turnips.) But then there was this ghastly vision, in a country cinema to which I was taken by mistake when still very young, that caused a new person to be born within me. I won't dwell on it—Dachau, with its bulldozers and its corpses, and everything that nowadays compels me to leave the room whenever I hear the slightest anti-Semitic remark and makes me incapable of tolerating a certain kind of talk and even a certain kind of cynicism—and God knows I've developed a deliberate cynicism of my own over the years, with the life I've led and the people I've known. It's a *sine qua non* for me—and I'm ashamed to say so in an age where everyone wears their fine sentiments on their sleeves as ostentatiously as their ignoble ones—that I would cheerfully (cheerfully is an exaggeration, but at any rate deliberately) face a firing squad rather than say or do certain things, or allow them to be done. It's also a *sine qua non* that I don't esteem myself one jot the more for this, having never cultivated in relation to myself anything other than the perpetual and diabolical desire to please. Never the desire to be respected. Respect leaves me cold, which is indeed just as well, since what with my driving Ferraris in bare feet, my drinking, and my dissolute life, it would be most extraordinary for anyone to consider me worthy of respect —unless at some time or other they have been struck by a phrase in one of my books and want to tell me so. But even then it always seems to me that this phrase, this affective missile has been fired at random and I can no more claim responsibility for it than for the air we breathe. I don't think it's all that important to preserve one's self-esteem or to think of oneself as an entity with precise distinguishing marks. I merely think that one shouldn't put oneself in a contemptible position (by contemptible, I mean very precisely a position in which one despises oneself). I'm not talking about other people, needless to say. In this instance, the opinion of other people is as vain and ineffectual as the foam that slides harmlessly off the rocks. That isn't what wears you down. What wears you down is the wave, and the wave is the reflection of yourself glimpsed a thousand times in a mirror, and that reflection is a thousand times truer, a thousand times harsher than the reflection, too often indulgent, that lurks in the eyes of those famous "other people." Of course there have been times when I've hated myself altruistically, so to speak, usually because I've done someone harm. Of course there have been times when I've despised myself because I've failed to be any use to someone or to myself. Of course there have been times when I've been left stranded, like a fish out of water, gasping for air and for happiness, or for what the English call "self-satisfaction." What of it? The truth was never anything else but myself alone, hating myself sometimes for being alive at dawn, just as it was equally myself peacefully aware of my life, of the air I breathe, of my own hand lying apart on the sheet, at dawn on the following day. But, in either case, alone.

Depression may be rather too fashionable a subject, but it's nevertheless fascinating. I began this novel-essay with a description of that state. Since then I've encountered fifteen similar cases and I myself only pulled through by virtue of this serious habit of stringing words together one after another, words that suddenly began once again to blossom forth in front of my eyes and echo in my head. And each time I came across this malady, this catastrophe —for it's no joking matter, and nothing to do with laziness or weakness of will—I was overwhelmed with sympathy. As a matter of fact, when you think of it, why write at all if not to explain to "other people" that they can escape this disease, or at any rate recover from it? The absurd, the naïve justification for any piece of writing, whether a novel or an essay or even a thesis, is always this outstretched hand, this frantic desire to try to prove that there's something to prove. It's this comic habit of wanting to demonstrate that forces exist, currents of strength, currents of weakness, but that in so far as any of this can be formulated it's therefore relatively harmless. As for the poets, my favorites, those who play games with their deaths, their feeling for words, and their sanity, perhaps they take more risks than we novelists do. It takes quite a nerve to write: "The earth is blue as an orange," and it requires colossal effrontery to write: "The dawns are desolating/every moon is anguish and every sun is gall." Because that is to play about with the only thing that belongs to us pen-pushers—words and their meaning—and it's tantamount to abandoning your weapons before the battle begins or deciding to hold them upside down and wait with your eyes already dazzled, half blinded, for them to explode in your face. This is what I have against the New Novelists. They play with blank cartridges, defused grenades, leaving their readers to create for themselves characters left undelineated between neutral words, while they, the authors, openly wash their hands of them. God knows, ellipsis is tempting. I don't understand the pleasure some writers get from using it to the extent that they do, but it's really a little too facile, possibly even unhealthy, to make people puzzle over obscurities when there's nothing to show that they've caused the author himself any real headache. Give me a Balzac, who weeps over his heroines, his tears falling into his coffee, or give me a Proust, who in his obsession with detail leaves no room for development.

After this little lecture on French literature, I shall return to my Swedes or, more prescisely, to my Swedish lady who with her long legs is striding along the pavements of Paris in the early morning. I still don't know why I flung Eleanor into the arms of that young whelp. (No doubt because I find it difficult to visualize the outcome of this escapade.) Perhaps it was because I like spinning out my stories or because, consumed with a jealousy foreign to my nature, I'm beginning to be slightly irritated by her integrity and her way of defending herself in a love affair, resorting to a technique as implacable and effective as Modesty Blaise's judo. One doesn't admire one's heroes or one's heroines, one doesn't even envy them, since that would be pure masochism and masochism isn't my strong point. Or my weak one. Nevertheless, Eleanor makes me feel small. It's really true: I want her to bite the dust, to toss and turn in bed, sweating and biting her knuckles, to wait for hours by the telephone in case this Bruno boy should deign to call her, but I genuinely don't know how to bring her to this. In so far as she does whatever she likes, her sensuality is kept under control, and her loneliness is neutralized by the presence of her brother. And she has no ambition whatsoever. I shall end up on the side of Bruno Raffet, who, being what he is, remains vulnerable. As a matter of fact, I've often found myself preferring second-rate people to supposedly superior people, simply and solely because of their uncontrollable tendency to bang themselves against the sides of life's vast lampshade like fireflies or moths. And my frantic attempts to catch them in flight without hurting them, without crushing their wings, have never been particularly successful, any more than my ludicrous efforts to switch off the lamp in time. And then, some time later, whether it's an hour in the case of insects, or a year in the case of human beings, I find them still clinging to the inside of the lampshade, as eager to stun themselves, to suffer, to bash themselves about as when I had tried to stop their pathetic merry-go-round. I may appear resigned to it all, but I'm not; it's the others, the newspapers and television, who are. "Oyez, oyez, good people. So many per cent of you are about to die in car crashes, so many per cent of cancer of the throat, so many per cent of alcoholism, so many per cent of a poverty-stricken old age. And don't say you haven't been warned." Except that, in my opinion, the proverb is untrue and prevention is not cure. I believe the reverse: "Oyez, oyez, good people, listen to me, so many per cent of you will experience a great love, so many per cent of you will understand something about your lives, so many per cent of you will be in a position to help someone, so many per cent of you will die (of course, a hundred per cent will die), but for so many per cent of you there will be someone in tears watching at your bedside." That is the essence of this godforsaken existence. Not the beaches that unreel in the film sets of our dreams, not the Club Méditerranée, not playmates, but something fragile, precious, that we systematically plunder in this day and age and that Christians call "the soul." (Atheists too, in fact, without using the same term.) And if we're not careful, the day will come when we'll be faced with this soul, panting, begging for mercy, and covered with bruises . . . bruises that we shall have richly deserved.

*L*ike most of us, Eleanor had been born in the dark with the sheets of her mother's bed pulled up over her head and, like all of us, bunch of fledgling owls that we are, she had tried to put off uncovering herself for as long as possible. Since she wasn't poor, no one had snatched the sheets away from her brutally at too tender an age, and she had had plenty of time to edge her way slowly towards the light, or life. The only thing was that she had never emerged into broad daylight. Long before her looks and her innate qualities would have led anyone to expect, she had begun to pull the sheets back over her head and retreat into the security of darkness. In fact, but for Sebastian, she would have had no contact with life other than those, at once inhibited and unbridled, which she had with another naked body, and which must be as remote as possible from the raw, harsh realities of existence, whether poverty, passion, or violence. She was a dreamer without imagination, and this explained her weakness for books and her harshness towards her lovers. Cats liked her more than dogs. They recognized in her a sort of fatalism, an impersonal warmth, a life at once intense and inert that they had in common with her. Bruno Raffet, who was quite a different sort of animal, wolflike, eternally ravenous, unsatisfied and, on occasion, savage, was too immature to perceive this. To round off yet another metaphor from the animal world, if there had been a fire somewhere and their characters were reduced to their most elementary state, Eleanor would have approached it purring, while Bruno would have fled with his teeth bared. Meanwhile, they were driving along together in an open car, elegant and hand-some as a pair of dummies, on their way to lunch at a rustic inn on the outskirts of Paris; and Bruno, unused to women of this sort, had adopted a manner that exasperated Eleanor in the extreme. He had thrown his keys to the gas station attendant, amiably it's true, but nevertheless "thrown," he had given each tire a knowledgeable, friendly kick, he had tapped the various dials on the dashboard of his little English sports car with a proprietorial air, he had even gone so far as to suggest to Eleanor that she light her own cigarette with the cigar-lighter. She found it incon-ceivable that a man shouldn't stop on the expressway to light her cigarette. She found it inconceivable that someone should throw his car keys to a garage attendant, or to any-one else for that matter, instead of calmly handing them over; she found the whole sporting-driver's act that in his euphoria he was putting on for her quite ridiculous; in-deed, she almost wondered why he hadn't cried, "Gee-up!" as he let out the clutch. To complete the picture, disregarding the buffeting wind that was ruining Eleanor's make-up, he had taken it into his head to find some seduc-tive tunes on his car radio which, he might have guessed, would be inaudible once he exceeded 70 miles an hour. The tiresome thing about a certain type of vulgarity (even if, in Bruno Raffet's case, it was mere childishness) is that it can suddenly be triggered off by a possession whose charm must at all costs be shared with someone who doesn't care two hoots for it. Bruno's ignorance about his African masks and his obvious indifference to them had endeared him to Eleanor, but he loved his car and, in her eyes, loved it in the wrong way. She had had many horses as a girl. It had never occurred to her to pat their heads or give them lumps of sugar. She had simply been concerned with treating their mouths well and schooling them. It was the best way she knew to pay tribute to their beauty, their strength, and their indifference. Now, years later, she wasn't going to go into raptures over a dashboard. Consequently, it was in a very bad mood that she took her seat at table in this pretentious inn, surrounded by what seemed to her ghastly people who talked either too loud or too soft and created, or sought to create, an atmosphere of exclusiveness or mystery out of these perfectly anodyne surroundings. Bruno was positively purring; he was delighted with the way things were going and privately thought himself rather admirable for having invited out to lunch, the day after he had "had" her, a woman who could be of no use to him; he was feeling very much the young lord of the establishment and of the highway and of his prey. He handed her the menu with a lordly gesture, putting on the patronizing, not to say slightly bored, air of a man who knows that women, because they are thinking as much of their figures as their appetites, take a long time to make up their minds. This attitude was not only for Eleanor's benefit but for the benefit of the restaurant staff, who had immediately recognized the famous Bruno Raffet, and he examined his fingernails with an unassuming and indulgent smile. He was therefore surprised to see Eleanor's gray, unblinking eyes coolly taking it all in and even more surprised when she handed him back the menu as though she were giving a baby its pacifier, got up from the table, and vanished. He just had time to push his chair back, his manager having told him it was the thing to do, and sit down again—imagining in his proprietorial glow that she had gone to tidy her hair. *Perhaps she was feeling a bit faint, perhaps he had driven too fast, but what was one to do with no fewer than 300 horsepower under the hood and a clear expressway for once? Anyway, Swedish women were supposed to have strong stomachs.* After ten minutes or so, he began to get restless and found himself in what was, for him, a novel situation. Only recently, and not without difficulty (via God only knew what beds and what pitfalls!), he had made the transition from peevish, graceless, avaricious youth to blasé young man. This too rapid adjustment, so to speak, meant that he lost his head, nearly shook the headwaiter by the shoulders, interrogated the cloakroom girl overanxiously, ran to his car, and then ran back again to telephone Paris, much to the amusement of the barman, who was already in on the story. This was the moment, while he was still totally unaware of her motives for deserting him, for him to make up his mind to forget her. According to the sort of clockwork mentality he had picked up from his managers, from newspaper articles, and from his various conquests, where a woman or a contract was concerned there shouldn't be the slightest chink in one's armor. But Eleanor had left in a taxi, and this put him back three years, to the time when he had gone hungry and thirsty, to the time when life was not, as it was now, simply what he wanted it to be. So, like the heroes in the storybooks, heroes he had always considered rather silly, he got into his car and sped back to Paris in hot pursuit. It was Sebastian, in a sweater, who opened the door. "Yes," said Sebastian, "she's here; yes, she found the wind too much; yes, you know how it is, she isn't too keen on rustic inns; yes, you know what it is, sometimes she finds it difficult to explain;

yes, she's asleep." Then he had the impulse that was to save him; almost pushing aside Sebastian, who put on an air of indulgent scepticism, he opened the door and found Eleanor stretched out on the bed placidly reading *Pickwick Papers.* As he looked at her, certain memories and anecdotes of friends came back to him and he told himself that here and now he must show her who was the boss. Give a woman a good hiding and she won't do it twice. Alternatively, ignore the whole thing and pretend you don't give a damn; but it was too late for that since he had followed her back and was standing there trembling with fear and anger at the foot of her bed, in this dingy little flat that suddenly seemed to him the most forbidding and best-defended of castles.

"I see you couldn't stand that dreadful place either," said Eleanor. "Listen, I've got to the bit where Pickwick and his friends are on a battlefield during a maneuver. I've never read anything so funny."

And as he stood staring at her, still windswept and stupefied with anger and amazement, she gaily patted the pillow beside her and, pointing to a passage in the book with her finger, virtually forced him to lie down beside her. He had never read *Pickwick,* and once his heart had stopped pounding and he could take in the sentences which she was reading to him in a low voice, punctuated with peals of laughter, he ended up by laughing too, snuggling against her, all tension gone, and so spent one of the best afternoons of his life. Around five o'clock, since they were getting hungry, Sebastian, who seemed to have abandoned his role of manager for the day, cooked them some spaghetti.

*I*t may seem strange to begin a chapter with a marginal note, but something has been puzzling me since yesterday evening, when I first noticed it: why is it that in every detective story, as soon as a man on the run turns down the good offices of a prostitute in the street, we read, "He repulsed her"? And, every time, the wretched woman hurls insults at him. Are prostitutes really so vain and resentful? Or do men take pleasure in the idea that, because they have refused their bodies or their money to women whose profession it is to solicit them (and often a very wearisome profession, I imagine), the latter must feel outraged and aggrieved? I don't know. In any case, as I say, it's an intriguing though minor point. On second thought, is it so minor? I believe men like to be desired by anyone, no matter who and for no matter what reason, even if it means dipping their hands into their pockets. Women, too, come to that. But it's more understandable in women: they're still, regardless of anything we may do or say, "the object"; and an object is dispassionate, practically invulnerable, and all the more invulnerable because it doesn't attack. But those great babies, our masters, our Samsons, whom the world wants to deprive of Delilahs —for, after all, it's obvious that quite apart from their strength, we're going to be the ones who cut their hair at the same time as their hearts—in my opinion, they're getting a bad press these days. If I understand it correctly:

(a) They're the breadwinners—but that's unfair because they earn more than women.

(b) They take their wives, three children, and a dog for a drive on weekends, and they're endangering their wives in doing so.

(c) They make love, true enough, but on the one hand it appears that it's overrated (see *Marie-Claire* on the relative unimportance of their sex in the matter).

(d) On the other hand, should there be a slip-up, who's going to suffer for it? Not them! And that's grossly unfair to us, even if we've forgotten to take that precious pill with our morning coffee.

(e) They're unfaithful to their wives, they drink, and finally, they often prefer one another's company, which it appears is a sign of utter contempt for us.

(f) Having bought a television set, they have an unfortunate tendency to flop down in front of it; and in spite of the fact that we more or less forced them to buy it, this is a sign of boredom.

And, after all, we don't ask much of them: not to overdo the male role in life, but nevertheless to *be* a real man, and at the same time notice when we're wearing a new dress, go into raptures over it, and want us all the more as a result. As for the idea that we should reassure them about themselves, they shouldn't count too much on that. They've had two thousand years, even if they were only born thirty years ago, in which to oppress us, to prevent us from achieving great things, and it's about time they paid for it. I'm joking, of course, but much as I detest the ostentatious virility of some men who, it must be admitted, bore most women (by night as well as by day), there are times, especially these days, when I begin to feel some sympathy with their gentle and puzzled protests. How tedious this mania for generalization can be! It isn't the man we live with who's going to decide about equal pay, any more than it's he who'll decide the number of children we're going to want, any more than it's he who's the symbol of this famous sex war that we're always hearing about. It's too easy to enumerate absurdities on that subject—and God knows there are plenty, on both sides—but it seems to me regrettable, or more precisely, stupid, that for the sake of certain abstract theories, two people whose lives together have been based on concrete reality should be reduced to totally irrelevant and sterile debate.

But what am I saying? Either a man and a woman are intellectually compatible and can discuss why they like an article in a newspaper, or a poem, or a piece of music, or a particular horse in the Tiercé (and God knows it's rare for this desire to talk to one another to last beyond a few years!) or else their relationship is a purely physical one. "Where are you? What have you been doing? I don't love you any more. I love you. I'm leaving. I'm staying." What will these theories lead to? Splitting the human race into two on the pretext of reconciling it or unifying it or putting it on the same level, when one knows that men and women have always attained or fallen short of or transcended this level, depending on their relative strength or weakness, and that it's ultimately absurd. I've seen brutes loved by sensitive women, ferocious women by tenderhearted men, and so on. I've never believed that the notion of sexual equality could be valid, except, of course, as regards wages, and the kinds of quasi-racial discrimination which exist and will, I fear, continue to exist for a long time to come. If one acknowledges that all human relationships are based on a fundamental inequality—an inequality that cuts across sexual boundaries and that for me has been summed up in the most accurate and terrifying way by Huxley: "In love, there is always one who loves and one who submits to being loved"—and if one accepts this cruel but inescapable truth, one cannot help but realize that inequality between the sexes isn't the real problem. And that's where a lot of intelligent and sincere women are taken in. The truth is that the married couple, or the individual, or the mass of people are completely deadened by a way of life that is designed to deaden them and that even if it weren't *designed* to do so would nevertheless succeed. And it follows from this, of course, in accordance with the prevailing technique—which is a technique of diverting the argument—that the inequality of the sexes is blamed for the mutual exhaustion of a married couple. For after all, which of us, man or woman, can come home after a full day's work and expect to feel anything but hungry, thirsty, and tired? (Except, possibly, during the first year of living together.) There was the same effort to misrepresent the profound and, to me, justified rejection by a generation of not unintelligent young people of a future that no forty-year-old, if he were honest, would accept. Oh yes, we hear them complain loudly enough today, our forty-year-olds: "It's a disgrace, you can't call them beaches any more! There's no countryside left! There's no longer any freedom!" And if they were offered their youth over again, do you really believe they'd choose their children's? They'd find it intolerable. They'd insist on a playback of the long tape recorder of life and they'd begin again at exactly the same point as before. And it isn't lack of curiosity or a hankering after the past that motivates them, but a profound horror of a future which, if present indications are anything to go by, will certainly be no fun. And thereupon—the same technique of evasion —they explain that this generation loves violence, that it hasn't any constructive ideas, that it isn't even interested in love. And yet I've seen very young people deeply in love, in an ultra-romantic way, but no one gives them credit for it: "No, no, if you don't mind my saying so, *my* generation knew all about feelings, we read Balzac and all the classics; and if my son cries himself to sleep, it's only because some little bitch who's been sleeping with all his friends anyway has cheated on him." As for eroticism: "These poor kids don't know the meaning of the word, whereas we, when we were twenty-five—d'you remember, Arthur?—we knew how to enjoy ourselves all right." It's time you got it into your thick heads, dear bourgeois, whatever your age or whatever your class (for when it comes to love, the French, on the grounds of their glorious past, are ten times more chauvinistic than any other nation), it's time you realized that love between twenty-year-olds is not merely the contact between two naked bodies. What you must fundamentally recognize is that these young creatures, with the same inner urges, also want the warmth and the poetry —these desires being perhaps more quickly assuaged between the sheets than in the days of their elders, but quite as imperative.

In any case, thank God, neither this government nor its successors will determine how these young people will turn out. Their roots are already spreading, and those roots are derision, contempt, and not, alas, hope—not yet. It's easy enough to tell them, "You wait, by the time you're our age, you'll be earning this much as an assistant manager and you'll pay that much for a family car; you'll see how quickly you'll be forced to change your tune—if not by us, then by circumstances or money, or rather the lack of it." But in my opinion it would be more natural, and more affectionate, on the part of their elders to say, "Go on, have a good time, but don't beat up your teachers or your pals—because really violence is an irreversible phenomenon and primarily a bourgeois one, and by practising it you'll wind up in the same mess as ourselves. Go and take a look at new places, go to the other ends of the earth, since that's what you're dying to do; forget all the folklore, go and visit the Hindus, hashish or no hashish, it's perfectly feasible; go and visit the English, too, and if you feel so inclined, treat the world as your playground since it's now yours for the price of a few dollars and a little time." It's not easy to say such things to kids who are high-strung, complicated and, in many cases, already bogged down. But if they're bogged down, we must remind ourselves that we left them to their own devices, and that, during the nightmare of the past twenty years, there's been nothing to drag them out of themselves. Any more than for us. But we've had our chance to bewail our fate, and God knows we took advantage of it. Now it's up to us to help. Amen.

Disaster! I'm horrified to discover that I've completely forgotten a character en route: the poor man who was so fascinated by the back of Eleanor's neck in the Rue Pierre Charron and who was destined to play a strange and obsessive role in her life. Now he's been overlooked and, having done my best to get interested in him again, I can see that he won't last the distance. Ah well, too bad. Whatever my original Machiavellian intentions, he'll have been a man who, in a sunny restaurant, once stared at Eleanor's profile. His role stops there. Anyone can mislay the odd protagonist along the way, but out of politeness and before expunging him forever from my pages, I'll give this one a name: he's called Jean-Pierre Bouldot, a bank clerk for the past twenty years, extremely badly paid and, as the saying goes, a good citizen. He pays his taxes on the dot, not without a struggle, his wife is frigid, his children rather below average, and he takes the Metro every day from Aubervilliers. At one time he anticipated being an engineer *manqué*, that the improvements on this line would be interesting from a technical point of view. He hoped that human intercourse would be simplified as a result and that it would be a joy to him to go down those steps every morning and climb them again every evening. Unfortunately, it was all a bit too complicated and technical, and his loudly voiced enthusiasm found no echo among his fellow passengers. Nevertheless, he's making out all right these days: he lives with his Metro ticket between his teeth and he gets home in the evenings in time to pacify or smack his children as the case may be. On the day he saw Eleanor, he had been squeezed in so many turnstiles, had taken so many wrong turnings, had sweated so much and got so out of breath in that labyrinth, which had become transmogrified into the most terrifying wilderness in the most savage western, that he had got out, defeated, at the Champs-Élysées. And there, a beneficiary of progress, no doubt, but unable to think up a better excuse for his boss, M. Colet-Roillard, than an attack of "flu" (an excuse that would in any case debar him from the office for the afternoon), he decided to lunch in a snack bar in the Rue Pierre Charron. It was there that he had seen Eleanor as one sees somebody one has always known and yet will never know. Long afterwards, having endlessly daydreamed between the Metro stations that bounded his habitual journey and the inexorable path of his destiny, he had succeeded, at the time of writing, in forgetting Eleanor completely. Exit Jean-Pierre Bouldot.

*B*runo, meanwhile, was blissfully happy. He had infiltrated the van Milhem camp. He was at once teased and supported by Sebastian, who was rather amused by him, and accepted by Eleanor, who no doubt confined herself to giving him her body. But when he awoke at her side and tried to awaken her too with little affectionate, interrogative nudges with his head, he marveled to see her look of surprise, to see her yawn and turn to him, flat stomach against flat stomach, hands on one another's backs, and he marveled, too, at the quickening of her breath—something that only his caresses could provoke. For none of his words or his thoughts seemed to annoy, to touch, or to humiliate Eleanor. Pressed against her, his blood coursing through his veins, he waited peacefully, unsuspectingly, for her to give him the push. It was then that Robert Bessy returned from New York. He had had a trying three weeks, business had been tough, and he had had to swallow large quantities of tranquillizers in order to keep going. He returned to Paris in no better shape than when he had left: viz., short, fat, and unsure of himself. His only solace was the thought of his friends the van Milhems, the beautiful van Milhems who had never in their lives felt the lure of the dollar, and of Bruno, rather too good-looking, rather too unstable, whom he had raised to his present not inconsiderable heights by dint of patience and generosity. His feelings for him were perfectly disinterested, inasmuch as he never expected any physical response from him and inasmuch as he, Robert Bessy, at the age of forty, had become as vulnerable and helpless as an infant. There was no one to meet him at the airport but there was a message in his flat, the flat in the Rue de Fleurus in which Eleanor and Sebastian had lived, the flat he had kept on because it was the scene of his first meetings with Bruno, a flat that was now empty, lifeless, without even any flowers, a thousand times more depressing in its Englishness than the van Milhems' present stark abode. There is a kind of comfort, of luxury and well-being which is perhaps only bearable when there are two or more people to share it, and which when you are alone, like Robert, becomes positively hostile. What was the use of those two Regency chairs in front of an empty grate, what was the use of that splendid view over the rooftops, what was the use of that impeccable, all-electric kitchenette, of the valet on which he hung his overcoat, of the suitcases with their exotic lables, TWA, NEW YORK, PARIS, and above all, what was the use of his unshaven face reflected in the mirror? He tried to pass off his depression as the effect of the famous jet lag which is a familiar excuse among traveling people. Petty astronauts, they have been quick to confuse the deficiencies in their blood stream with the great clichés of the day: time, distance, nervous exhaustion. He took some pills, half stimulant, half sedative, and went through the motions of bathing, shaving, and changing his clothes, like a sleepwalker. He had arrived at three o'clock in the afternoon, local time, but he felt as though it was midnight, the witching hour. Instead of telephoning his office, he sat down on his bed, incapable even of unpacking, and waited. An hour later, an hour in which it seemed to him that he had plumbed the depths of misery and loneliness, the telephone rang. It was Sebastian, Eleanor, and Bruno calling from a bar: they hadn't wanted to disturb him earlier, so that he could get a bit of rest. (Good intentions have much to answer for.) He made an effort to sound cheerful and bright, but when Bruno said (his voice seemed different, somehow), "If you like, 'we'll' come and pick you up . . . if you like, 'we'll' meet somewhere . . . if you like 'we'll' come to you," he knew there and then, without a shadow of doubt, that the faint blows to the heart he received with each "we," and the absence of a single "they," were merely the prelude to a great, painful tattoo that would leave him no peace. They were "other people," and therefore hell. He was himself alone, washed, dressed, and shaved, awaiting his summons, in other words his sentence, an hour and a half later. What was more, he told himself bitterly, it was really nobody's fault, not Bruno's because he knew perfectly well that Bruno preferred women, not Sebastian's, because *he* had never been able to take such matters seriously, not Eleanor's, who had never hesitated to take anyone she wanted, and who, had he mentioned it to her, would certainly have handed Bruno back to him at once. But no one can ever give anyone back to you: *finders keepers,* that's the rule. Something that he, Robert Bessy, nice, kind Robert Bessy, had never been able to manage. In going out to meet this formidable trio, he felt like Daniel on his way to the lions' den. Except that Daniel was handsome and slim and young and soon had the lions at his feet. These lions of his would buffet him gaily and kindly with their elegant pads, bristling with claws that were never sufficiently clipped and filed. Without knowing what they were doing, they would cut him to shreds and send him back alone to this flat where there was no living thing left to look at except his suitcase. As a precaution, he put two extra pills into his waistcoat pocket and then sat down to wait; looking down at his feet, at the black tips of his beautifully made shoes, bought for thirty dollars at Saks Fifth Avenue, splendid moccasins of which he had, as it happened, brought back an identical pair for Bruno, he waited for nightfall and the sacrificial hour.

The town is empty and I wonder, half fascinated, if the people will ever come back. I know they're all on the roads, in their different machines, driving towards pleasure or possibly death, while I feel comparatively free and safe. I compare myself to the bird which lives just opposite me, my nearest neighbor in fact, and which has pitched its tent in a tree that has been sawed to the bone, a tree that nevertheless looks horribly alive, more so, even, than the rest—those burgeoning with leaves, buds, and promises. This particular tree, being totally bare, looks mutilated yet is nothing of the kind. At any rate, for this reason or for reasons of comfort which the cuckoo understands but I don't, this tree is thronged with birds. In the spring, to my intense displeasure, more aural, I admit, than senti-mental, they came with a buzz saw—I think that's the term —to amputate my neighbor. For trees are always pruned at dawn, in Paris. Daring workmen, perched at heights that made me tremble as much from fear for their safety as from rage at my loss of sleep, cut these poor chestnut trees to pieces.

As though to reassure it—I'm still speaking of my tree— the birds chose the forks between its sawn-off members as so many sanctuaries. It is much more popular than the other, living trees. Which reminds me, I wonder where I shall take refuge later on. There are so many different ways of dying and so few of them are elegant. To be sure, there's always "the ceremony of crumpled steel," as Blondin wrote of Nimier;* there's an old-fashioned, peaceful old age by the fireside somewhere in the country with obstreperous grandchildren climbing over your knees; there's suicide, that slippery slope that mustn't be talked about; there are also farcical solutions. If I've always refused to be a member of any kind of jury or to take on what are called responsibilities in the literary world, it's not so much out of principle as out of a laziness which has become a principle it itself. Today, however, perched on my balcony and watching a snarling dog, an exasperated father, and a tearful child go by, I can well see myself in years to come, an amiable old lady covered in decorations of every kind, and still a bit confused in my diction (there's little hope that things improve with age), sitting in state at a banquet at Drouant's, or at Maxim's, I'm not fussy. I'm seventy-four years old. My fourth husband has just died, stupidly as they say, so I'm dressed in black and my decorations show up all the better. I've just finished a little sole with lemon juice, because my doctor forbids all excess. Some television commentator or other interviews me, not without difficulty as my glass of Chablis has gone to my head. Nevertheless, I tell him how praiseworthy the latest prize-winning novel is and how delighted we are, my colleagues Duras, Mallet-Joris, and myself, to have honored a new talent. At which point I begin to squawk, because I haven't had my raspberry flan and I've grown very greedy with age. Benoît IV, my latest chauffeur, impassively helps me on with my Pomeranian stork coat

* Writer Roger Nimier died in a car crash and his obituary was written by his friend Antoine Blondin. (Tr.)

(the latest fashion-fur in 2010). The prize winner, decked out in Moa-feathers, covers my hands with kisses. Benoît IV opens the door of our aerocar and, after passing other aerocars belonging to friends on the way, we alight on the terrace in the Rue Guynemer. For some time now, the Invalides–Champs-Élysées hop has come to resemble Zola's Champs-Élysées without the horse droppings. Lecanuet is still in power, thanks to the remarkably efficacious injections by Dr. Jekyll. On the Côte d'Azur, because of pollution, vacationers are not allowed within five miles of the shore. Ah, the things I've seen, the things I shall see before I die! I've seen women turned savages burning their bosses' files on the Place de la Concorde. I've seen children threatening their parents with the whip, refusing to allow them the slightest sexual deviation. "Beware of traumas!" they cried, and the happy, docile parents, relieved of responsibility at long last, trailed behind these little self-intoxicated gnomes whose principal object it was to deprive them of all sustenance. I've seen "the hourglass of earth and sky turn upside down" (cf. Éluard). I've seen exotic plants growing happily in Paris. I've seen people madly in love accept the fact that their love is unilateral. I've seen people give the shirts off their backs to their friends, knowing that the latter would never know. I've seen farmers reading poetry as they lolled beside their grazing cows, and shouting to me as I passed, "You know, the earth is blue as an orange!" I've seen fish drunk with despair (usually gudgeon, I don't know why) fling themselves, eyes upturned, onto the hook. I've seen owls hide and refuse to open their eyes for nights on end, so fed up were they with our bliss.

ow about some caviar?" asked Robert.

He was one of the last survivors of an underfed generation for whom the words "caviar" or "champagne" still had festive connotations. Eleanor, unfortunately, had never liked caviar. Sebastian found it didn't agree with him. As for Bruno, now that he knew he could have it whenever he wanted, he no longer had more than a condescending flicker of interest. The three of them surrounded him, as in a dream, affectionate but very remote, and he tried to ingratiate himself with each of them in turn, like an unpopular little boy in a school playground. Bruno first, of course. Superb, dazzling Bruno, blonder and more blue-eyed than ever, like one of those characters in Proust, of whom he had only read the biography; as though his new passion for Eleanor had, by some strange alchemy, intensified his natural coloring, making it more resplendent. For there could no longer be any doubt that he was now very much in love with

Eleanor. All his gestures were directed towards her, and the restrained graciousness with which she received his compliments was even more disquieting to Robert. Her attitude clearly revealed that she was not yet in love with Bruno, that she lagged behind him, in other words had the edge on him. And as Robert knew only too well, having always fallen in love too soon, this small time lag was generally irrecoverable. Sebastian was doing his best to understand poor Robert's troubles, but he had a natural tendency to take things lightheartedly; and in any case there were a thousand possible explanations for the panic-stricken expression that occasionally came over his friend's face: the journey, exhaustion, irritation, possibly even the affair between Bruno and Eleanor, an affair to which he personally attached little importance but which might turn out to be more serious than he thought. After all, Robert must have known that Bruno preferred women, that Eleanor wasn't his first mistress, nor his last, and that the nonchalance with which his sister treated her love affairs was a guarantee of safety for the future. As for Eleanor, she was doing her utmost (out of consideration for Robert) to channel, even to stifle, the exuberance of her young lover, and her aloofness was more accentuated than ever. This naturally made Bruno even more passionate than usual, and more impatient. He could think of no explanation for this coolness which he found so hurtful, and it never occurred to him that Eleanor might know of his former relationship with Robert. Young people, however cynical, have these prudish inhibitions and assume that everyone else shares them. By the same token, not having the remotest idea why he was being made to suffer in this way, he now decided that it was Robert's fault, he being the extraneous element introduced into their charmed circle after a fortnight's absence. All of them were right in their way and all of them behaved well. But alas, there was this crucified animal on the pink tablecloth, in this restaurant, and that animal was Robert. The caviar having been turned down, they were offered *caneton aux olives* and then cheese, also turned down, followed by a *sorbet*, which was unanimously accepted. Each of the courses, and especially the intervals in between, was an additional torture for Robert Bessy. At one point he fumbled for his tranquillizers (the ones he had had the foresight to slip into his waistcoat pocket) and swallowed them with a hearty laugh, explaining that American food, however healthy, gave him heartburn. They decided on a final drink in a night club, and the word "final" made Robert jump as though it were an obscenity. Nevertheless, he caught himself picking up the bill for his expense account, conscientious businessman that he was, and it made him smile. What an incredible farce it all was! His whole life had been just that. His natural good will, his ebullience, his infatuations and, a little later on, his inclinations had combined to make a horrible jumble of the remainder of his life, each moment of which could only wound him further. He sat there in the taxi with his eyes open, perfectly clear-headed for once, no longer looking at, no longer even seeing, Bruno's hand clasped over Eleanor's in the shadows. The club they had chosen because it was "fun" was like Dante's Inferno or something out of Hieronymus Bosch. But he said "hello, hello" nevertheless, he shook hands all around, and when an old crony pointed to Bruno with a wink, he smiled gaily with a knowing air, just as he had done three years before. The music, the smoke, the alcohol were no longer pleasantly vertiginous excitements but cruel and unavoidable compulsions which would never again be capable of breaking his fall. An hour went by that seemed an eternity, Sebastian dozing, Eleanor dancing as little as possible and finding even that too much because Bruno plagued her with questions as soon as they were alone. Robert waited.

He waited for the *coup de grâce* that couldn't be long in coming. When they left, the van Milhems, deafened and rather jaded, announced that they would walk home together, by themselves, and having embraced him warmly, vanished into the night. Bruno, without looking him in the face, hurriedly explained that he had a longstanding date with some friends and that he would ring him next day. Left alone, Robert called a taxi, and as it drove off he saw, without experiencing the slightest additional pain, that Bruno had walked around the block and was running like a madman towards Eleanor's flat, that little flat that he, Robert, had unearthed one day the previous August thanks to his concierge, not knowing that this somewhat seedy abode would become his lost paradise.

Whether from exhaustion due to the effects of those apparently fatal time zones, or from some deeper compulsion that he could suddenly no longer ignore, Robert Bessy killed himself that night. He swallowed, without difficulty, the rest of his pills, and by sheer chance the dose happened to be sufficient to do the trick. As they say in detective stories, he knocked himself off. A rather vivid piece of slang in the sense that, having knocked up against life, he had been unable to rise above it. Often, on a racetrack, superb thoroughbreds knock into a fence, are unable to get up again or damage themselves in doing so, and the vet has to come and put them out of their misery. Robert Bessy was neither superb nor thoroughbred, and he dispensed with a vet.

I have placed my heroes, then, in the most hellish, the most unbearable, and the most odious position: that of feeling responsible for a death one has in no way desired and in no way foreseen. When, earlier in this book, I wrote an apologia for imagination, it was of course for this reason: happiness and unhappiness, recklessness and gaiety are all perfectly wholesome states of mind, perfectly valid and necessary, but they make one blind. The situation of my two Swedes and my young Frenchman, learning, at dawn, of the death of their friend from despair and desertion, is one from which there is positively no escape. Sebastian was sad and accused himself of being more imperceptive than he really was, of being brutal even, for in such situations one prefers to invent faults for oneself than to acknowledge one's failing. Eleanor felt out of place. As for Bruno, the most closely involved, having the cruelty and honesty of youth, he thought of one thing and one thing only: the consequences that

Robert's death would have upon his relations with the van Milhems. I shall have more to say about that later on, but meanwhile it would be as well for people who commit suicide and don't allow you to ignore it to realize once and for all that it isn't sorrow, real sorrow, that they generally leave in their wake; nor is it remorse. And yet that is always their aim. What they produce is a defensive reaction or at any rate a desperate attempt at self-justification. This means that those most closely affected, whatever their genuine distress, are much more concerned with explaining to others how they hadn't realized, how they couldn't have realized ("You know what she was like"), in other words more concerned with forging an alibi for themselves than mourning the dead. God knows I've seen plenty of suicides in my life. Admirable ones, tidy ones, sordid ones, unsuccessful ones, second attempts. It's a subject on which I no longer know what to believe. It isn't true that people never try again after an "unsuccessful attempt." It isn't true, in my opinion, contrary to that of the psychiatrists, that there are born suicides. On the other hand, I certainly think that once a person has made up his mind to draw attention to himself in this particular way, all other ways are closed to him. Given that the aim of ninety-nine per cent of human beings (and I'm being generous) is to draw attention to themselves, one could almost draw up statistics, and in the more extreme and frenetic cases define quite precisely, by means of some mock national opinion poll, how many had chosen sleeping pills, how many seduction, how many pride. But there's a real nightmare for those left behind, and that is the "if." The conditional, the conditional tense as it is conjugated, has always irritated me in the extreme. As far as I'm concerned, the phrases "if only I'd known" or "if only I'd understood," etc., have always been meaningless, conjecture without the benefit of experience, and thus patently inadmissible. "If pigs might fly . . ." has always seemed to me the height of idiocy, mockery, and contemptibleness, because after all, if we knew why we were alive, if we knew why someone we love dies, or, which is perhaps even sillier, if we knew why someone we love no longer loves us, then we'd really be getting somewhere! The real horror of a friend's suicide is that the "if" one propounds yet once more is suddenly fixed, or at any rate locatable in space and time: "It's ridiculous, when I left Arthur at three o'clock, he seemed perfectly all right. If I'd known that. . . ." "It's absurd, I passed him just opposite the Flore, he was brown as a berry, and he waved at me. If. . . ." And the multitude of tiny memories that everyone digs up for your benefit begins to seem like a bunch of sharks determined to have the hide off you, and the bones. All these memories are pinpointed, and are therefore unbearable. For instance, supposing I read in the newspaper that Arthur has been killed in a car accident (since it appears to be the most fashionable way to die); well, depending on my relations with Arthur, either I bang my head against the wall, or I telephone his mother, or I weep, or I simply say, "Poor old Arthur, he always was a bad driver." But if the same Arthur has finally decided that life isn't worth living—and my life too, in a certain sense, since he's a friend—and if no one has been able to prevent him from putting an end to it, neither his friends nor my friends nor even me, and Arthur is lying dead and cold somewhere, I end up by wondering sometimes whether Arthur, my Arthur or yours, didn't have the right idea. When you kill yourself, you not only shatter people's hearts, their affection for you, their sense of responsibility towards you, you also undermine their basic reason for living, which, if they really think about it, is no more than an intake of breath, the flutter of a pulse, and now and then a moment's ecstasy at the contemplation of a garden, a person, or a plan, however ridiculous. It undermines everything. Suicides are very brave and very blameworthy. I have loved too many of them to pass any definitive judgment, and in any case, who am I to judge anyone? But certain decencies, such as a simulated accident, in private of course, still seem to me more humane, nicer—the word is inadequate and that's what I like about it—than this business of flinging your corpse in people's faces as much as to say: "There you are, you couldn't do a thing to stop me." If only my neurotic friends would leave me in peace nowadays, if only they'd put some Schumann or some Wagner into their mini-cassettes in their *deux-chevaux* or their Ferraris, if only, in the name of heaven, they'd pretend! Decorum, let's have a little decorum! Just because life is inelegant doesn't mean we have to behave likewise. Why can't they spare us the pills, the pistol shots, and above all that disfiguring gas; why can't they spare us all that and do us the kindness of allowing us to believe that life for them was a thing of charm and beauty and exotic delight, that it's only by an unhappy chance that it has been wrested from them, and that now, six feet underground, overgrown with weeds, they envy us for still being there to enjoy it. That seems to me to be the least one can do for the people one loves, the people one has let down. However, I can't lay down the law on this subject because like everyone else, circus dogs that we all are, I've jumped through the burning, golden hoops of that temptation, like everyone else I've felt fear and longing, and like everyone else I would gladly, at times, have made further attempts at those hoops and trampolines. Since then, something has happened to change me, either a faint distaste for the whole business or a faint renewal of my taste for myself or, quite simply, fear. The imbroglios that people contemplating suicide involve themselves in are both the most high-minded and the most obscene conceivable. If I've chosen to speak

rather boldly about this poor man's death, it's because I
have a horror of this sort of self-pitying scream, a scream
which in his case would doubtless have been "Bruno,"
"Mother," or "My God," or "I'm in pain," or "I'm thirsty,"
a scream which means that death is never triumphant.

The rain was coming down in buckets, and in a gloomy
church in the 16e *arrondissement*, endeavoring to follow
a ritual unfamiliar to them as Protestants, stood the van
Milhems, upright, blond, and pale with exhaustion, not
knowing when to raise or lower their heads and caring
even less. A few rows away was Bruno, who hadn't seen
them again till then. For the rest, there was that delightful
cohort which, on various pretexts, is to be seen at every
christening, wedding, or funeral in Paris and would, if it
could, attend divorces as well. Press photographers went up
and down the aisle taking what they call discreet flash
photographs. And the priest, who had clearly got the
message that suicide was no longer an impediment to a
Christian burial, said Mass in French. In his sermon he
explained to all the long-faced people in the congregation,
in a theatrical idiom one would no longer dare attribute
to any lady professor at the Comédie-Française, that
they would never again see their friend Robert Bessy on
this earth, that he would disappear into the clouds but
that, thanks be to God, there would be someone somewhere to take him in, comfort him, and ensure his eternal
happiness. To anyone who knew that for Robert Bessy, this
eager, fond comforter had been and could only be that
frivolous young nitwit Bruno, the idea was calculated to
provoke a smile or floods of tears. The Parisian approach
to funerals is both solemn and grotesque. People arrange to
meet beforehand, lunch together, and hold each other's
hands. After which they whisper a few lugubrious comments on the absurdity of the priest's sermon, and then

comes the extraordinary moment, undoubtedly the only genuine moment, when they see the person who believed himself or herself to be the Robin Hood or Joan of Arc or God knows what of their generation, pass by in a cramped little wooden box. They are well aware that this little box awaits them too, and that one day, as a result of smoking or driving or suddenly succumbing to one of life's innumerable hazards, they will find themselves therein, horizontal in the midst of vertical people who will have been whispering more or less continuously throughout the Mass. As the coffin goes by, it's the one moment when you see people's faces crumple, whether because they've lost someone they've loved and are now remembering, or because they're afraid for themselves. The van Milhems were afraid of nothing, and in any case they had lost something that was, for them, irrecoverable: this corpse was nothing less than the corpse of their luck, the corpse of their good nature, the corpse of their insouciance, and worst of all, of their nobility of soul. They had inadvertently allowed one of their friends to kill himself, and although they had never mentioned it between themselves, even at the time the blow happened—and it was a real blow—for anyone who knew them well their demeanor betrayed a hundred unspoken comments, each more terrible than the last. Robert Bessy, like so many typical Parisians after they had died, turned out to have a father and a mother in the provinces who were as nondescript as every other provincial father and mother, and who bore themselves with dignity. Everyone, impresarios, producers, film directors, actors, friends, went up to pay their respects to this somehow exotic couple who had no idea that their son was homosexual, solitary, and snobbish and that that was why he had killed himself. And Robert Bessy's mother thought that the most friendly, the "nicest-looking" person in the congregation was Bruno Raffet. Afterwards, everyone went out onto the forecourt. The coffin was swiftly embarked—since undertakers in France have this in common with the Sanitation Department: they work at top speed—and then, in the driving rain, some people went off to find their cars—because after all, a car is always useful even when one is grief-stricken (especially when one is grief-stricken)—while others looked for taxis. Bruno, his hair soaked to the scalp and looking handsomer than ever, came up to the van Milhems, who were standing there, aloof, remote, and abstracted, like two exotic birds, and for a moment he hoped their lack of involvement in that appalling Mass, their apparent indifference, meant that he still had a chance. But as he lifted his woebegone face to Eleanor's, as though somehow imploring her help—in an almost childlike way, as though to say, "You know I've done nothing wrong; anyhow you can't blame me for loving you, for having loved you"—at that moment gently, almost tenderly, Sebastian pushed him away with one hand, like a commissionaire, and wagged a finger at him that was not at all a sign of complicity, but, on the contrary, a sign that meant that he really must give up there and then. Eleanor didn't even look at him. She had an old muff dug up from God knows where, and an ancient toque drenched by the rain, and altogether the van Milhems, apart from the proud carriage of their heads, it goes without saying, were less elegant than usual. Bruno was never to see them again. He knew perfectly well that it wasn't his fault, and that they didn't regard it as his fault or theirs either; it was simply that the van Milhems had failed somebody who was their friend, who had looked after them like a friend, and to forgive themselves for this was out of the question. In any case *she* couldn't forgive herself for it in the arms of his executioner. Even if he had only become an executioner because of her.

pril 1972

I met them that same night. They were getting deliberately drunk and so was I. They looked fairly battered and I was too. I didn't know their problems, but I had enough of my own. I began to tell them about a house in Normandy that was windswept, ringed by trees, full of dogs and cats—I should say one dog and one cat, since one shouldn't have dogs and cats in the plural: that amounts to a denial of animal jealousy, a denial I deplore. Anyway I was telling them about this house. I told them that the wind made the shutters bang like mad, that sometimes it was fine during the day, that the sea was nearby, and that all things considered it was, or could be, an ideal refuge. We left the date fairly open and so I was very surprised when, the day before my departure, they telephoned, still wanting to come. In the meantime, I had heard their story, or at least the story of

Robert Bessy. I'd heard of Bruno Raffet's incessant and fruitless telephone calls, I'd heard what people said about them, about what was called their "arrogance," and I liked what I heard. So we set off in a hired Mercedes, with luggage that was almost as frayed-looking as its owners, and took the road to Normandy. Nothing much was said during the journey. For reasons I didn't know and never had time to discover, the chauffeur was the most talkative, the gayest among us. It was as though we were all trying to find some elementary form of politeness and niceness. Each of us, it seemed, needed bandaging all over.

They liked the house. It's a big house and the wind does indeed howl around it. And it isn't very elegant, so everyone can put their feet on the sofas. The first night was odd. We recognized one another, of course. But each of our words and gestures might have been interchangeable, so much so that we spoke to one another with extreme politeness and almost avoided one another. Drink had become a balm, music a "background" as they say. As for the dog, clumsy and affectionate, gazing steadily at us and evidently puzzled by these three humans who should have been dictatorial but were merely speechless with fatigue, he seemed the only living creature among the lot of us. My own scar being the least serious, during the course of this evening overclouded with politeness and reciprocal wariness, I made up my mind to try to help them. "Tomorrow," I told myself, "everything I can give them shall be theirs. I shall give them the grass, my precious grass, I shall give them the goat with no ears, who's bound to make Eleanor laugh. I shall give them a sort of peace, a sort of rebellion, anger, and indignation, I shall give them everything I've been able to do or to achieve over thirty-seven years; I shall try to give them, if I can, some way of coming to terms with themselves at the same time as I myself try to do the same." But tomorrow was tomorrow and I think that the night seemed long to each of us in our separate rooms.

From then on it rained without ceasing. Sebastian and I, too weak to resist, got into the habit of sleeping together with or without good reason. At all events we spent our days at Eleanor's feet, while she remained as ever engrossed in her detective stories, looking oh, so elegant compared with us, so dirty, so disheveled, so human. From time to time she would run her beautiful long fingers through our hair, comparing the texture, the softness, and thus we became, he, her brother, and I, the stranger, rivals in laughter and more affectionate than ever. We listened to nothing but opera: *La Bohème, Tosca, La Traviata,* and the sublime voices of the singers allied to the simplicity of their emotional problems pierced our hearts. The trees along the drive dripped with rain, to such an extent that the dog preferred to play indoors with us rather than out of doors with his sticks. The fire crackled, inviting from one and all confidences that we never brought ourselves to exchange. It could have been a life, perhaps—a strange life but nonetheless genuine because utterly free of compulsion, and when Eleanor's slender hand brushed my cheek and Sebastian's head rested on my shoulder as he hummed *"Mi chiamano Mimì,"* yes, it added up to something. Something quiet, tender, and doomed from the start. There should be reserves for the pure of heart, as for Red Indians. My country house was close to being that, because I watched over it as scrupulously as my over-affectionate dog and my over-watchful cat.

Then came Stockholm. A telegram from Stockholm. I remember that afternoon. I was sitting, as usual, on the floor, between Eleanor's and Sebastian's knees, all of us helpless with laughter, and I heard the postman arrive. The telegram said that Hugo had been released at last and that he, the only man who had never, even for one minute, doubted Eleanor or her love, was waiting at Stockholm airport for her to come back to him. She got up and I understood her. I understood at once her desire to go back to this man who was wrong about her, her desire to go back to this interminable misunderstanding and this reassuring madness. For I could tell from her eyes, from her gestures, that she was at the end of her tether, that she had had enough of the shoddy Paris of 1972 that her brother had tried to enliven for her. With the telegram, she breathed again, they both breathed again. Back to the peaceful rivers of Sweden, back to Hugo, so generous in his foolishness, back to worlds I had never known. Nevertheless, the last evening was painful. We were all three of us in the little sitting room, the cat in Eleanor's lap, the dog stretched out on the floor still breathing God knows what scents of the chase, but breathing heavily between Sebastian and me. Then, overcome by tiredness and tension, we said, "Goodnight, see you in the morning," knowing that the morning would bring one of those farewells made hectic by the pressure of time and urgency, for the train left at a quarter past twelve and we were not the sort of people who are wide awake by a quarter past twelve. It was indeed a painful journey—from my house to Deauville station. When I say painful I mean silent. We had five minutes to spare and we spent them with our noses buried in one another's necks. I didn't know who was who any longer, nor did they. And then that stupid train began to puff and smoke and make trainlike noises. And suddenly, peering over that thing like a bannister rail, I saw those two faces once more, very distant and yet at the same time so tender that I knew I would never see their like again. I raised my hand. It was pouring rain but neither of them begged me to go, and I said in a rather faint voice, "Au revoir, au revoir." Eleanor van Milhem leaned forward (and the Normandy countryside shimmered around her in the window pane) and she said to me, "No, not au revoir, goodbye," in a voice so gentle and so final that I could have taken it the wrong way if I hadn't known better. The spring had been very cold in Deauville that year. Nevertheless, as I left the station, alone and feeling rather sick at the thought, it cleared up, thanks to one of those happy storms peculiar to Normandy skies and, on my way to my car, I received a pitiless shaft of sunlight on my face and I knew that Eleanor was right, that it was the last time I should see the van Milhems face to face, and perhaps myself as well.

VGM Opportunities Series

OPPORTUNITIES IN HUMAN RESOURCE MANAGEMENT CAREERS

William J. Traynor, SPHR and J. Steven McKenzie, SPHR

Foreword by
Michael R. Losey, SPHR
President and Chief Executive Officer
Society for Human Resource Management

VGM Career Horizons
a division of *NTC Publishing Group*
Lincolnwood, Illinois USA

Cover Photo Credits:
(*Clockwise from top left*) Pacific Bell; Photo Network; Rush Presbyterian–St. Luke's
Medical Center; Photo Network.

Library of Congress Cataloging-in-Publication Data
Traynor, William J.
   Opportunities in human resource management careers / William J.
Traynor and J. Steven McKenzie.
     p.   cm. — (VGM opportunities series)
   Rev. ed. of: Opportunities in human resources management careers.
© 1989.
   Includes bibliographical references.
   ISBN 0–8442–4092–3 (hard): ISBN 0–8442–4093–1 (soft).
   1. Personnel management—Vocational guidance—United States.
I. McKenzie, J. Steven. II. Traynor, William J. Opportunities in
human resources management careers. III. Title. IV. Series.
HF5549.2.U5T73   1994
658.3′0023′73—dc20   93–46084
                                          CIP

Published by VGM Career Horizons, a division of NTC Publishing Group
4255 West Touhy Avenue
Lincolnwood (Chicago), Illinois 60646-1975, U.S.A.

4 5 6 7 8 9 0 VP 9 8 7 6 5 4 3 2 1

ABOUT THE AUTHORS

William Traynor has worked and instructed in human resource management and development. Currently a professor emeritus at California State University, Long Beach, Dr. Traynor served as faculty personnel administrator at San Fernando Valley State College (CSU Northridge) and director of personnel at Pepperdine University. A graduate of the U.S. Naval Academy, he also holds a master's degree in personnel administration from the George Washington University and a doctorate from Brigham Young University. He is a senior professional in human resources (SPHR). Dr. Traynor served 27 years in the navy, including submarine command.

He is active in the Society for Human Resource Management (SHRM) and has conducted sessions at its national conferences. He served on the Research Committee and is currently on the Training and Development Committee. In 1981, 1984, 1986, and 1990, he received grants (including Fulbright and Asia Foundation) to design and conduct training at the University of the South Pacific in Fiji.

J. Steven McKenzie has spent his entire career in the field of human resource management. Currently the manager of training and employee education at Arkansas Louisiana Gas Company, a regional gas utility with more than 1,600 employees in four states, Steve also is an instructor in the executive MBA program at Centenary College of Louisiana in Shreveport.

A graduate of the University of Wisconsin–Whitewater, he also holds a master's of business administration degree from Louisiana Tech University. Additionally, he is a certified senior professional in human resources (SPHR) and a certified manager of suggestion systems (CMSS).

The author has a broad generalist background in the field of human resources. He is very active in the Society for Human Resource Management (SHRM) and the American Society for Training and Development (ASTD). He currently is a member of the SHRM Training and Development Committee.

FOREWORD

Years ago, when I first entered this profession, the field was very different from what it is today. It was a relatively new addition to the corporate structure and still somewhat ill-defined and underutilized. But because it existed to serve people, with all their contrasts and complexities, it was a fascinating and rewarding job to have.

It is definitely still rewarding, but the times have changed. Today the field of human resource management (HRM) is firmly entrenched in the workplace hierarchy. It is one of the most pivotal and indispensable departments in an organization, as lively and dynamic as the work force it seeks to serve.

Today's work force is among the most diverse, best educated, and most motivated in our country's history. People at work today want more than a paycheck. They seek employment that is fulfilling as well as challenging. They want jobs that are significant within the organization and to the economy at large. HRM professionals work to accommodate the needs and goals of both the worker and the employer, and, more than ever, the success of any organization depends now on the individual productivity, efficiency, and well-being of each worker.

Organizations in both the public and private sector require the services of professionals in human resource management. HR managers must possess the knowledge, skills, and attitudes to perform effectively in the modern workplace. Technical expertise is needed to design and execute sophisticated programs involving employee training and development, benefits and compensation administration, and compliance with government-mandated laws and regulations.

Human resource professionals must be sensitive to the requirements of sound management and the occupational needs of working people. They are part of the management team but also serve to bridge the gap between management and its employees. Excellent interpersonal skills are crucial to dealing sensibly with individuals and groups, labor and management, and the internal and public affairs of an organization.

The role of the Society for Human Resource Management (SHRM) is to assist those who are pursuing productive careers in HRM. The Society exists to help individual HR professionals understand our body of knowledge and attain the qualifications required to perform effectively in our demanding profession. We provide an information and communications network that promotes individual and organizational development through our publications, seminars, conferences, and training courses. And our more than 400 local professional and 300 student chapters offer the opportunity to meet and learn from each other.

SHRM was founded in 1948 by 28 personnel managers who anticipated growth in human resource management that would require professional development guidance and support. They were right. Today the Society has more than 56,000 student and professional members from around the world. The phenomenal growth in membership is a reflection of the increased influence of our profession and our members' dedication to excellence. The growth of our field and quality of our management is dependent on that dedication.

Human resource management is as vibrant and ever-changing as the population at large. For that reason, it is uniquely challenging and stimulating and will continue to grow in the years ahead. If you are looking for a career that promises abundant professional opportunity and great personal satisfaction, let me heartily encourage you to consider human resource management. Good luck in all your educational and professional endeavors.

Michael R. Losey, SPHR
President and CEO
Society for Human Resource Management

DEDICATION

This work is dedicated to Dale Yoder, Ph.D. (1901–1989), who served the field of personnel and industrial relations (now called human resource management) in many capacities and won many awards. Dedicating this book to him recognizes Dr. Yoder for the person he was: a courageous professional who led the way in developing the field. He gave unstintingly of himself to aid the progress of others who were struggling to find their way in a challenging and changing profession. These efforts endeared him to his colleagues and won him the respect and gratitude of many, many others in this vocation.

CONTENTS

About the Authors . . . . **iii**

Foreword . . . . **iv**

1. **The Function of Human Resource Management** . . **1**

Human resource management terms. Human resource
management in the economy. Development of human resource management. Labor-management relations. Equal
employment opportunity. Present status.

2. **Human Resource Management as an Occupation** . **17**

Formulation of human resource management policy. Aid-
ing supervision. Supervisor-employee relationships. Role
of human resource management in organizations. Functions of an enterprise. Specialty areas of human resource
management.

3. **Features of the Field** **72**

Salaries. Working conditions. Satisfactions. Working levels. Characteristics of successful personnel workers.

4. **Requirements and Preparation** **87**

Required qualifications. Standards for employment. Educational requirements. Starting your career. Self-evalu-
ation. Possible resources. Choices: job or school?
Counseling. Applying for a job.

5. **Launching Your Career** **107**

The resume. Locating the job opportunities. The job interview. Success and advancement. The occupational outlook. Career expectations.

6.   Today's Issues in Human Resource Management . 133

Work/family benefits. Minimum wage. AIDS. Health care. OSHA reform. Labor law reform. Electronic monitoring. Drug/alcohol testing. Diversity management. Controlling worker's compensation costs. Compensation. Right to know. Technology. Older worker recruitment/retention.

7.   Additional Information about HRM 147

Organizations. Additional sources of information.

Bibliography **151**

CHAPTER 1

THE FUNCTION OF HUMAN RESOURCE MANAGEMENT

The function of managing human resources is performed in all organizations: large and small, private and public, profit and nonprofit. It is the "people" aspect of work. Just as the success of organizations depends on the sound management of finances, production, and other functions, it also depends on the sound management of people—organizations' human resources. The field of human resource management involves the dynamics of people at work and their infinite diversity.

Today the management of human resources concerns all managers and workers. The human resource manager, however, is the professional expert in the field who designs and manages the programs that mold an effective work force in support of the objectives of the organization. Currently, the senior HR manager carries the responsibilities and enjoys the compensations that go with top management positions, with salaries for top-level managers often exceeding $100,000. HR managers are "big wheels" in organizations, and they influence the directions that agencies or companies take in pursuing their goals. They also formulate the policies and programs that constitute the human resource function of the organization.

As a career field, human resource management is growing and maturing. Its status is elevating as its areas of responsibility are broadening. Each year, thousands of new workers find employment in personnel and labor relations. They may start their career at the bottom rung of the career ladder and work up to the top level, achieving high-salaried positions. Education and related experience help them attain suitable positions in their organizations.

HUMAN RESOURCE MANAGEMENT TERMS

Before going on, we should review the terms and definitions that are used in the human resource management field.

Human Resource Management

The term *human resource management* refers to the broad aspects of managing people in work organizations. In business organizations, employees are seen as resources, just as money, buildings, and equipment are resources that require management in order for an organization to function effectively. HR management is concerned with employee as groups and as individuals at work, and it includes such matters as recruitment, pay, training, retirement, health insurance, grievances, and advancement. In the public sector, the term *personnel administration* is used more frequently, but it is intended to mean substantially the same thing. Often the terms *human resource management, personnel management, personnel administration, HR management,* and *HRM* are used interchangeably.

Labor Relations

Labor relations is a term that is used in two senses. First, it means relations with the work force as an entity or groups of employees in a plant or multiplant organization. It can also mean relations with individual employees. Second, it denotes those matters covered by the labor agreements between labor and management within a company, dealing with wages, hours, and conditions of work.

Industrial Relations

The expression *industrial relations* is falling into disuse in America, though it is used widely in Britain and many other countries. It is occasionally used to mean all aspects of personnel management, but usually it means the relationship between management and organized labor—what we would now call *labor relations*.

HUMAN RESOURCE MANAGEMENT IN THE ECONOMY

In the 1990s, workers' social awareness has resulted in an emphasis on quality of their work life. The rights of individuals at work demand more attention from society and federal legislation. Organizations are realizing that their most important investment is their employees. People spend a major portion of their lives in their places of work, and increasingly they are becoming involved in those decisions at work that influence their livelihoods. While organizations consider that it is important to get the most out of their workers, employees believe it is just as important that they get as much as they can from their employment. When employees are hired, employers make a serious investment in them in terms of wages, training, vacations, unemployment insurance, disability, worker's compensation, and retirement commitments. Employees also make a commitment to the organization in terms of time, effort, and future promise. There is a moral contract that management must pay for the work employees do, and employees must do the work they were hired to perform. These mutual obligations are carried out through a set of personnel programs that constitute the management of human resources.

There are several major factors shaping the current evolution of the field of human resource management.

The Climate of Work

Among the major elements in the contemporary system of working organizations is the working and managing environment, including the structure of working organizations and the economic, social, and political systems in which organizations exist and operate. Another is the working people—the individuals who manage and supervise and are employed to perform work.

Managers accomplish their missions through leadership by guiding the efforts of their subordinates in support of the goals of the organization. According to Dale Yoder and Paul D. Staudohar, authors of *Personnel Management and Industrial Relations,* this is accomplished within the framework of dynamic work situations and the working relationships in them.

The Decade of Diversity

The 1990s will become known as the decade of diversity. Never before in the history of America has the composition of the work force been made up of so many different types of people. All types present a different challenge to the HR manager to assimilate them into the established work force.

For example, high school graduates who are functionally illiterate and unable to read the simplest safety precautions are applying for work. Because these people may be the only ones available, many organizations are hiring them and training them to an acceptable level of literacy. Currently, this is a major long-range problem.

Women constitute an increasing percentage of the work force. Many of them have been homemakers for years and thus have plenty of social experience and have shouldered important responsibility rearing children, but they may not be attuned to the work environment. When they join the work force, they must adapt to a different life-style from what they are accustomed to.

With both legal and illegal immigration soaring, a great many people are entering the work force who cannot communicate in English, who come from social backgrounds that are radically different from mainstream America, and who do not readily adjust to the environment of the industrial workplace. They may be intelligent and skilled, but they are very different types of people. Many come from cultures where the work they are accustomed to performing was far different from the work culture in today's industrial America.

Young, new workers may bring with them new ideas, expectations, and values. Many of them are products of the "me generation," and they see things in a different light from older, more experienced workers. They are bright and conscientious in their work, but they may perceive their role at work as being more personal-oriented than organization-oriented. They may bring with them different attitudes toward holidays, overtime, or profit sharing, and they may expect greater economic security. In keeping with the trends of the times, they may want more freedom in planning and organizing their work and more opportunity to suggest changes.

There are many experienced older workers who have become unemployed by virtue of layoffs, reductions in force, and mergers. These are skilled workers who must start in a new organization or industry in order to provide for their livelihood. These people have suffered a setback in their working careers, and their outlooks and expectations are different from other workers'.

There are racial, cultural, and religious differences in today's work force that require greater understanding. One of the primary efforts of human resource management in America is to accommodate all the differences.

Today's supervisors may require training in order to deal effectively with the diversity of people in the workplace. They must have patience and understanding to lead these new human resources as well as a continuing knowledge of the technical aspects of job assignments.

Trends of the Times

Changes in organizational cultures and individual expectations influence conditions of employment and present continual challenges to contemporary human resource managers. Some of the major trends of the day include the following.

- Cultural diversity in the work force demands more tolerance and more imaginative approaches to acceptable interrelationships at work.
- With rapidly advancing technology, the demand for increasing the skill levels of the American work force has become urgent. Education, training, and retraining are becoming a part of the work scene.
- The size of work organizations continues to increase through growth, merger, and acquisition. At the same time, though, many of the work forces of these organizations are downsizing. But expansion and globalization require more sophisticated and speedier communications.
- Continuing governmental intervention in the management of work organizations deprives industries of the freedom to manage their affairs. While seeking to improve the lot of the working person, government is, at the same time, tying the hands of managers who strive to improve the production of goods and services in an increasingly competitive marketplace. Thus, management is pressured to find innovative ways to improve productivity while at the same time enhancing the welfare of its employees.
- An explosive population growth has necessitated a continuing employment effort in America and throughout the world. People at work contribute more to society than those who remain unemployed (see table 1.1).
- Levels of formal education continue to rise as less formal programs—literary, radio, television, and travel—contribute to a spread of sophistication. While jobs are harder to get, young people are spending more time on their education, and employers are expecting higher levels of education.
- Organizations are experimenting with new structures and new styles of management and communications. Telecommunicating is being used more widely. Computer networking is affecting work patterns and permitting more work-at-home situations.

Table 1.1. Populations and Labor Forces (in millions)

Year	United States		World	
	Population[6]	Labor Force[5]	Population	Labor Force
1960	—	—	3,289[1]	774[4]
1965	194	77	—	—
1970	205	86	3,575[2]	1,499[7]
1975	216	95	—	—
1980	228	107	4,258[3]	1,781[7]
1985	239	115	4,865[8]	NA
1990	252	127	5,423[9]	NA

[1]World Population Growth and Response Population Reference Bureau. Washington, D.C., 1976.

[2]*The World Almanac and Book of Facts.* New York: Newspaper Enterprise Association, 1981: 731.

[3]*Information Please Atlas and Yearbook.* 36th ed. New York: Simon and Schuster, 1981.

[4]*World Tables.* Baltimore: Johns Hopkins University Press, 1976: 514–16.

[5]Bureau of the Census. *Statistical Abstract of the United States, 1992.* Washington, D.C., 1992: 380.

[6]Bureau of the Census. *Statistical Abstract,* 8.

[7]*Labor Force and World Population Growth.* Geneva, Switzerland: International Labor Organization, 1974: 64.

[8]Bureau of the Census. *Statistical Abstract of the United States, 1988.* Washington, D.C., 1988: 522.

[9]Bureau of the Census. *Statistical Abstract of the United States, 1992.* Washington, D.C., 1992: 819.

DEVELOPMENT OF HUMAN RESOURCE MANAGEMENT[1]

The field of human resources management has been recognized formally as a functional specialty and area of practice for just over half a century, but its roots are embedded deep in the past. The management of personnel has been necessary ever since there have been groups of people organized to achieve common work. Individuals responsible for

[1]This section derived from *Managing Human Resources* and *The Management of Personnel Relations* (see bibliography).

leading and managing organizations have always had to provide some type of management, motivation, leadership, remuneration, and training for their employees.

Early personnel programs existed in the Middle Ages when the growth of towns and villages created new demands for goods and services. They also provided employment opportunities for those seeking to escape their status as serfs in the feudal system. Skilled artisans organized into guilds, which established controls and regulations pertaining to their respective trades. The guilds of that day were the forerunners of the employer associations of today, and they helped provide standards of craftsmanship and foundations for apprentice training.

Until the Industrial Revolution began, most goods were manufactured in small shops or handcrafted in the home. The revolutionary times stirred the growth of factories when cheap labor, capital, power-driven machinery, and improved production techniques became available. There was also an increase in the demand for manufactured goods. With the introduction of the factory system, work became specialized, and jobs became repetitive, monotonous, and unchallenging. Craft workers enjoyed some degree of economic security by virtue of their having a marketable skill, while factory workers, being unskilled, lacked security, had little power to improve their situations, and could easily be replaced.

In those days, factory labor was considered a commodity along with money, machinery, and materials necessary for the production of goods. Employees were hired at the lowest possible wage, given minimal training for their unskilled jobs, and discarded when their services were no longer required. It was the employer who had all the power of hiring and firing, and employees had to accept the conditions of employment on a take-it-or-leave-it basis.

The extension of voting privileges and free education to all citizens in America helped workers gain more political influence leading to the passage of legislation that offered them some degree of protection. Early on, state laws regulating the hours of work for women and children were enacted. Later, protective legislation covered hours of work for all labor as well as working conditions, employee safety and health, and compensation payments for injuries suffered through industrial accidents. This legislation, combined with increased workers' collective bargaining power, helped bring about substantial improvements in employment conditions.

Other developments began to impact the place of work. The mass production and assembly of standardized parts introduced changes in work methods. Then, as industrial organizations grew, ownership was spread among large numbers of stockholders who delegated management responsibilities to a new and expanding group of professional managers.

With the improvement of production techniques and labor-saving machinery, worker productivity increased, but so did overhead costs and wage rates. This led to greater attention being paid to improved utilization of equipment, facilities, and labor.

Rising labor and overhead costs forced managers to devote more effort to achieving greater production efficiency. This need stimulated a movement referred to as "scientific management," which entailed improved work methods and the establishment of production standards. These changes had a serious impact on personnel/industrial relations. The new movement stimulated the use of new personnel management tools, such as time measurement, with which to measure and motivate employee productivity. The increased pressure on labor introduced challenging human resources problems for managers.

The development of human resource management into a professional field of endeavor was aided by the knowledge and research contributions made by industrial psychology. Early research highlighted the contributions that psychology could render in the areas of testing, training, and improved work efficiency. Psychological research stimulated by World War I and World War II work and testing programs helped bring about further advances in psychological testing, performance appraisal techniques, and learning theory. In later years, research and training centers made significant progress in the areas of sensitivity training, group dynamics, personnel assessment, and organizational behavior. The contributions of industrial and organizational psychology are now utilized to achieve more effective results in the management of human resources.

LABOR-MANAGEMENT RELATIONS

The development of labor-management relations in America has been an integral part of the history of human resource management.

Union Organizations

Through the affiliation of 25 craft unions, the American Federation of Labor (AFL) was formed in 1886. It sought to improve employment conditions for its membership, and it became the first association of unions to weather depressions and employer opposition. It was a loosely organized group of autonomous national unions composed mainly of skilled craft workers.

On the other hand, the Congress of Industrial Organizations (CIO) was formed to organize the mass-production industries, and once established, these unions initiated vigorous organizing drives. Competition for members brought on bitter jurisdictional conflicts between the AFL and the CIO. However, in 1955, they united into a single AFL-CIO umbrella organization with a membership of 15.6 million. AFL-CIO membership now stands at 13.3 million.

Labor Legislation in the Private Sector

Labor legislation in America is now viewed as consisting primarily of three basic acts. The Wagner Act of 1935 (National Labor Relations Act) placed federal protection behind employee efforts to organize and bargain collectively with management through representatives of their own choosing. It established the National Labor Relations Board (NLRB), and it imposed severe penalties on employers for committing specified unfair labor practices. The Taft-Hartley Act of 1947 modified the Wagner Act and listed unfair labor practices on the part of labor. This had the effect of balancing the power of management and labor across the collective bargaining table. The Landrum-Griffin Act of

1959 (Labor-Management Reporting and Disclosure Act) attempted to correct some racketeering and corrupt practices, but most importantly, it established a "Bill of Rights for Union Members," protecting the individual member's right to vote and take part in the governance of a union.

Labor Relations in the Public Sector

Public sector labor relations are governed by executive orders, legislative acts, and state laws. Executive Order 10988, issued in 1962, provided federal employees the right to form unions, choose representation, and bargain collectively within government agencies. In 1971, Executive Order 11491 defined more precisely the bargaining rights of federal employees and created the Federal Labor Relations Council to hear appeals relating to unfair practices and bargaining issues. The Civil Service Reform Act of 1978 brought regulation of federal labor relations more in keeping with the National Labor Management Relations Act, which governs relations in the private sector, and established a Federal Labor Relations Board similar to the NLRB. Even with this act in place, labor organizations representing federal employees do not have the legal right to strike, as the Professional Air Traffic Controllers Organization (PATCO) found to its misfortune in 1981 when it struck and its members were fired. State laws provide a wide variety of provisions to govern labor-management relations in each area of jurisdiction.

EQUAL EMPLOYMENT OPPORTUNITY[2]

The matter of Equal Employment Opportunity (EEO) permeates all facets of an organization, its operations, and its human resource management. Brief descriptions of some of the major EEO legislation follow.

---

[2]This section derived from *Personnel/Human Resource Management* and *Managing Human Resources* (see bibliography).

Equal Pay Act of 1963

The Equal Pay Act is an amendment to the Fair Labor Standards Act and is administered by the EEOC. The act forbids discrimination in the areas of pay, benefits, and pensions based upon a person's gender by making it illegal for employers to pay one gender at a lower rate than the other gender for jobs of equal work. *Equal work* is defined as two or more jobs which require the same skill, responsibility, and effort within the same company under similar working conditions. For example, a city cannot pay male police dispatchers more than female dispatchers unless one of these criteria applies:

1. Pay differences for men and women are legal if they are based upon seniority, merit, or quality or quantity of work. Seniority systems are typically utilized in manufacturing settings. Historically, more men work in manufacturing than women, and men may therefore have more seniority. Thus, it is legal to pay men more than women since the pay is based upon length of service, not sex.

2. Merit pay systems are legal because pay differences are based upon skills, abilities, and performance, not sex. Pay based upon quality or quantity of work is permitted because everyone is different, and each person may produce to the best of his or her ability. Women usually have better dexterity than men, and therefore women may earn more than men under a quality/quantity system.

Civil Rights Act of 1964, Title VII

Discrimination in employment against many groups is now prohibited by law. For example, the Civil Rights Act of 1964 provides:

"It shall be unlawful employment practice for an employer (1) to fail or refuse to hire or to discharge any individual or otherwise to discriminate against any individual with respect to his compensation, terms, conditions, or privileges of employment because of such individual's race, color, religion, sex, or national origin; or (2) to limit, segregate or classify his employees in any way which would deprive or tend to deprive any individual of employment opportunities or otherwise inadvertently affect his status as an employee because of such individual's race, color, religion, sex, or national origin."

This act helped to bring about equality in hiring and job opportunity practices.

Age Discrimination in Employment Act

The Age Discrimination in Employment Act (ADEA) was enacted in 1967 and amended in 1978 and 1986. The act declares it illegal for an employer to discriminate against persons 40 years of age or older in compensation, terms, conditions, or privileges of employment. Provisions of this act may not apply if age is a job-related, bona fide occupational qualification or statutory limit.

Vocational Rehabilitation Act of 1973

This act is concerned with workers who are disabled or limited due to various physical and mental handicaps. The Vocational Rehabilitation Act and its amendments and other related legislation require contractors to take affirmative action to hire qualified handicapped people, to inform employees and unions about their affirmative action plans, and ensure that buildings financed with public money are accessible to the handicapped. Private businesses without federal contracts are not covered by the act; however, they may be subject to state laws prohibiting discrimination on the basis of physical or mental handicap.

Vietnam-Era Veterans Readjustment Act of 1974

This act requires that affirmative action in hiring and advancing Vietnam-era veterans be taken by federal contractors having contracts of $10,000 or more.

Pregnancy Discrimination Act of 1978

This act is an amendment to the Civil Rights Act of 1964. It requires that women employees affected by pregnancy, childbirth, or related medical conditions be treated equally for all employment-related purposes. The act forced changes to maternity leave policies and employee benefit programs. Pregnancy must now be treated the same as any other medical condition.

Immigration Reform and Control Act of 1986

The Immigration Reform and Control Act of 1986 prohibits employers from knowingly employing illegal aliens. It requires employers to examine applicants' identification documents and complete verification forms concerning new employees' eligibility to work legally in the United States.

Americans with Disabilities Act of 1990

The act prohibits discrimination against individuals with physical or mental disabilities and the chronically ill. The Americans with Disabilities Act (ADA) defines a disability as:

1. a physical or mental impairment that substantially limits one or more of the major life functions
2. a record of having such an impairment, or
3. being regarded as having such an impairment

An example of a person regarded as having an impairment would include a person sharing living quarters with a person of the same sex who has AIDS (Acquired Immune Deficiency Syndrome). Employers are required to provide reasonable accommodations to employees or applicants who are disabled but qualified to do the work. The accommodation must be made unless it is unreasonable or causes an undue hardship on the employer. What is unreasonable? It depends on the size of the business. A large multimillion-dollar conglomerate will be required to do more than a small sole proprietorship. Consideration includes making facilities accessible and useable, restructuring jobs, permitting part-time work, reassigning to a vacant position, or changing equipment.

Employers must now also ensure that all employees and applicants can perform the "essential functions" of the job. Essential functions can be described as the reason the job exists. For example, a clerk/typist must be able to type as one of the essential functions. That is why the position was created.

The act is now in effect for employers with 25 or more employees. Those with 15 but less than 25 employees will be covered on July 26, 1994.

Civil Rights Act of 1991

This act had several provisions that affected employers, but none had more impact than those allowing compensatory damages and jury trials. Until the 1991 Civil Rights Act (CRA) was passed, all civil rights cases were tried by judges. Now, employees or applicants could have a jury trial. Employers have a more difficult time winning these lawsuits since juries tend to side with the employee rather than the employer because of the "deep pockets" syndrome. Juries usually feel sorry for the employee and award damages even if the employer did nothing wrong. Damages allowed under the CRA include compensatory and punitive damages. These were previously available only to racial and ethnic minorities. They are now available to all victims of sex, religion, or disability discrimination. Damages are capped from $50,000 to $300,000, depending upon the size of the work force of the employer.

By now it should be evident that human resource managers must be well aware of the contents of all legislation pertaining to all aspects of people at work. HR managers must design and execute programs that comply with the requirements of law and are in keeping with good business practice. This is one of the greatest challenges in the field of HRM.

PRESENT STATUS

The field of human resource management is presently enjoying unprecedented prestige, growth, and development. Top HR managers are being moved to the vice-presidential level in increasing numbers of firms. Federal, state, and local legislation all require greater attention to the processes of management related to people at work. Conducting and supervising these processes is a major concern of the human resource managers of public and private organizations.

CHAPTER 2

HUMAN RESOURCE MANAGEMENT AS AN OCCUPATION

Service in the occupational field of human resource management entails many different functions and relationships. The HR manager serves as part of management but also advises management on personnel/HR matters. He or she is in the unique position of counseling managers and employees concerning work-related matters. There are many aspects of service in HRM.

FORMULATION OF HUMAN RESOURCE MANAGEMENT POLICY

The human resource department has tremendous influence over the day-to-day activities of everyone in an organization through its relationship with top managers in their policy formulation procedure. The top management of a company is a small group of its most important executives—usually officers—held responsible by the board of directors for operating the enterprise efficiently. One of top management's primary duties is determining policy, deciding the rules under which the organization will be managed. One of the chief responsibilities of the HR director is that of advising top management while it is in the process of formulating human resource policy.

Suppose, for example, that management is putting together a new employee vacation policy. We say, "Joe has a two-week vacation each year." But we seldom consider the thought and care that have gone into determining exactly what rules govern the length of Joe's vacation, when he gets it, and other aspects of it.

Is he eligible for a two-week vacation no matter how recently he came to the company, or must he have been employed for a certain length of time? If he has been on the payroll half that long, is he entitled to a one-week vacation? Will he always be eligible for just two weeks each year, or will he be entitled to more as his length of service with the company increases? Is his vacation to be with or without pay? Instead of taking time off, would Joe be permitted to work as usual during his vacation period? If he is allowed to do this, will he receive both his regular wages and his vacation pay? Can he take his vacation whenever he chooses, or is he assigned a time for it? Is his vacation a "gift" from the company as an expression of appreciation for loyal service, or is it something Joe has "earned"? If it is a gift, is he entitled to vacation pay even if he quits his job the day he leaves for vacation? If it is earned, and if Joe is fired for stealing company property, is he eligible at the time of discharge to receive the portion of vacation pay earned as of that date?

These questions have many implications; several pages could be written about each. And so it is with all of the personnel policies that must be established if the organization is to function smoothly—policies relating to wages, leaves of absence, pensions, transfers from job to job, disciplinary matters, promotions, employee grievances, and many others. It is the responsibility of the HR director to consult with and advise top management in the formulation of such human resource policies.

AIDING SUPERVISION

Not infrequently, a personnel worker is called upon to advise a group leader or perhaps a major executive how to improve her or his relationships with subordinates. In one office, a clerk says he quit his job "because the boss never even says 'hello' in the morning or 'good night' when I leave. I don't mind his criticizing my work when this is justified, but I'm tired of being ignored." The personnel worker investigated the situation and found that other clerks in the department felt the same way. The personnel worker tipped off the supervisor, who was amazed to discover how quickly employees responded to a cheery "good morning" and to an occasional kind word for a job well done. The atmosphere in the office changed completely, and each day employees accomplished more work. The single most valuable contribution a personnel worker can make is that of helping supervision at all levels to cement the boss-employee relationship.

SUPERVISOR-EMPLOYEE RELATIONSHIPS

It is a truism that a chain is only as strong as its weakest link. In the same way, an organization is as strong—as effective—as the individual relationships between its supervisors and the employees reporting directly to them.

How an employee and boss get along together, the extent to which they enjoy mutual respect, and the degree to which each spontaneously backs up the other in time of crisis—these are the keys to determining whether an organization will function smoothly and how effective it will be in attaining its objectives. This is why the relationship between worker and supervisor must be regarded as highly personal and why the most important obligation of the personnel worker is to use every opportunity to help build, maintain, and cement these relationships throughout the organization. Human resource workers must, at all costs, guard against interfering with them.

Joan was a fine administrative assistant and was recognized throughout the company as one of the best. She was among the few people who could get along harmoniously with her immediate supervisor, an absent-minded, cantankerous curmudgeon who forgot important details unless reminded of them—usually by Joan. One day, obviously upset,

Joan came to the HR department: most of the other administrative assistants had received salary increases, but she had not. She was sure she merited one and that her boss merely had neglected to take care of the matter. What could be done? Without a moment's hesitation, the personnel worker told her to take the problem to the man for whom she worked. The employee relations worker emphasized that the matter rested solely between Joan and her boss and that the human resource department had nothing to do with it. She had considered going to her boss, Joan responded, but could not bring herself to do so. Her boss was difficult at best, and now was not a time to approach him on a matter of this kind, for he was deeply absorbed in a demanding engineering problem of vital importance to the company. If facing that boss was her only alternative, she would have to consider seeking a job elsewhere. She left the human resource department disappointed, though understanding why the personnel worker would not intercede in her behalf as she had hoped.

The next day, the personnel worker happened to see Joan's boss in the corridor and, without mentioning her visit, said casually that in going over the records she had noticed that it was past time for Joan to have a salary increase if she merited one. Joan's boss thanked her for the reminder. A week later, Joan received a raise. She rushed to thank the personnel worker. She chided Joan, however, saying, "Thank your boss, not me. You work for him, not me. He gave you the raise, not me. Apparently he is deeply engrossed in this project right now and was simply not aware of the oversight. He is certainly appreciative of your merits and is willing to reward you for them."

In another company, at the end of a highly successful year in which exceptionally high profits had been realized, management decided to give all employees a bonus—an unprecedented thing for the corporation to do. The announcement was to be signed by the president and posted on the bulletin board. But the HR department objected. Though the final announcement made it clear that the bonus came from the company, each employee's copy of the announcement was signed by an immediate superior.

There are many ways in which the relationship between an employee and an immediate supervisor can be improved, and personnel workers should take advantage of each opportunity to strengthen the organization.

ROLE OF HUMAN RESOURCE MANAGEMENT IN ORGANIZATIONS

The human resource office of any organization performs several functions. One of its primary duties is to keep the organization staffed with the best-qualified personnel available. Another vital function is to perform administrative matters related to personnel—record keeping, promotions, wage and salary classifications, and processing and keeping track of vacation credits and sick leave taken. The personnel office is also responsible for dealing with the human resource aspects of the overall management of the organization.

FUNCTIONS OF AN ENTERPRISE

The term *function* means an ongoing activity that must be performed in order for an enterprise to continue its operation. For example, training is an ongoing function necessary to the development of personnel. There are certain basic functions performed in all organizations.

Financing

Financing, or capitalizing, means obtaining funds necessary to establish and continue operating an enterprise. In the public sector, the government provides funds to establish and operate the various government agencies. The California State University at Long Beach, for example, is allocated a certain amount of money each year in order to carry out its duties and obligations to faculty, administration, students, and the general public.

Budgeting/Accounting

A budget is a plan stating the intended utilization of allocated funds in order to carry out the duties and responsibilities assigned the enterprise. Budgeting is the process. Within the Nissan Motor Corporation in the United States, for example, a certain amount of money is allocated (budgeted) for the purchase of training equipment. Another sum is assigned for maintenance of buildings. While budgeting is a process that states the intention of the agency for the allocation of funds, accounting is the process of keeping track of how the funds are actually spent. The budgeting function results in a statement of intent (budget) concerning how to use the funds available to carry out the responsibilities of an organization. The accounting function keeps track of how funds are actually expended during the period of the budget— usually a year, At the end of the budget period, a comparison can be made between the intended allocation of funds and the actual expenditures. In a well-managed organization, free from natural disasters and other uncontrollable forces, the allocations and expenditures should match closely. Managers review the effectiveness of the budget or allocation plan. They may ask, "Did the funds allocated actually achieve the purpose for which they were intended?"

Production/Service

The purpose of an organization can be viewed as either production or providing a service. Some organizations make a product such as television sets or machine parts. Others provide a service such as transportation, banking, or education. The missions of many organizations include both production and service. All managers must keep in mind the mission of their organization so that the performance of their duties supports that mission. Telephone manufacture, for example, is quite different from telephone service.

Marketing

Marketing means selling a product or service and includes such aspects as pricing, distributing, and advertising. In the private sector, it is easy to understand the marketing function in relation to such matters as selling clothes or repairing automobiles. In the public sector, agencies may have to charge for part or all of the services provided and also must advertise to make the general public aware of the availability of the service.

Human Resource Management

There are many activities concerning the management of personnel or human resources in any organization. These are considered in more detail later in this chapter.

Management/Administration

There are many activities that must be carried out in order to make an enterprise operate. For example, there are decisions to be made such as whether a clothing store will deal only in street wear or take on a line of sports wear. Enterprises must operate within the provisions of current legislation: "Does our pay schedule meet established guidelines? What about safety? Racial balance?"

Human resource management is one of the central functions performed in the management of all enterprises, private or public, profit or nonprofit, large or small.

SPECIALTY AREAS OF HUMAN
RESOURCE MANAGEMENT

In a large enterprise, the human resource department might be divided into two managerial categories—personnel relations and labor relations—and further divided into specialty or functional sections. Eight sections are used in this book to illustrate a possible structure. Typical tasks performed within these sections of the human resource department are shown in the organization chart appearing later in this chapter and are briefly described below.

Employment and Placement

This section has principal responsibility for finding and placing employees, including recruitment, interviewing, testing, selection, placement, promotion, transfer, and termination.

There are specialized techniques for recruiting job applicants, and there is an art to selecting those best suited for job openings. The employment interviewer must identify the most qualified candidates, and from them, the supervisor makes a final choice. Supervisors must have confidence in the interviewers, because they depend on their judgments to find the right person for each job opening.

The size of a company plays a part in determining which member of the personnel department team performs the interviewing function. Usually in a large department, it is the duty of one or more specialists, while the personnel manager maintains general supervision. In all cases, of course, the manager establishes the basic policies and procedures to be followed. In a smaller company, the manager may do some or all of the interviewing. The personnel department serves as a filter, screening job applicants who will ultimately be hired by the supervisor in whose department a vacancy exists.

An interview is not merely a conversation, though a skilled interviewer tries to make it seem so. The interviewer must endeavor to elicit information that reveals the applicant's character, note clues to personality makeup, ascertain what the applicant's schooling and work experience have been, and determine what the applicant's career objectives are. Though much of this latter information can be gleaned from the application form or resume, the interviewer must be familiar with questioning techniques designed to bring out specific information and reveal the applicant's personal feelings in areas important to the company if he or she expects to determine the candidate's potential. For some jobs the candidate's dress, attitude, and general behavior may be important; for others these may be of little importance. The procedure must be performed carefully and within Equal Employment Opportunity (EEO) guidelines, which will be discussed later.

The value of using psychological tests in the course of interviewing is controversial, and psychologists justifiably frown upon their use by persons not trained to administer them properly and to interpret results accurately. Certain tests have been devised specifically for the use of those untrained in psychology, and in some companies employment interviewers are called upon to use them. Test ratings should be used sparingly, however, and never exclusively, to determine whether an applicant is qualified to be hired.

Typical titles for the person who conducts initial employment interviews are employment manager, employment supervisor, or personnel assistant. This person's principal duties include planning for staffing requirements; recruiting personnel for sales, technical, nonprofessional, professional, supervisory, and managerial positions; analyzing jobs and preparing job descriptions; processing transfers, promotions, terminations, layoffs, returns from layoffs, and claims for severance pay; and conducting exit interviews.

When you apply for a job, you can expect to complete a form. Then you will be interviewed and possibly tested. If you are selected for the job, it is usually because you have received approval from the person who will be your immediate supervisor. The duties you perform in the job will be determined by the supervisor and the employment manager, who get together and decide the kinds of work that must be performed in that position.

Determining Personnel Requirements. Considerable lead time is required to recruit, select, and train employees for many of the jobs in an organization. Therefore, job vacancies must be anticipated as far as possible in advance. A company's work load and personnel requirement are determined by the product, sales, or services provided. Effective planning helps the company anticipate customer demand. The pressure of unions for stabilized employee turnover has caused many companies to devote more time to human resource planning in an effort to minimize fluctuations in the work force.

Through the use of forecasting techniques, a company may be able to discover cyclical trends affecting sales and organizational growth and to project these trends into the future as a means of predicting its own business activity. Temporary fluctuations in the rate of production need not necessitate any changes in the size of the regular work force. Adjustments to temporary increases in the work load can be accomplished through the use of overtime, by subcontracting some of the work, or by utilizing the services of companies that supply temporary personnel.

Public agencies such as educational institutions and hospitals must also operate efficiently within established budgets. Many of these public enterprises experience fluctuations in the demand for their services.

The personnel requirements of an organization, which are determined by the volume of work being performed by it, must be translated into specific job allocations. Authority to fill positions is limited by departmental payroll budgets that specify the positions to be filled and the wages to be paid to each new worker.

Recruiting Personnel. An organization can develop an effective work force only if it is able to recruit the best-qualified people. Such individuals may already be employed in other positions in the organization or they may be recruited from the outside.

An employer should neither neglect nor rely too heavily upon internal sources for personnel. The use of internal sources can be beneficial to morale and can enable an organization to realize a return from the training investment it has in its employees. Computerized information systems have made possible the use of data banks covering the qualifications of each employee. An organization can screen its entire work force quickly to locate candidates who have the qualifications required to fill a specific opening. These data can also be used to prepare personnel reports pertaining to work force statistics, labor costs, absenteeism, and employee turnover by job classes, department, or for the organization as a whole. Computerized data can be used to plan the career paths of people in organizations and to anticipate the openings and staffing requirements that will result from attrition.

There are many sources from which personnel may be recruited. The major external sources of applicants include the following:

Advertising
Educational institutions
Employment agencies
Employee referrals
Unsolicited applications
Professional organizations
Labor unions

The effectiveness of advertising as a recruitment device depends on the nature of the appeal that it makes to readers. The growing demand for people with the advanced education required for jobs in the scientific, technical, or administrative fields has prompted many employers to do more recruiting at educational institutions. These institutions screen out many of the less interested or less capable students. Most schools and colleges operate placement services that provide the personal history records of those graduates who seek employment. These services can be of assistance to recruiters by helping them to locate and to arrange interviews with qualified candidates and to disseminate company brochures, handbooks, and other literature about the company to interested persons.

Employment agencies differ considerably in terms of their policies, services, costs, and the type of applicants that can be obtained through them. Some agencies are publicly supported or are operated on a nonprofit basis, while others operate as profit-making enterprises and charge a fee to the applicant or the employer. Public employment offices are maintained in most of the larger communities throughout the nation, and part-time offices are located in many of the smaller ones. Because they charge fees, private agencies tend to provide more specialized employment services than public agencies, and they often cater to a specific type of clientele. The growing need for people with proven managerial ability and experience has encouraged the growth of consulting firms that specialize in the recruitment of management personnel.

Employees may help their employer locate qualified applicants by referring friends and acquaintances to job openings. High morale can make employees boosters of their organization and can contribute to the recruitment effort.

Most companies receive inquiries about employment from people representing a variety of backgrounds and qualifications. Unsolicited sources may not yield a very high percentage of acceptable candidates, but they should not be ignored. The fact that individuals take the initiative to apply for employment may indicate that they have a definite interest in the company.

Many professional organizations operate a placement service for the benefit of members and employers. The regional and national meetings of technical and professional societies attract many recruiters. Labor unions are a principal source of applicants for blue collar jobs.

Generally underdeveloped sources of workers include the culturally and economically disadvantaged. Because of their lack of education or job skills or because they had a past record that was considered undesirable, disadvantaged members of society have had little chance of being selected for employment, much less being sought for it. Contemporary programs now seek people for jobs.

Women can be recruited through both conventional and special sources. It should be understood, however, that all recruiting must be performed within the provisions of the following legislation: 1964 Civil Rights Act, Title VII; Executive Orders; Age Discrimination in Employment Acts; Vocational Rehabilitation Act of 1973; Vietnam-Era

Veterans Readjustment Act of 1974; Immigration Reform and Control Act of 1986; and state and local employment laws.

Wage and Salary Administration

This section of the personnel department has principal responsibility for coordinating the wage and salary program in an organization.

Although a company need not deal with all of its employees in precisely the same manner, all want to be treated equitably. It would not do, for example, for salaries to be increased every twelve months in one department and only every eighteen months in another. Nor would it be fair for one supervisor to increase the hourly pay rate of machinists in a department by five cents while another supervisor in the same shop gives an eight-cent raise to workers doing the same type of work. There are special techniques for avoiding inequities of this kind, and the essence of wage and salary administration is the application of these techniques.

When an employee of a small company receives an increase in her or his compensation, usually the employer has made the decision to grant it. But when those on the payroll of a large company are recipients of such an increase, they seldom have any concept of its cost to their employer or the amount of time and deliberation that has gone into determining how large the raise is to be.

The wage and salary administrator must make a detailed study of the company's pay rates compared with those of nearby firms that depend upon the same labor market. This calls for a community wage and salary survey. For this to be accurate, comparison cannot be made on the basis of job titles alone; an accounting clerk in one firm, for example, may be performing far more difficult or much easier tasks than an accounting clerk in another. Instead, a comparison is made between the amount paid in the personnel worker's company for performing a specified combination of tasks—no matter what the job title—with that paid in other companies for (as nearly as possible) the same mixture of duties. The degree of similarity between jobs is determined by matching previously prepared job descriptions item by item.

The result of such a survey is not the only factor upon which the personnel director's recommendations are based. Any increases or decreases in cost of living that may have occurred since the last pay adjustment was made as well as changes in compensation contemplated by nearby companies and other pertinent factors in the labor market must also be considered.

The wage and salary administrators must compile the statistics that the personnel director needs to decide policy recommendations. The personnel director will be expected to furnish top management with statistics to help them make the final determination. For example, let us assume that there are 4,000 hourly wage earners in the company and that they work an average of 40 hours per week. Each must be paid for 2,080 (40 × 52) hours per year, including vacation time. If each receives a pay increase of one cent per hour, the cost to the company will be $20.80 (2,080 × .01) yearly per person, or $83,200 ($20.80 × 4,000) yearly for all hourly paid employees.

Now let us further suppose that there are 300 clerical workers in the company on the pay scales indicated.

From this demonstration you see that when the personnel director undertakes to prepare annual wage and salary adjustment recommendations, he or she is faced with a sizable task.

150 workers	$5 per hour =	$750 per hour
50 workers	$6 per hour =	$300
50 workers	$7 per hour =	$350
50 workers	$8 per hour =	$400

Total   = $1,800 per hour
$1,800 per hour × 40 hours per week   = $72,000 per week
$72,000 per week × 52 weeks per year = $3,744,000 per year
                              (wages for clerical workers)

In a small organization, it may be feasible to manage wages and salaries informally. However, in order to administer them equitably when there are several thousand employees on the payroll, in order to provide a realistic basis for the hiring of personnel, and in order to get and keep the best personnel possible, the duties involved in each job must be spelled out in writing. This means that each job in a company must be evaluated in relation to what is being paid for identical and differing tasks in the same company as well as in neighboring concerns. In addition, each employee's job performance must periodically be appraised to ensure that it is being maintained at specific standards.

Thus, a job evaluation is a technique of judging the worth of similar and different kinds of jobs. It can rank the importance and value of one job as opposed to another within an organization. Or a job evaluation can compare similar jobs within different enterprises. It is important to note that a job evaluation does not measure the worth of the performance of the person doing the job; it simply establishes the range within which the salary or wage paid for the job should be pegged.

Before such an evaluation can be made, however, the job must be broken down into its component parts and a formalized description of it set forth on paper.

The benefits of a written job description are manifold. It clarifies for the employee and the boss precisely what is involved in the job—what is expected of the worker. It serves to inform a job applicant of the duties he or she will be expected to perform if hired. It is a basis for evaluating the performance of an employee on the job. And, as previously pointed out, it is the basis also for evaluating the job itself in terms of the salary or wage range established for it.

Once again, the role of the HR director in such a job evaluation and job description program depends on the company. In a large concern, the HR director is likely to have someone on the employee relations staff who specializes in wage and salary administration. On the other hand, consultants in this aspect of personnel management may be called in, with the HR director acting as liaison among consultant, employees, and management.

Typical titles for this individual are wage and salary administrator, salary administrator, or assistant personnel director.

This person coordinates the evaluation of jobs for compensation purposes, assigns labor grades or classifications to jobs, establishes and maintains wage and salary structures, conducts wage and salary surveys, checks compensation policies and practices for compliance with laws and regulations, and maintains records and files dealing with wages and related data.

Do you think you should be paid more for the work you are doing? Maybe you should. But the wage you are paid is based on the classification or job rating of the position you hold.

Importance of Financial Compensation. Money that employees receive for their services is important to them not only for what it buys but also for what it provides in terms of status and recognition within the organization. Money represents a quantifiable measure of worth; therefore, employees are sensitive about the amount of their pay and how it compares with other employees'. Wage payments must be equitable both in terms of an employee's performance and in terms of what other employees are receiving for their performance.

Compensation forms a basis for judging whether the money an employee receives is fair in terms of the employee's perceived contributions. According to equity theory, every employee expects that a certain relationship will exist between personal input—what the employee contributes to the job in terms of skill and effort—and personal outcome—what the employee receives from the job in terms of pay and other rewards. If the outcome doesn't match expectations, the employee experiences a feeling of inequity and resentment.

Effective communication is necessary to assure employees that they are being treated equitably in terms of their compensation. An effective communication system facilitates feedback from employees concerning the relative importance that they attach to the various financial and nonfinancial rewards.

Determining Compensation. An effective compensation system contributes to the achievement of the overall objectives of an organization by motivating employees toward this end and by providing adequate controls that keep labor costs and employee productivity commensurate with each other. The most common system by which employees are paid is based on time. Blue collar jobs traditionally have been paid on an hourly or daily basis and are commonly referred to as day work. Workers compensated on this basis are classified as hourly employees or wage earners. Those employees whose compensation is computed on a weekly or monthly basis, on the other hand, are classified as salaried employees. Traditionally, hourly employees are paid only for the time that they work, whereas salaried employees are compensated for performing the work they are hired to do regardless of time.

Day work is the most common system of compensation because it is easy to understand and administer. It enables both management and employees to compute wage payments readily. In order to provide employees with a financial incentive that may increase their productivity, they may be paid according to the number of units they produce under a system of piecework.

There are many factors that may help to determine the wage rates established for various jobs. Wages for jobs requiring specific qualifications may be affected by the availability and demand for personnel with these qualifications. However, restraints created by such factors as government regulations and union bargaining power will prevent the forces of supply and demand from operating freely. Data obtained from community wage surveys help personnel managers determine how closely their wages conform to the pattern in the community.

Because of continued inflation during the past three decades, wage rates have been adjusted upward periodically in order for employees to maintain purchasing power. These adjustments have been accomplished through formulas that tie wage increases to the Consumer Price Index (C.P.I.), according to an escalator clause in a labor agreement, or as the result of collective bargaining. Or they may result also from employer efforts to maintain equity and fairness in compensation.

Other factors affect compensation. A company's ability to pay is influenced by such economic conditions as its competitive position within its industry and the prosperity that exists within its geographic region. If the work force is unionized, wages and other conditions of employment are determined primarily through the process of collective bargaining. Bargaining arguments based upon prevailing wage rates, cost of living, ability to pay, or any other factors may favor either one party or the other. The wage rate that is finally agreed upon is likely to be due more to the comparative economic pressures that the two parties are able to exert upon each other than it is to the logic of their arguments.

Job Evaluation. The relative worth of a job may be determined by comparing the job with others within the organization or by comparing it with a scale. Methods of comparison may be made on the basis of the jobs as a whole or on the basis of the factors comprising the jobs.

The point system is relatively simple to understand and to use. This system permits jobs to be evaluated quantitatively on the basis of the elements that constitute the demands of the job. The skills, efforts, responsibilities, and working conditions that a job usually involves are typical of the more common major factors that make one job more or less important than another. The point system requires the use of a point manual that indicates the number of points allocated to each factor and to each of the degrees into which these factors are divided.

The factor comparison system is a system in which the specifications of the jobs to be evaluated are compared with the specifications of key jobs within the organization that serve as the job evaluation scale. The factors of skill, mental effort, physical effort, responsibility, and working conditions are typical of those comprising the factor comparison scale. Key jobs include those of varying difficulty for which complete and accurate descriptions and specifications have been developed.

The job grade or classification system permits jobs to be classified and grouped according to a series of predetermined wage classes or grades. The system has the advantage of simplicity since the job is evaluated as a whole. The federal civil service job classification system is possibly the best known system of this type. The descriptions for each of the job classes contain the elements for comparison. The number of classes that are required for the system will depend upon the range of duties, responsibilities, skills, and other requirements that exist among the jobs to be evaluated and the degree to which finances are to discriminate one class from another.

The simplest and oldest system of job evaluation is the job ranking or order of merit. In this system, jobs are arrayed on the basis of their relative worth. One technique that is used to rank jobs consists of having the raters arrange cards containing the specifications for each job in their order of importance. Differences in the rankings made by the raters can then be reconciled into a single rating.

Rate Structure. The evaluated worth of each job in terms of its rank, class, points, or monetary worth must be converted into an appropriate wage rate. The rate of pay that is established for a particular job also must give recognition to such external factors as labor market conditions, prevailing wage rates, living costs, union negotiated rates, and legal minimums.

The relationship between the relative worth of the jobs and the rates they are paid can be represented by means of a wage curve or conversion line. The wage curve normally will indicate the relationship between the evaluated worth of jobs and the wages currently being paid.

It may be preferable to group the jobs into wage classes or grades and to pay all jobs within a particular class the same rate or rate range. The relation between wage classes and rates also may be determined by means of a conversion table.

The final step in the job evaluation process is to determine the proper wage class into which each job should be placed on the basis of its evaluated worth. Job evaluation and classification traditionally are concerned with the job rather than the qualifications of the person performing it.

Government Regulation of Wages. One of the principal laws affecting wages is the Fair Labor Standards Act of 1938. It covers employees who are engaged in the production of goods for interstate and foreign commerce, including those who work in areas closely related to such production. The major provisions of the act cover minimum wage rates, overtime payments, and child labor. The minimum wage prescribed by the law has been raised from the original figure of 25 cents per hour to the present rate of $4.25 per hour. An overtime rate of one-and-a-half times the base rate must be paid for all hours worked in excess of 40 during any single week. The act forbids the employment of minors between the ages of 16 and 18 in hazardous occupations such as mining, logging, woodworking, meat packing, and certain types of manufacturing,

Training and Development

The duties of this section include principal responsibility for planning, organizing, and directing training activities. Although the broad field of training is now frequently referred to as human resource development (HRD), the process and function are usually still called training.

Many personnel departments administer training programs to help rank-and-file workers improve their job skills and perhaps be upgraded into jobs requiring greater skill. Some companies have programs, entirely independent of those devoted to training, designed to develop executive potential among those in lower-echelon supervisory positions. Other companies recruit potential executives from college campuses, and still other companies provide comprehensive training for all new employees regardless of rank.

A company's training program is commonly the responsibility of the HR director. Since training is a highly specialized area, the HR director usually has within the department a specialist in this field. However, when certain employees within the organization are to be trained, the HR director does not select them, since line supervisors are the ones who know the employees' capabilities and how they perform on their current jobs. It is these supervisors who can best evaluate the potential of those who report directly to them.

Typical titles for this position are director of training, manager of human resource development, manager of personnel training and development, and training coordinator. The principal duties of this person are directing and coordinating the training programs that may include the following types of training: on-the-job, apprentice, supervisory, sales, and management. This person consults with other managers concerning training and development needs, prepares manuals and other materials for use in training sessions, and counsels employees concerning training opportunities.

If you worked in the training and development section of the HR department, what would you do if management decided there was a need for more welders? Set up a training program? How much would a program cost? Who would instruct? You would find that if there were a need to train only a few people, outside schooling might be better than internal instruction.

Employees require continuous development if their potential is to be utilized. Employee development programs usually include a wide variety of activities. The primary purpose of these activities is to encourage the development of employees so they will contribute more effectively to the goals of the organization and will gain a greater sense of satisfaction from their work.

An orientation program should give new employees an understanding of how their jobs contribute to the success of the organization and how the services or products of the organization contribute to society. The personnel department is ordinarily responsible for coordinating orientation activities and for providing information concerning conditions of employment, pay and benefits, and other matters not directly under the supervisor's direction.

In a large organization, the personnel department provides managers and supervisors with considerable assistance in conducting training, organizing classes, selecting and training instructors, procuring equipment and other aids, and working with educational institutions and government agencies. Frequently, in larger organizations, these activities are handled by separate training divisions within the personnel department. In smaller organizations, however, most of the training is arranged by the managers and supervisors of the departments that are concerned.

Managers should be alert to signs indicating that employees require training. If production records show that workers are not achieving production standards, additional training may be required. Similarly, an excessive number of rejects or material waste may be caused by inadequate training. An increase in the number of accidents may be an indication that employees need safety training.

While training represents a positive approach to the improvement of performance, it cannot provide the solution to all such problems. For example, if production has fallen off because workers are disgruntled and resentful over inadequate pay, additional training is not likely to increase production.

Training Methods. Several different methods of training are available. In large organizations, most of these methods will be used.

On-the-job training. This kind of training is conducted by the supervisor right on the job as it is being performed. It has the advantage of providing firsthand experience under normal working conditions. It also provides an opportunity for the supervisor to build a good relationship with the new employee.

Vestibule schools. Large business organizations frequently provide what are called "vestibule schools" as a preliminary to actual shop experience. As far as possible, shop conditions are duplicated, but instruction, not output, is the major objective, with special instructors provided.

Conference training. This is individualized instruction by a supervisor where the training involves primarily the communication of ideas, procedures, and standards. This method allows for considerable variation in the amount of employee participation.

Apprenticeship training. In apprenticeship training, the young worker entering industry is given thorough instruction and experience, both on and off the job, in the practical and theoretical aspects of a skilled trade. These programs require cooperation between management and labor unions, industry and government, and the company and the school system.

Classroom training. Training in the classroom provides for teaching the maximum number of trainees with a minimum number of instructors. It lends itself particularly well to areas of instruction where information can be imparted by lectures, demonstrations, films, and other audiovisual materials.

Programmed instruction. Organizations are making increasing use of programmed instruction in both employee and executive development. Programmed instruction breaks down subject matter content into highly organized, logical sequences that demand continuous responses on the part of the trainee. After being presented a small segment of information, the trainee is required to answer a question either by writing an answer in a response frame or by pushing a button on a machine. If the response is incorrect, the trainee is given further explanatory information and is instructed to try again. Computer-assisted training programs are now being used extensively.

Simulators. By simulating hazardous conditions, personnel may be given training and experience under safe conditions. Simulator design emphasizes realism in equipment and its operation so that the trainee learns how to perform the tasks in a setting as close to the actual circumstances as possible.

Development of Managers. Management development programs tend to be broader and longer range in nature than those for operative employees. Rather than trying to develop skills to perform specific jobs, management programs are mainly concerned with development in the broader sense, including skills, knowledge, attitudes, abilities, perceptions, and personality traits that are considered essential to the performance of assignments. Management development programs have become well established and accepted in the more progressive organizations as an essential personnel function.

Current emphasis in management development focuses on individual redevelopment and the needs of all management personnel rather than just those at the lower levels. There is also a trend to place more emphasis upon organization development in order to further individual and team growth. Organization development is concerned with the environment and culture of the organization, with locating and solving organization problems, and with making the changes necessary to achieve growth. Management organization development programs are considered a subsystem closely integrated and interrelated with human resource planning, management assessment, performance appraisal, and human resource accounting systems that comprise the total personnel management system. Management development programs generally provide a variety of activities and experiences for participants.

Coaching. Coaching is the process of assisting people perform their managerial duties and responsibilities more effectively. It permits individuals to profit fully from work experiences as they receive assistance from those who have acquired greater wisdom and experience. Coaching is frequently used in conjunction with a management-by-objectives (MBO) program, which focuses attention on work achievements rather than individual characteristics.

Understudy. Staff assistant jobs can provide development opportunities for those assigned as understudies to senior executives. An understudy has the opportunity to learn much about her or his superior's job and techniques for handling it. The benefits to the understudy depend on the time and interest devoted by the superior.

Rotation. Job rotation is intended to provide a greater variety of work experience for the manager. Rotation usually is among jobs on the same organizational level and for short periods. The value of rotational training depends in large part upon the amount of supervision that trainees receive and upon the seriousness with which they pursue their assignments.

Projects. Projects or task force assignments provide managers the opportunity to become involved in studying current organizational problems or in planning and decision-making activities. These can be both interesting and profitable for the participants.

Staff meetings. Participation in staff meetings offers another means of increasing knowledge and understanding. These meetings enable participants to become more familiar with problems and events that are occurring outside of their immediate area and expose them to the ideas and thinking of other managers.

Organizational training courses. Many large organizations have formal training courses of their own for management personnel. While these courses usually are lectures or conferences, some are conducted on a home-study basis. Frequently covered subjects include courses dealing with human relations, supervision, personnel administration, labor relations, general economics, general management, and communications. Case studies are useful for helping executives learn how to obtain and interpret facts, to be conscious of the many variables upon which management decisions are based, and in general to improve their decision-making skills.

In-basket training. This is another way to simulate a problem situation. In this technique, the participants are given several documents, each describing some problem or situation, the solution of which requires an immediate decision on the part of the trainee.

Management games. Case situations are brought to life through the development of management games. Participants who play the game must make a continuing series of decisions affecting the enterprise. The simulated effects that each decision has upon each functional area within the enterprise is determined by a computer that has been programmed for the game.

Role-playing. Role-playing consists of assuming the attitudes and behavior of and acting out the roles of the individuals who are involved in a personnel problem—usually those of a supervisor and a subordinate. Role-playing helps participants improve their ability to understand and to cope with the problems of others.

Sensitivity training. One of the executive training methods that has grown rapidly in popularity is sensitivity training. This method is used with small groups whose members work together for a number of days. Sensitivity training once had primarily a psychotherapeutic orientation as far as management development is concerned. Its emphasis more recently has been sociological. Current sensitivity training programs have tended to produce more organization and job-oriented discussion with less probing into personal feeling and behavior than they did in the past.

Professional reading. Many larger organizations maintain extensive business and technical libraries for their personnel. Executives are encouraged to make maximum use of these facilities as a means of improving their knowledge and of keeping abreast of the latest management practices.

Performance Evaluation. Performance evaluation is an integral part of any total personnel development program. Performance evaluation occurs whether or not there is a formal evaluation program in an organization. Employers and supervisors are constantly observing the manner in which subordinates carry out their job assignments. They also form impressions about employees' relative worth to the organization. Most of the larger and many smaller organizations have developed formal programs that are designed to facilitate and to standardize the evaluation of employees.

Merit rating is a term still used in referring to evaluations of employees in jobs that are typically paid on an hourly basis. However, with the extension of performance evaluation programs to personnel in white collar and managerial jobs, such terms as *performance appraisal* and *performance evaluation* have become popular. Although performance evaluation programs may serve many purposes, they are designed primarily to improve job performance.

Employee Benefits and Services

Duties here involve principal responsibility for programs of benefits and employee services, including communications, recreation, counseling, and others.

Typical titles of this position include manager of personnel services, assistant HR director, or director of employee benefits and services.

The person's principal duties include administering company insurance, disability, pension programs, and a variety of other benefits and services for employees; recording sick leave credits, reviewing requests for vacations and claims for worker's compensation, unemployment insurance or severance pay; and possibly representing the company at hearings related to these claims. Other functions include responsibility for employee communication, including newspapers, suggestion systems, handbooks, and the maintenance of bulletin boards; directing recreational or social programs for employees; and, in some instances, directing food service and advisory services for veteran's affairs. This person may counsel employees on work-related personal problems.

If you are assigned to the employee benefits and services section, you will deal with an almost endless variety of personal problems, all of which are vital to the interest of the individual employee concerned. A man approaches you hesitantly and explains that his wife has worked for the company for twelve years. Yesterday she was hospitalized as the result of an off-the-job automobile accident. What should he do? You will have to advise him concerning the rights and benefits of the employee in this situation.

The most important form of income security for employees is that achieved through continuous employment. However, every person employed must at some time leave that employment—through retirement, layoff, discharge, injury resulting in disability, resignation, death, or termination of the job. To guard against the disastrous effects of such eventualities, provisions are made to provide for the security of the employee. In this sense, security is meant to be providing some income for people when their regular source of income is cut off for any of the mentioned reasons. Other benefits accruing to employees under the heading of benefits and services include those intended to make employment attractive and to provide incentives for high productivity and faithful service.

Unemployment Income. The primary source of income for individuals whose employment has been terminated is that provided by the unemployment insurance portion of the federal Social Security program.

State unemployment compensation. Employees who have been working in employment covered by the Social Security Act and who are laid off may be eligible for unemployment compensation during their unemployment. The period of time the eligibility lasts may vary, according to the state law and the economic conditions of the times, from 26 weeks to 52 weeks and in some instances longer. Eligible persons must apply to their state employment agency for unemployment compensation, register for available work, and be willing to accept any suitable employment that may be offered to them.

The amount of the compensation that a worker is eligible to receive varies among states. It is determined by the worker's previous wage rate and period of employment. Funds for unemployment compensation are derived from a payroll tax based on the wages paid to each employee up to an established maximum. A separate account record is maintained for each employer, and when the required reserve has been accumulated in this account, the rate of tax is reduced. Because of this sliding tax rate, the employer has an added incentive not to lay off personnel, since the unemployment compensation that these personnel will receive will deplete this reserve account and cause the payroll tax rate to increase again.

Supplemental benefits. Supplementary Unemployment Benefits (SUB) are paid by those firms that have agreed to it as a result of the collective bargaining agreements between the managements and unions. The SUB plan permits an employee who receives a layoff to draw, in addition to state unemployment compensation, weekly benefits from the company that are paid from a special fund created for this purpose. Employer liability under the plan is limited to the amount of money that has been accumulated within the fund from employer contributions based on the number of hours of work performed.

Disability Income. There are several ways in which employees may be compensated during periods when they are unable to work because of illness or injury. Most of those in public employment as well as many in private industry, particularly in white collar jobs, receive a set number of sick leave days each year to cover absence for health reasons. Loss of income during absences resulting from job-incurred injuries can be reimbursed, at least partially, by means of worker's compensation insurance. Laws providing for such compensation have been enacted by each of the fifty states. These laws, however, vary somewhat among states in terms of the exemptions in their coverage and benefit provisions.

Worker's compensation laws may be classified as compulsory or elective. Under a compulsory law, every employer subject to it is required to comply with its provisions for the compensation of work injuries. These acts are compulsory for the employee also. An elective law is one in which the employer has the option of either accepting or rejecting the act. If employers reject it, they lose the customary common law defenses—assumed risk of the employment, negligence of a fellow servant, and contributory negligence.

Benefits. Worker's compensation laws typically provide that the injured employee will be paid a disability benefit that is usually based on a percentage of wages. Each state also specifies the length of the period of payment and usually indicates a maximum amount that may be paid. In addition to the disability benefits, provision is made for payment of some medical and hospitalization expenses and some costs of rehabilitation, and in all states, death benefits are paid to survivors of the employee.

Financing. The worker's compensation benefits prescribed by law in the various states generally are financed by the employers through insurance. A few states require employees to make a small contribution.

Retirement Income. The source of retirement income upon which most workers depend is that provided by the federal Social Security program. In most government as well as certain private employment, however, benefits are provided for employees by means of other private pension plans. Pension plans continue to grow. A recent Bureau of National Affairs study revealed that over 90 percent of the production workers in manufacturing were covered by pension plans. The economic downturn of the 1990s, however, is casting some doubt on the reliability of the coverage.

Pension size. Numerous factors affect the amount of pension employees receive. One of the most important factors is the amount of funds the employer allocates for pensions. The share of this fund that is to comprise a particular individual's pension usually is determined by such factors as years of service, the earning level attained by the employee, and in some instances, the amount of that person's Social Security payments. The size of the pension also will be affected by the amount, if any, that the employee contributes to it.

Abuses. In the past, many private pension plans have proven to be illusory because employees covered by them have received benefits much smaller than had been promised or have received no benefits at all. Such conditions led to the passage of the Pension Reform Law, officially entitled the Employee Retirement Income Security Act of 1975 (ERISA). The provisions of this act are discussed later in this book.

Social Security. Social Security is not a pension system but rather an insurance system designed to protect those covered by it against loss of earnings resulting from various causes. In addition to protecting those covered against the loss of earnings due to retirement, Social Security insurance is intended to protect employees against losses caused by unemployment and disability. It also protects their families against loss of income in the event of their death.

Coverage and financing. In order to receive benefits under the Social Security Act, an individual must have been engaged in some form of employment that is covered by the law. Most employment by private enterprise and most types of self-employment including farming, active military service after 1956, and employment in certain nonprofit organizations and government agencies are subject to coverage under the act.

The Social Security program is supported by means of a tax levied against each employee's earnings up to a maximum limit. This amount is matched by the employer. In recent years, upward adjustments have been made periodically, both in the tax rate and in the maximum amount of earnings subject to the tax, to cover increases in the benefits provided under the program.

Retirement benefits. To receive retirement benefits, a person must have reached retirement age, must be retired, and must be fully insured. Whether an individual is fully insured is determined by the number of quarters in which he or she has received a prescribed amount of earnings. The exact number of quarters that a person must obtain in order to be classed as fully insured will depend upon date of birth or, if one becomes disabled before reaching retirement age, upon the date of disability. Retirement benefits consist of those benefits workers are entitled to receive in their own behalf, plus additional benefits for eligible dependents.

Disability benefits. The Social Security program provides benefit payments to workers who are too severely disabled to engage in gainful employment. In order to be eligible for such benefits, however, an individual's disability must have existed for at least five months and must be expected to continue for at least twelve months. Those eligible for disability benefits must have worked under Social Security for at least five out of the last ten years before becoming disabled. Benefits are computed on the same basis as retirement benefits and are converted to retirement benefits when the individual reaches the age of 65.

Survivors' benefits. Major features under Social Security are:[1]

- Lump-sum death benefit—$255 maximum
- Monthly benefits for widows/widowers with full benefits starting at age 65 and reduced benefits starting at age 60
  widows/widowers at any age if caring for dependent children under 16
  dependent parents 62 years or older
  unmarried children under 18, or under 19 if a full-time student in elementary or secondary school

---

[1]U.S. Department of Health and Human Services, Social Security Administration, SSA Publication No. 05-10084, June 1993.

- Remarriage after 60 (50 if disabled) will not prevent the payment of benefits
- Reduction in benefit payments for annual earnings in excess of $8040 if under 65 and $11,160 if over 65.

Health insurance or Medicare. Health insurance is the most recent addition to the Social Security program. This insurance provides for hospital insurance and medical insurance for persons over 65. Hospital insurance is financed by employer and employee contributions and covers most of the expenses of hospitalization for a given period. Medical insurance coverage requires the payment of a monthly fee by those who elect to be included. This coverage pays a major portion of the doctor's fees for medical services, including office calls, home visits, surgery, and various laboratory services.

Other Benefits. There are many other benefits and services that can be provided by employers that are not directly related to the security aspects of work. The cost of these benefits to employers has been on the rise and currently runs between 30 and 40 percent of payroll.

Health services. Most organizations of any size provide some form of health service such as first aid, treatment of minor illness by nurses, and routine services administered or supervised by a physician. The extent of the service varies considerably, but it generally handles minor illnesses and injuries and provides preventive measures against such nonoccupational illnesses as polio, colds, and influenza. In many organizations, health services have been expanded to meet the requirements of the federal Occupational Safety and Health Act (OSHA). This will be described in greater detail later in this book. One of the main objectives of company health programs is to educate personnel in the principles and practices of good physical and mental health.

Insurance programs. One of the oldest and most popular employee benefits is the group life insurance program, which provides death benefits to beneficiaries. As a rule, the amount of life insurance coverage for an individual employee depends solely on the salary level; however, in many industries there are plans to provide the same amount of insurance regardless of salary. Group medical, surgical, and dental plans and prepaid drug programs are also popular services provided by the employer through a master or group policy written by an insurance company, by an association such as Blue Cross or Blue Shield, or through some type of prepaid medical practice such as the Kaiser Foundation Health Plan.

About 9 out of 10 persons in the United States under 65 are covered by private health insurance, chiefly group insurance plans connected with employment. Plans negotiated by unions through collective bargaining with employers account for almost half of the employees covered by health benefit plans in private industry.

Financial services. Credit unions have been established in many organizations to serve the financial needs of employees. The credit union encourages thrift by offering interest or dividends on deposits at a higher rate of interest than that paid by most commercial banks. It also serves as a lending institution from which the employee may borrow money at relatively reasonable rates of interest.

Counseling services. While most organizations expect supervisors to counsel subordinates, it is recognized that there will occasionally be employees with personal problems that require the services of qualified counselors. Many organizations refer such individuals to outside counseling services such as church organizations, family counseling services or marriage counselors, and mental health clinics. Some organizations, however, retain a qualified person, such as a consulting psychologist, a counselor, or another qualified individual to whom employees may be referred.

Legal and accounting services. Some organizations make the services of professional persons on the staff available to employees at no expense. An attorney can contribute immeasurably to employee effectiveness by providing help in drawing up a will, giving advice on contracts, and assisting employees in locating qualified personnel to handle complicated legal cases. Similarly, the talents of an accountant can be made available, at least on a limited basis, to employees who need assistance in completing tax returns.

Recreational services. Many organizations have recreational programs. To be effective, the extent of these programs and the specific types of recreation should be determined largely by the expressed desires of the employees.

Most organizations offer some type of sports program in which personnel may participate voluntarily. Bowling, for example, is popular because a large number of employees may participate on an intramural basis. Many organizations have teams that represent them in athletic contests with other local organizations.

Other services. In addition to the services described above, other services have become popular with employees and serve to meet their needs. These include such services as assistance with purchasing housing, moving and transportation, child care facilities, and food service.

Safety and Health

Personnel in this section direct the accident prevention and safety and health programs.

Typical titles for this position include safety director, safety manager, safety engineer, safety coordinator, safety and health officer.

This individual's principal duties include coordinating the accident prevention program; investigating causes of accidents and recommending corrective measures; making safety and sanitation inspections; advising supervisors on the application of safety rules; and establishing safety rules, regulations, and standards. This person also conducts safety education programs, prepares safety manuals, works closely with the medical services department in providing emergency treatment for injured employees, and checks occupational safety and health policies of the organization for compliance with federal, state, and local regulations.

In order to prevent electrocution of an employee, you may be required to check the possible hazards in all the electrical outlets. This is obviously a job that requires a great deal of responsibility.

Employee and Labor Relations

The power of employees as individuals to bargain with their employer and to protect themselves from arbitrary or unfair treatment is limited. Because of this, many employees find it to their advantage to bargain collectively with their employer through a union.

HR workers in employee and labor relations have principal responsibility for collective bargaining, preparation for contract negotiations and administration, and grievance settlement as well as preparation for arbitration.

When company executives and supervisors are contemplating action that will almost certainly result in unfavorable employee reaction, they consult HR personnel. Consider, for example, what is likely to happen when the sales of one of the company's products have declined, with the result that a backlog of inventory has accumulated and made it necessary to lay off those employees engaged in the production of the overstocked item. Surely this will have an adverse effect upon workers suddenly thrown out of jobs as well as upon the morale of those still employed. Repercussions can be minimized, however, if the layoff is preceded by a careful study of the situation.

How many of those whose jobs are affected can be put to work temporarily elsewhere in the plant? Will the employees thus transferred receive their usual compensation or the rate of pay for the jobs to which they are assigned during the layoff? How will the company select the ones to be laid off? Will only those go who have been with the company for a short time, or will those with more seniority go? Will layoff time be added to length-of-service credits (which help determine the amount of vacation time, pension, and other benefits to which an employee is entitled), or will these credits not be permitted to accumulate for laid-off workers while they are gone? Since there are several holidays, like Christmas and Fourth of July, for which employees customarily are paid without working, will those laid off be compensated for holidays that occur during the layoff? Will each worker be notified when to return to work, or must the employee check in occasionally to find out? Will the company try to help those affected find work with other employers during the layoff?

The employee relations worker is expected to know, or sense, that these and perhaps other questions will be on the employees' minds. He or she may be given the responsibility of composing a written notice that explains the reason for layoff and answers questions before they are asked. This carefully prepared explanation, signed by the production department head and posted on bulletin boards throughout the plant, will help to alleviate the blow. It will have a salutary effect upon employees who are retained but who, without such an explanation, might assume they would be the next to go. In addition, it will do much to maintain the goodwill of workers the company will want back when the time comes for resumption of normal production.

Often a trained personnel worker will foresee bad worker reaction when others in management, less attuned to employee thinking, do not. One corporation, looking forward to expansion, announced that it had acquired land for a new plant to be located some distance from the old one. Management thought this would be greeted with enthusiasm, but it was not, Employees were upset, assuming that the new facilities would replace the old and result in the loss of their jobs. Production tapered off. It resumed, however, when—belatedly—workers learned the facts. Had the personnel department been consulted before the announcement was written, it would have been made clear that the new plant would not affect current employees but would mean further hiring. And there would have been no loss in production.

Typical titles for this employee are director of industrial relations, manager of labor relations, labor relations director, employee relations manager.

This person's principal duties include representing the company in collective bargaining negotiations and arbitration hearings, preparing briefs and exhibits for use in negotiations or arbitration, possibly approving final contract at close of negotiations, interpreting contract provisions to all levels of management, dealing with union representatives on matters of contract interpretation and administration, and representing the company in the grievance procedure. This worker also participates with management in formulating labor relations policies, reviews industrial relations policies and practices for compliance with federal and state labor laws, sometimes prepares and distributes handbooks and manuals explaining clauses in collective bargaining agreements, assembles and analyzes information on trends in labor relations, and prepares studies on personnel problems dealing with seniority, layoff procedures, and related subjects.

If you are assigned a position in the labor relations section, your duties will be viewed by others as being extremely important and responsible. You may be called upon to brief the management negotiating team on any one of a number of vitally important subjects. You might be expected to extract from the latest area wage survey the data relevant to the occupational skills employed by your firm. You will have to be up to date on inflation and wage trends in the industry and in the community.

If employees are not unionized, the employer's personnel policies and practices can affect employee desires to unionize. Every employer, therefore, must be concerned with unions either because of the need to negotiate with them or because there is always the possibility that employees may decide to unionize.

But, unionized or not, there are many facets of dealing with the work force as a whole that come under the heading of employee and labor relations. Under the pressures of today's social forces, most employers find it advisable to treat all their employees with the same consideration they would apply if the work force were unionized. Most of the comments that follow in this section relate to unionized workers, but they might apply equally to a nonunionized work force.

A major function of a union is to negotiate and administer the labor agreement that covers the conditions of employment for its members with their employer. Its function also is to protect members from unfair treatment and to assist them in resolving grievances they believe may exist in connection with their employment. By providing employees with a sense of security, power, and importance in their relations with managers, a union can exert a significant influence upon management.

Impact of the Union upon the Employer. When a union is recognized and certified as the bargaining agent for employees, an employer will have to use time that was previously devoted to other personnel functions to negotiate labor agreements and discuss with union representatives the problems and grievances relating to its administration. Accurate personnel and financial records also are necessary to support the company's position during contract negotiations or grievance hearings. Wages, hours, and conditions of work are, by law, all proper subjects for collective bargaining between management and unions. In keeping with current trends in personnel management, unions typically seek to achieve participation in those company decisions that affect the employment, security, and welfare of their members.

Appeal of the Union. Identification with the union can give the employees an added feeling of security and equality in relations with their boss. As members of a union, employees may feel less hesitation in challenging those actions of their employer with which they disagree or in expressing their sentiments freely about their jobs since they know that the union is obligated to provide protection from possible retaliatory action.

Among the benefits for union members are the economic ones that unions can offer their membership. By bargaining collectively with an employer, workers have far greater strength than they would ever have as individuals in their demands for higher wages, improved fringe benefits, greater job security, and a shorter work week.

Union Leadership. To interpret the behavior of union leaders, one must understand their backgrounds and ambitions and recognize the political aspects of the offices they occupy. The leaders in many of the national unions have developed political machines that enable them to suppress opposition and to perpetuate themselves in office. Tenure in office for the leader in a local union, however, is less secure. In local unions, officers periodically must run for re-election, and if they are to remain in office, they must be able to convince a majority of the members that they are serving them effectively.

Some unions recognize that the practice of obtaining leaders from the ranks can serve to weaken the organization. Therefore, they bring in persons with advanced education to become union officers rather than just employed staff specialists.

Government Regulation of Labor Relations. Relations between the union and the employer are governed by state and federal laws. These laws evolved from common law and legislation and from legal interpretations rendered by the National Labor Relations Board and the courts. Contemporary interest in labor legislation is centered on three specific acts of federal legislation.

The Wagner Act. The essence of the act is contained in Section 7, providing employee bargaining rights as follows:

> Employees shall have the right to self-organization, to form, join, or assist labor organizations, to bargain collectively through representatives of their own choosing, and to engage in concerted activities, for the purpose of collective bargaining or other mutual aid or protection . . .

Other provisions of the Wagner Act stipulate unfair labor practices on the part of employers. In addition, the Wagner Act provided for the establishment of the National Labor Relations Board to consider cases brought before it.

The Taft-Hartley Act. The Taft-Hartley Act modified some of the provisions of the Wagner Act. Primarily, though, it lists those actions on the part of unions that are considered unfair labor practices. One of the major effects of the act was to relax the restrictions that the Wagner Act had placed upon an employer's freedom of speech. The act also increased the conditions under which court injunctions might be issued in labor disputes as well as the opportunities to obtain court injunctions against certain illegal strikes and other unfair practices by unions.

The Landrum-Griffin Act. One of the most important provisions of the act is the bill of rights for union members, which requires that every union member must be given the right to nominate candidates for union office, vote in union elections, attend union meetings, participate in union meetings, and vote on union business. Another provision of the act establishes certain ground rules governing the use of members within the trusteed locals. Additionally, an important provision concerns the reports that unions and employers are required to submit, including financial reports of the operation of the union.

Current Labor Issues. The many conflicts and strains that are occurring within this nation's social structure are having a significant effect upon union policies and practices and upon the attitudes and behavior of union members. Union problems resulting from today's rapidly occurring social, economic, and technological trends are very different from those that confronted unions when they were in their formative years.

Changing character of the union member. In the early days of the labor movement, unions tended to consist of members who knew firsthand what employment conditions could be like without unions and what personal sacrifices were required to organize and make a union survive. As subsequent generations entered the unions, their memberships have contained fewer individuals who are dedicated to the social causes of the unions. Furthermore, union members no longer may be categorized as being from a downtrodden working class, but rather they are identified with the American middle class.

Unions and civil rights. The gains achieved by organized labor have helped to plant the seeds of some very significant problems for both unions and their leaders in the area of civil rights. Members of African American and other protected groups have become frustrated because they believe that they have not been accorded fair, equal opportunity to participate in the gains being realized by organized labor as a whole. Frustration over alleged injustices by unions, whether real or perceived, has led to militant actions by African American labor leaders aimed at increasing African American leadership control in labor organizations and in enlarging the membership and employment of African American workers in crafts and other jobs with higher pay.

Unionization of white collar groups. Traditionally, white-collar employees tended to identify themselves with the owners or managers and to perform similar work activities in proximity with them. As a group, they enjoyed certain privileges and socioeconomic status that blue collar workers did not have.

In recent years, however, growth in the size of organizations in which white collar groups are employed has tended to impersonalize their work and to isolate them from and reduce their identification with management. The lack of job security during layoffs resulting from automation or declining sales, together with growing difficulties encountered in attempting to resolve grievances, has helped to push them toward unionization.

Collective Bargaining. Employer recognition of a union constitutes the first stage in the establishment of a bargaining relationship. Such recognition often is the result of a unionizing campaign initiated either by employees with the organization, by an outside union acting on its own, or at the invitation of the employees. The success or failure of an organizing campaign depends largely on the working climate and morale that exist within the employer's organization.

Recognition Procedures. Union elections are usually conducted by the National Labor Relations Board. Ballots permit the employees the choice of "no union" as well as the names of the contending unions. The union receiving a majority of the votes is certified by the NLRB as the bargaining agent for a period of at least a year or for the duration of the labor agreement.

Recognition gives a union the right to represent employees within a particular bargaining unit that may or may not encompass the entire organization. The bargaining unit may be defined as a group of employees recognized by an employer or designated by an agency as appropriate for representation by employee organization for purposes of bargaining. The key factor in considering the composition of the bargaining unit is the basis of common occupational interest.

Negotiations. After recognition is achieved, the parties must get together for the purpose of negotiations. Collective bargaining is the process by which the employer and the union negotiate the conditions under which the members within the bargaining unit are to be employed. These conditions are described in the labor agreement that results from such bargaining.

In the bargaining process, sometimes negotiations break down. Then the union may try to bring pressure to bear on management to meet its demands. Several tactics are available to the union.

Strike. A strike involves the refusal of a group of employees to perform their jobs. It is the withholding of services of that part of the work force on strike.

Picketing. When a union goes on strike, it is general practice for the union to picket the employer by placing persons at the entrances to the premises to advertise the dispute and to discourage persons from entering or leaving these premises. A picket line can result in the refusal by employees of other organizations to cross the picket line to deliver and pick up goods.

Boycotting. Another economic weapon of unions is the boycott. This results when a union refuses to allow its members to patronize a business enterprise where there is a labor dispute.

Lockout. Under special circumstances, when labor and management cannot come to agreement, management may choose to lock its workers out. This is done by simply shutting down the plant or place of business.

Overcoming Deadlocks. When labor negotiations are deadlocked, that is, the parties cannot come to agreement, a third party may be called in so that agreement can be reached. There are several degrees of third-party participation.

Conciliation. A conciliator provides a catalytic service by keeping the negotiations moving and thus helping the two parties arrive at their own solution. No attempt is made by the conciliator to impose solutions or force compromises. The effective conciliator simply keeps the talks going until the parties eventually reach solutions.

Mediator. A mediator exercises a more positive role in helping to resolve a deadlock by suggesting compromises, solutions, or making suggestions that will lead to agreement. Both the conciliator and the mediator help the principals retreat from their deadlocked positions without suffering a loss of face. Actually, there is little difference between conciliation and mediation.

Arbitration. In arbitration, both parties to the dispute agree to permit an impartial umpire or arbitrator to consider the relative merits of their respective positions and resolve the dispute through the award that the arbitrator makes for the case. The decision or award is binding on both parties.

Fact finding. Government pressure may be exerted in some circumstances through the appointment of a fact-finding board to investigate a bargaining deadlock. The board has no power, but it can make public its findings, thus bringing pressure to bear on the principals to the dispute.

The Labor Agreement. After agreement has been reached through collective bargaining, it is put in writing and signed by the representatives of both parties. The major portion of the agreement is concerned with conditions of employment. These conditions include wages, hours, fringe benefits, and various provisions covering discipline and other personnel actions.

In the negotiating process, management strives to preserve its rights or prerogatives. In a sense, management's authority is supreme in all matters except those it has expressly conceded in the collective bargaining agreement or in those areas where its authority is restricted by law. The inclusion of a management's rights clause in the work agreement represents a "no trespassing" notice that the employer hopes will deter the union from encroaching on its exclusive territory.

Union security is as important to the union as management rights are to the employer. Union security determines the extent to which the jobs within its representation area will be held by the union members and the extent to which the union will be able to maintain disciplinary control over members. Within these provisions are the various degrees of security determined by the kind of shop agreed upon in the work agreement.

The union shop provides that any person who is hired, if not a union member at the time, must join the union within a prescribed period —usually thirty days—as a condition of employment. The agency shop does not require employees in the bargaining unit to join the union, but it does require that they pay dues to the union that serves as their bargaining agent within the organization. The closed shop requires that an employer hire only those who are union members. Additionally, under a checkoff provision, the employer withholds union dues from the paycheck of each union member who signs an affidavit agreeing to such a deduction.

Employee Grievances. No matter how carefully and conscientiously a union and an employer may negotiate a labor agreement, differences over its administration and application are almost certain to arise between the two parties. Typically, union grievances are a response to actions that it believes the employer has taken or failed to take in living up to the terms of the labor agreement or the policies of the organization.

Grievances can result from a variety of causes. Many of them involve the agreement and result from omissions or ambiguities in its provisions that cause each party to interpret differently the meaning of a particular provision or how a particular personnel decision should be made. Sometimes grievances stem from a failure of employees either to meet the demands of their jobs or to gain satisfaction from performing them or both. Employees who are placed in the wrong job, for instance, are more likely to perform unsatisfactorily. Another source of grievance lies in supervisory practices. The supervisor's attitude and behavior toward individual workers and the union may provide a fertile source of grievances.

Most large organizations have formal grievance procedures that provide for an airing of the grievance and consideration of it at various levels of the organization until the grievant is satisfied or the solution sought is finally denied. In a unionized shop, it is the union officer, such as the steward, or the grievance committee that will represent the interest of the aggrieved worker. Management is represented in these discussions by, first, the first-line supervisor, then probably the company personnel officer, then finally someone at the top management level such as the general manager or the president of the firm.

If a solution is not forthcoming within the structure of the grievance procedure as provided, the union has two alternative courses of action if it wishes to pursue the matter further. It can call a strike, or it can submit the grievance to arbitration. Most grievances are settled at the first level among the worker, the supervisor, and the union steward in the shop.

Disciplinary Action. The purpose of a disciplinary program is to provide the means for securing employee performance and behavior that is necessary to meet organizational goals. While one of its purposes is to provide corrective action, a more important purpose is to prevent the need for such action in the first place.

Definite policies and procedures for handling disciplinary matters are essential for ensuring fair treatment of offenders. While it is usually recommended that disciplinary action be handled on an impartial basis without regard for the specific circumstances involved, most individuals rebel against the imposition of inflexible rules.

Before taking any disciplinary action, supervisors should interview the employees with a view to obtaining the reasons for their behaviors and attitudes and any information that will enable the supervisors to understand the infraction. A record of offenses and disciplinary action taken is usually maintained in the employee's personnel file. Supervisors must be able to distinguish between what does and does not constitute a valid disciplinary case. Furthermore, they must learn how to document their case against an employee so that the evidence supporting their action will not be refuted by evidence that the union presents in the arbitration hearing. In considering the facts in a disciplinary case, the arbitrator or other person hearing the appeal usually will seek to determine the extent, if any, to which the disciplined employee was at fault and the extent, if any, to which management may also have been at fault.

Any necessary disciplinary actions should be administered only after the case has been reviewed thoroughly to ensure that the individual being disciplined is completely responsible for her or his actions, that every possible effort has been made to make the employee aware of the deficiency and what is expected, and that he or she is being counseled in order to improve performance and behavior. Not only will the respect of the employees and the union be increased by the proper handling of disciplinary problems but also any action that is taken is less likely to be reversed subsequently through the grievance procedure or through arbitration.

Personnel Research

The duties of this section are to collect and analyze all kinds of data related to personnel and employment, including numbers of personnel, wage levels and trends, human resource planning needs, and new developments in the field.

Most progressive personnel departments are continually conducting at least some research on such problems as accident proneness and causes of absenteeism and on such subjects as employer-employee communication, wage incentives, and the most effective methods of utilizing the services of the physically handicapped. These studies help to determine personnel policy. Sometimes they are carried on by full-time researchers.

The typical title for this individual is director of personnel research.

The principal duties of the director of personnel research are to conduct systematic investigations into current personnel problems of the organization; to investigate new and improved methods of management, including testing, training, compensating, and other functions; and to maintain records of employment and investigate indications of increasing turnover rates.

If the turnover rate in the purchasing department has suddenly increased, that bears looking into, and the director of research conducts an investigation in conjunction with the purchasing officer.

Research can be defined as systematic and purposeful investigation of facts with the object of determining cause and effect relationships among such facts. From research personnel workers hope to establish principles that define the relationship between two or more phenomena. Managers then attempt to use these principles in their philosophy, approach, attitude, and specific practices.

Two general types of research are usually identified as basic or exploratory and operational or applied. Exploratory research is concerned with the discovery of knowledge for its own sake. The scientist builds conceptual models and tests various hypotheses against them. Operational or applied research is directed toward the solution of particular business problems. The payoff of operational or applied research is immediate, observable, and tangible.

A wide variety of people and institutions engage in either pure or applied research. Some of these are described here.

Colleges and Universities. These institutions are set up to operate at both the pure and applied levels of personnel research. It is common to see bureaus of business research that engage in personnel projects as well as investigations in other fields of business management. Among the outstanding university centers of personnel research are the Institute for Social Research of the University of Michigan, Personnel Research Board of Ohio State University, Institute of Industrial Relations of the University of California, the Behavioral Sciences Group of Carnegie Institute of Technology, and the Center for Industrial Relations of the University of Minnesota.

Government Agencies. Various governmental agencies conduct basic and applied research. Units of the U.S. Department of Labor are particularly interested in research dealing with personnel management. For example, the *Dictionary of Occupational Titles* was prepared by the United States Employment Service for the general use of industry.

Figure 2.1

ORGANIZATION CHART
Human Resource Division of a Major Industrial Organization

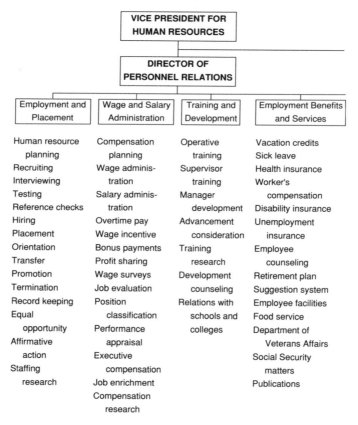

Employment and Placement	Wage and Salary Administration	Training and Development	Employment Benefits and Services
Human resource planning	Compensation planning	Operative training	Vacation credits
Recruiting	Wage administration	Supervisor training	Sick leave
Interviewing	Salary administration	Manager development	Health insurance
Testing	Overtime pay	Advancement consideration	Worker's compensation
Reference checks	Wage incentive	Training research	Disability insurance
Hiring	Bonus payments	Development counseling	Unemployment insurance
Placement	Profit sharing	Relations with schools and colleges	Employee counseling
Orientation	Wage surveys		Retirement plan
Transfer	Job evaluation		Suggestion system
Promotion	Position classification		Employee facilities
Termination	Performance appraisal		Food service
Record keeping	Executive compensation		Department of Veterans Affairs
Equal opportunity	Job enrichment		Social Security matters
Affirmative action	Compensation research		Publications
Staffing research			

Figure 2.1

(Continued)

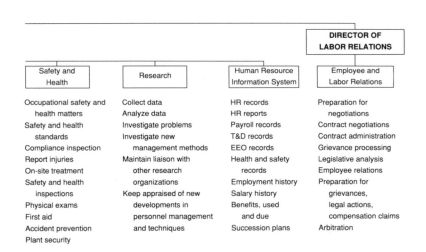

			DIRECTOR OF LABOR RELATIONS
Safety and Health	Research	Human Resource Information System	Employee and Labor Relations
Occupational safety and health matters	Collect data	HR records	Preparation for negotiations
Safety and health standards	Analyze data	HR reports	Contract negotiations
Compliance inspection	Investigate problems	Payroll records	Contract administration
Report injuries	Investigate new management methods	T&D records	Grievance processing
On-site treatment	Maintain liaison with other research organizations	EEO records	Legislative analysis
Safety and health inspections	Keep appraised of new developments in personnel management and techniques	Health and safety records	Employee relations
Physical exams		Employment history	Preparation for grievances,
First aid		Salary history	legal actions,
Accident prevention		Benefits, used and due	compensation claims
Plant security		Succession plans	Arbitration

Private Research Organizations. These organizations take a number of different forms. Some are employers' associations that accomplish particular projects of special interest to an industry. For example, industry wage and salary surveys may be conducted by an employers' association on a continuing basis. In addition, there are larger employer groups like National Association of Manufacturers and the Chamber of Commerce of the United States. Other associations are established strictly for the purpose of conducting business research. Such organizations as the Conference Board, the RAND Corporation, and the Stanford Research Institute are examples.

Individual Companies. Individual companies also do personnel research, particular of the operational or applied type.

Research Methods. All research involves the application, in some manner, of the scientific method. There are various specific forms that individual research projects can take.

Controlled experiments. Controlled experiments conducted by private concerns are relatively rare. Perhaps the most famous experiment of this type was the Hawthorne study of the Western Electric Company, begun in 1927. In this experiment, the work force was divided into two groups, experimental and control. In the experimental group, there was an attempt to keep extraneous variables constant and then to introduce one variation into the situation. The resulting acts could then be attributed to the single variant factor. In this manner, changes that sought to improve lighting, rest periods, and air conditioning showed immediate results in terms of improved productivity. No similar results were observed in the control group. To validate the discovered relationships, the conditions were returned to their original status in the expectation that productivity would drop. To everyone's great surprise, productivity did not drop and in some instances continued to improve. Obviously the conditions of the experiment had not been rigidly controlled. In personnel research, it is impossible to keep all other factors constant and then isolate them one at a time. What was not controlled were the minds and attitudes of the participating workers. They liked working in the experimental group; they felt very important. Regardless of what was done to them, they attempted to produce more. Recognition of the importance of these personnel resulted in marked increases in productivity.

Surveys. The survey is a commonly used research method. It usually takes the form of a questionnaire or structured interview. Its object is to determine present practices or approaches and to attempt to relate certain results to particular causes. For example, we may wish to know certain things about employee profit sharing. Can such plans survive a profitless year? If so, how many profitless years? Certain hypotheses must be established around which survey questions can be phrased. What criteria can be established so that we can judge the correctness of such hypotheses? When the actual survey is taken, companies are asked questions concerning the possible causes of the absence of profits. As a result, certain generalizations deducible from the study can be made.

Historical studies. There is a wealth of useful information in the files of most firms, including valuable records about personnel. Suppose, for example, that a manager wishes to do research on a problem of high labor turnover. The manager can study turnover experience on the basis of such variables as sex, age, department, home ownership, marital status, and stated causes for leaving.

Case studies. The case study approach is considered by many to be a separate method of research. Quite frequently, however, case studies result only in the creation of further hypotheses requiring additional research to validate. Case studies are intensive, in that a great number of subjects is investigated in detail in a relatively limited number of firms.

Simulation. In recent years, simulation of performance has become an increasingly popular method of research in many fields. Simulations have been used in business environments for studying problems of production control, inventory control, purchasing, and marketing.

Systematic and purposeful research is an obvious and continuing necessity in the field of personnel management. The future is never certain, but on the basis of an analysis of present trends, we can foresee certain events in the field of human resource management. Among them we can anticipate the following: a continuing emphasis upon human relations, with a switch to an emphasis upon creativity and productivity as contrasted with happiness and satisfaction; a greater role in helping to meet the private business firm's broader responsibility to society, including the need to adapt to the cultural diversity of the work force; expansion of the field of HR management to include organizational planning for growth; an increased acceptance of the responsibility for effective personnel management on the part of all managers; and a marked effort on the part of the human resource manager to assist the organization and its members to adjust to the inevitability of automated processes. The most dynamic element of the business economy is people. The expert in people, the personnel manager, has both an opportunity and a challenge in the business management of the future.

Human Resource Information System[2]

Years ago, the handling of personnel information, as with most data, was done manually. With the advent of computers and the personal computer (PC), personnel information is now entered, stored, and retrieved electronically by computer. A human resource information system (HRIS) is usually a computerized system that manipulates data into useable forms and allows individual users of the information to access it when and where they need it. An HRIS can be small or large. It can be organized on a department, division, or corporate-wide basis. It can be run on a mainframe computer, a PC, or a combination of both. The main function of an HRIS is to gather, create, and produce necessary data so the HR department can function effectively. There are three

---

[2]This section derived from *Strategic Human Resources Management* (see bibliography).

types of HRIS systems. These include the centralized, the decentralized, and modified systems.

The centralized system provides control and accountability for the system in one department or centralized place and generally ties a main computer to satellite units directly with on-line access or access via modem. This feature allows a centralized department to control the input of data while allowing other users to access the data for their own use. By having one main computer with satellite terminals, costs are reduced while providing the manager of the system with greater control. The main drawback of this type of system is the reduced flexibility of the satellite users. They are dependent upon the controlling department for access to the data.

An independent, or decentralized, system is generally a stand-alone system but may include some satellite facilities. This set-up would typically be a PC-based system tied together via a PC network. This type of system offers the greatest user flexibility since each user can make changes to fit individual needs. However, duplication of work can result since more than one person may design the same system.

A modified system combines the needed elements from all three systems to maximize the company's resources and provide the right amount of flexibility and control. Modified systems can be very expensive since one or more applications will be developed or purchased to meet HR needs.

HRIS and the Corporate Strategy. An HRIS is a very important element in the strategic management process. It can be used as a planning tool for future staffing needs as well as to monitor turnover, productivity, and labor and benefits costs. The applications of an HRIS are limited by how the company decides to use it. As companies become aware of the many uses of an HRIS, they place more emphasis on the importance of utilizing this strategic capability.

Type of Data Input into an HRIS. The type of information stored in an HRIS depends upon the uses of the system: the more extensive the use, the greater the variety of information stored. The types of data usually include

- basic employee information such as Social Security numbers, job titles, job classification, and employment history
- salary information, such as salary range, salary grade, and salary history
- benefit information, such as benefits used and earned
- EEO information, such as race, sex of employees and applicants, and the applicable demographic information by EEO job category
- promotion and transfer information, including positions open and job bid files
- training and development information, including programs available, courses completed by each employee, and training planned for the future
- labor relations data on union contracts, grievance information, and seniority information
- succession planning information about possible retirements and which employee may be qualified for advancement based upon skills and experience
- health and safety data, including accident frequency and severity rates; worker's compensation data, including cost of accidents; and other information required by the government or insurance companies
- access to external data bases such as the Human Resource Information Network (HRIN), an on-line data base of HR-related information available through Executive Telecom System, Inc., Indianapolis, Indiana

Once all of this data is entered into the system, it can be manipulated to create reports and provide information to the HR department so that it can effectively perform its function. A few examples of output derived from the data include a full succession plan for the company, overtime hours worked during a pay period, a training and development plan for a division or department, EEO compliance information, and benefits costs.

By properly utilizing an HRIS, a human resource manager will have access to the necessary data to position better an HR department to support the overall strategic objectives of a business. Personnel data in an HRIS are confidential and not permitted to leave a human resource department. They are referred to constantly for a variety of purposes but only by authorized people.

CHAPTER 3

FEATURES OF THE FIELD

All personnel/human resource managers perform common management functions, including planning the objectives and programs of the personnel department, organizing the work to be done, and filling the positions needed to perform the work. They also direct the efforts of the division of human resources by controlling the work activities, reviewing performance, and taking necessary corrective action.

SALARIES

Salaries in the field of human resources differ a great deal from one position to another. Factors causing variations include the size of the firm, level of responsibility, length of service, locality, and the nature of the organization. Because job titles are far from uniform and because a position described as personnel manager in one enterprise might be called director of human resources in another, specific salaries by job can only be described in terms of averages or ranges. The following tables list the titles most commonly used in human resource departments and show the salaries for each.

Different surveys will result in different figures for various human resource/personnel job titles depending on the populations surveyed.

Table 3.1. Human Resources Job Titles and Salaries, 1990

Job Titles	Salary Ranges
Personnel Clerks/Assistants	$15,368–26,366
Personnel Specialists	26,344–71,262
Personnel Supervisors/Managers	47,085–92,676
Directors of Personnel	45,032–97,381

Source: U.S. Department of Labor, Bureau of Labor Statistics, *White-Collar Pay: Private Goods-Producing Industries,* March 1990, Bulletin 2374, Washington: Government Printing Office, 1990.

This salary information is published in the *Occupational Outlook Handbook.*[1]

The median annual salary of personnel, training, and labor relations specialists was about $30,000 in 1990. For managers, the median annual salary was almost $36,000. However, salaries varied widely. The lowest 10 percent of specialists earned under $19,000, while the highest 10 percent of managers earned over $65,000.

According to a 1990 survey of compensation in the human resources field, conducted by Abott, Langer, and Associates of Crete, Illinois, the median annual salaries for selected personnel and labor relations occupations were: Industrial/labor relations directors, $63,500; training directors, $50,300; safety specialists, $39,200; compensation supervisors, $35,400; EEO/affirmative action specialists, $32,300; and personnel records specialists, $27,000.

A 1991 survey of salaries in selected white-collar occupations in private industry also indicated that salaries in the personnel field varied widely depending on the complexity of the job and level of responsibility. The median annual salary for personnel specialists ranged from

---

[1]U.S. Department of Labor, Bureau of Labor Statistics, *Occupational Outlook Handbook, 1992–93,* Bulletin 2400, Lincolnwood, Illinois: VGM Career Horizons, 1992.

$23,900 to $71,500; personnel supervisors/managers, $48,300 to $93,200; and directors of personnel, $44,800 to $99,900.

In the federal government in 1991, persons with a bachelor's degree or 3 years' general experience in the personnel field generally started at $17,000 a year. Those with a superior academic record or an additional year of specialized experience started at $21,000 a year. Holders of a master's degree started at $25,700, and those with a doctorate in a personnel field started at $31,100. There are no formal entry-level requirements for managerial positions. Applicants must possess a suitable combination of educational attainment, experience, and record of accomplishment.

Labor relations specialists in the federal government averaged $45,900 a year in 1991; personnel managers, $43,500; equal employment opportunity specialists, $43,100; position classification specialists, $41,000; and personnel staffing specialists, $38,500.

Similar to other workers, personnel, training, and labor relations specialists and managers receive fringe benefits that typically include vacation and sick leave, health and life insurance, and pension plans, among others.

A separate salary survey was conducted in 1993 by the Society for Human Resource Management and William M. Mercer, Inc., selected results of which are indicated in table 3.2.

WORKING CONDITIONS

Employees in personnel offices generally work about 40 hours a week. During periods of intensive recruitment or emergency, they may work much longer. As a rule, they are paid for holidays and vacations and share in retirement plans, life and health insurance plans, and other benefits available to all professional workers in their organizations.

Working conditions for personnel workers are generally very favorable. The offices are usually well lighted, ventilated, and pleasant places in which to work.

Table 3.2. Selected Human Resource Management Salaries

		Top HR Mgmt Executive $173,700		
Top Corp. Labor Relations Exec. $109,000	Top Corp. Security Manager $71,400	Top Corp. Employee Relations Exec. $84,300	Top Corp. Organizational Development Exec. $103,100	Top Corp. Compensation & Benefits Exec. $90,500
Labor Relations Supervisor $75,600	Security Specialist $31,400	EEO Manager $63,200	Employment & Recruiting Manager $59,100	Employee Benefits Manager $69,000
		HRIS Manager $59,000	Exec. Recruiting Specialist $49,800	Compensation Manager $67,900
		Employee Assistance Program Manager $58,300	Training & Development Manager $72,200	Sr. Compensation Analyst $43,800
		Managment Development Manager $62,600		

Source: Human Resource Compensation Survey, conducted by the Society for Human Resource Management and William M. Mercer, Inc., published in *Bulletin to Management*, July 22, 1993, by The Bureau of National Affairs, Washington, D.C.

Personnel workers meet and work with all types of people—employees, job applicants, union representatives, local officials of the community, educators, and other community groups and company executives. They may address meetings held with the firm's employees, supervisors, or civic groups.

SATISFACTIONS

There are many personal and professional satisfactions to be derived from working in the field of personnel/human resources. Particular aspects of the work may well have more meaning for some, but every HR worker finds most of the work very rewarding.

Personnel work is basically office work, located close to management. There is a complexity to the work that adds to the challenge of the assignment. It is brain work rather than manual labor and requires intellectual rather than physical effort.

Personnel assignments provide a professional status since the job requires responsibility and specialized technical training. Other workers' recognition of the responsibility of the job gives status to the position.

Personnel workers derive psychological rewards from the degree of professionalism of the work and the long-range improvements they are able to accomplish for the good of the organization, its employees, and the community. They also derive social satisfaction from the extent of human relations involved in the assignment. The wide range of personal contacts—with managers, supervisors, and individual employees—and the opportunity to be helpful to all of them are sources of social satisfaction.

The broad field of human resources is open to new applications of developing technologies. For example, electronic data processing is now widely used in personnel record keeping.

It is satisfying to know that salaries paid to workers in human resource management equal or exceed other comparable fields. Personnel workers are now receiving monetary recognition for their responsibilities and effort.

WORKING LEVELS

The organizational structure of a large industry is comprised of five levels of personnel workers. These levels are clerical, specialist, technical, managerial, and executive. The first two are white collar, hourly wage employees. The others represent three different levels within the management structure of the organization.

Clerical Level

The clerical level is the lowest employed in the personnel office. It is the beginning level for white collar workers in the occupational field of human resource management.

Duties. If you were a personnel worker at the clerical level, you would be engaged in usual office tasks such as typing, filing, phoning, and other typical work. In a personnel office, these tasks would be related to maintaining personnel files, processing papers, compiling lists, and digging out information related to organization employees in the personnel files.

Wages/Salaries. The current federal minimum wage is $4.25 per hour. As a beginning clerical worker, you could expect this wage or a little more at the start. With time and demonstrated proficiency, you could expect some increases in wages on a periodic basis.

Conditions. As a personnel worker, you would usually work in an office that is well lighted, ventilated, and pleasant. Until familiar with the work of the office and the rules governing the personnel processes, you can't expect to do much other than routine paperwork. As you gain experience and knowledge of the processes of personnel administration, your assignments may be broadened to include more contact with applicants and others who come into the office for assistance.

Hours. You will probably work an eight-hour day, forty-hour week. Some firms are shifting to four ten-hour days per week. Most personnel offices are open by eight o'clock in the morning and remain open until five or six in the afternoon. This usually means there will be some staggering of the work shift to have the office continually staffed during the day. You may have to work the second, or swing, shift in order to process the day-shift time cards or other pay and time-related matters.

Satisfactions. At the clerical level, you will derive satisfaction from learning more about the job and the importance of carrying out your duties with accuracy. You will also feel satisfaction from the growing skills you develop as you carry out the duties of your assignments. When you get to know your colleagues and feel comfortable in the workplace, you will feel more a part of the work force.

Specialist Level

Workers at this level are experienced in personnel work. They are white collar workers—wage earners who have worked for a considerable time and developed skills in which they have become specialized. They perform a special function in this regard. Examples include interviewers, testers, and benefits counselors.

Duties. At the specialist level, you will have accumulated a thorough working knowledge of all the personnel processes, rules, and regulations. You will perform duties requiring a knowledge of terms and usage of personnel information. Also, you may extract information from a variety of sources and combine data in ways that are useful to the office in the compilation of reports and other applications. At this level, you will be expected to operate a computer terminal.

As a specialist, you may have a number of clerical-level helpers. You will probably perform many duties under some supervision, such as interviewing, counseling employees on benefits, and preparing reports.

Wages/Salaries. An experienced personnel worker at the specialist level can expect $30,000 per year or more. Variations from this amount will depend on the size of the organization, pay scale, amount of experience, extent of responsibilities, time on the job, and other factors. As a personnel specialist, you are a very valuable employee who contributes much to the satisfaction of the work force.

Conditions. Your working conditions are the same as for all personnel workers. As a specialist, however, you may require a semiprivate office or location in order to conduct interviews, counsel, or perform other tasks requiring freedom from noise and interruption.

Hours. You will probably have to observe the same hours as other white collar workers, the standard 40-hour week. At peak periods of the year, some paid overtime may be involved.

Satisfactions. At the specialist level, you will find satisfaction in being able to perform those services that meet the needs of the office and the individual employee who comes to you for assistance. Frequently you will be the one who keeps the routine of the office functioning smoothly. The management of the office and the organization depend on you for special treatment of data and other information and functions that you are peculiarly able to provide.

Technical Level

Work at the technical level involves those duties usually associated with the first line of supervision. The technical level is the lower level of management in the occupational field of personnel/human resources.

Duties. As a relatively new personnel manager, you may serve in the capacity of a personnel technician. The title *personnel analyst* is frequently used in connection with positions at this level. You might head up a technical section of the human resource office such as the training section.

Job analyst is a typical technical title. Also called compensation analysts, they do very exacting work. They collect and examine detailed information about job duties in order to prepare job descriptions. These descriptions, or "position classifications" explain the duties, training, and skills each job requires. Whenever a large organization introduces a new job or reviews existing ones, it calls upon the expert knowledge of the job analyst. Accurate information about job duties also is required when an organization considers changes in its pay system.

Wages/Salaries. At this level, you will be salaried. That means that you are not paid by the hour but rather are paid on the basis of doing a particular kind of work and carrying out the duties assigned. You may receive salary increases on a periodic basis. The reward for doing a job very well is not so much an increase in pay but rather improved chances for promotion when the opportunity arises. Current salaries are approximately $41,000 per year.

Conditions. Working conditions for technicians in personnel will be comfortable but probably not spacious. You may spend a great deal of time in your office or, depending on the assignment, you may spend much time on the plant floor or in the field, investigating personnel matters.

Hours. Most managers are not restricted as to the number of hours they work. You are expected to work approximately 40 hours each week, but if the job takes only 35 hours one week, you are not expected to sit around and twiddle your thumbs. Probably the next week the work will require 45 or 50 hours of your time. Like all young managers, you are expected to be on the job when the office opens in the morning, typically eight o'clock. You will usually stay on the job until all the principal members of the management structure in the personnel department have left for the day. One of the best ways for the novice personnel manager to learn is to spend time on the job hammering away at problems until they are solved.

Satisfactions. You and other managers at this level will derive satisfaction from solving the technical problems confronting you. It is the source of much satisfaction to see how your own efforts mesh with other technical managers' and contribute to the total personnel program. There is always plenty of action for the young manager in a personnel office.

Managerial Level

This is the middle-management level in the division of human resources of a large enterprise.

Duties. At the managerial level, your duties encompass a broader range than at the lower levels. You may have to direct the overall personnel program and coordinate subordinate programs, such as the training program, the benefits program, and others. At the managerial level, you become involved in planning for the future direction of the enterprise as well as overseeing the subordinate programs. You may become involved in advising other managers in the organization concerning their interests in the personnel program and in the management of their personnel.

Wages/Salaries. The higher you go in the organizational structure, the more difficult it is to pin down salaries and duties. There is much more variation between companies in the range of responsibilities assigned, titles utilized, and salaries paid. Directors of personnel in medium-sized firms can expect to be paid something in excess of $50,000 per year. If you head up the personnel program in a very large firm and serve under a vice-president for industrial relations, you may be paid upwards from $85,000 per year. Directors of labor relations may be paid more.

Conditions. At the managerial level, you can expect very comfortable working conditions. Typically you will have a well-appointed office in which you can carry on the business of the personnel program with considerable privacy. You need facilities to accommodate the other managers, who will frequently be visiting the personnel director's office. A modern office may provide you with a computer terminal so you can call up personnel data. Some managers with a great deal of responsibility for the personnel program will not have adequate accommodations. Much depends on the view the organization holds of the personnel function and the space available to accommodate it.

Hours. At the managerial level, you can expect to work something in excess of 40 hours per week. Like all managers, you are paid to get the job done. If it takes more than 40 hours some weeks, that is only what is to be expected.

Satisfactions. With the current mushrooming of personnel/human resource law at the federal and state levels, there may be some satisfaction in not being hauled into court for violation of the ambiguous requirements. In reality, however, you will find there are many sources of satisfaction in being a personnel manager. A stable work force contributing to high productivity is a very satisfying condition. Being able to meet the challenge of changing requirements without upsetting the morale of the work force is surely a source of satisfaction.

In this occupational field, there is little standardization of titles and job responsibilities. At the managerial level, the personnel manager might be titled director of personnel or something else. At the executive level the top personnel manager might be titled director of personnel or vice president for human resources or another term. However, the general job description that follows under the title director of personnel is applicable to managerial-level personnel directors in very large corporations.

[Director of personnel] Directs a personnel management program for a company or a segment of a company. Serves top management officials of the organization as the source of advice and assistance on personnel management matters and problems generally: is typically consulted on the personnel implications of planned changes in management policy or program, the effects on the organization of economic or market trends, product or production method changes, etc.; represents management in contacts with other companies, trade associations, government agencies, etc., dealing primarily with personnel management matters.

Typically the director of personnel for a company reports to a company officer in charge of human resource/personnel management activities or an officer of similar level. Below the company level the director of personnel typically reports to a company officer or a high management official who has responsibility for the operation of a plant or a segment of the company.

For a job to be covered by this definition, the personnel management program must include responsibility for all three of the following functions:

1. *Administering a job evaluation system:* i.e., a system in which there are established procedures by which jobs are analyzed and evaluated on the basis of their duties, responsibilities, and qualification requirements in order to provide a foundation for equitable compensation. Typically, such a system includes the use of one or more sets of job evaluation factors and the preparation of formal job descriptions. It may also include such related functions as wage and salary surveys

or merit rating system administration. The job evaluation system(s) does not necessarily cover all jobs in the organization, but does cover a substantial portion of the organization.

2. *Employment and placement function:* i.e., recruiting actively for at least some kinds of workers through a variety of sources (e.g., schools or colleges, employment agencies, professional societies, etc.); evaluating applicants against demands of particular jobs by use of such techniques as job analysis to determine requirements, interviews, written tests of aptitude, knowledge, or skill, reference checks, experience evaluations, etc.; recommending selections and job placements to management, etc.

3. *Employee relations and services function:* i.e., functions designed to maintain employees' morale and productivity at a high level (for example, administering a formal or informal grievance procedure; identifying and recommending solutions for personnel problems such as absenteeism, high turnover, low productivity, etc.; administration of beneficial suggestions system, retirement, pension, or insurance plans, merit rating system, etc.; overseeing cafeteria operations, recreational programs, occupational safety and health programs, etc).

In addition, positions covered by this definition may, but do not necessarily, include responsibilities in the following areas:

- Employee training and development
- Labor relations activities
- Equal Employment Opportunity (EEO)
- Reporting under the Occupational Safety and Health Act (OSHA)

Personnel workers at the managerial level who are charged with responsibilities related to labor relations are frequently titled director of labor relations. Their duties include all aspects of labor relations including collective bargaining, interpreting the work agreement, and speaking for the company at arbitration hearings.

Executive Level

This is the top management level. This is the highest level in an organization where the personnel/human resource manager serves.

Duties. This is the top level for any personnel manager with experience in any of the functional areas. Whether your title is vice-president for human resources or director of personnel, as the top personnel manager in the organization you are included in the long-range planning of top management. Here you are in a position to influence company policy. You will recommend organization policy concerning personnel matters. You are a respected member of the top management team, and as such you have great influence in the firm, the industry, and the community. Your duties are so broad they will often take you away from your office.

Wages/Salaries. A recent survey made by the Society for Human Resource Management indicates that top-level HRM executives can expect a salary in excess of $170,000 per year.

Conditions. It is safe to say that at the top level of management your working conditions are very comfortable. You will be located in the executive suite. Also, your responsibilities are very great and vital to the operation of the organization. As the top personnel executive, you will spend a great deal of your time dealing with people from outside your office and outside your organization.

Hours. At the executive level, you may be sure that you will devote many hours in excess of 40 per week in carrying out the responsibilities of your assignment. Your time schedule may have enough flexibility, though, so you can get on the golf course in the middle of the week occasionally. To make up for it, you may frequently be working in the office until eight or late at night to keep up with the work, especially the volume of reading that is required at top levels of management.

Satisfactions. As the executive level personnel manager, you will derive satisfactions from noting the progress the firm is making in terms of worker stability, low turnover rate, low accident rate, high productivity, and high morale. The major contributions you as an executive can make to your company include such things as anticipating personnel needs brought about by changes such as plant expansion. Another contribution would be the handling of labor relations to minimize labor strife at work. The strength of many firms lies in the loyal support of a satisfied work force.

CHARACTERISTICS OF SUCCESSFUL PERSONNEL WORKERS

Personnel work is office work. The work is performed in pleasant surroundings in comfortable places that are generally clean and free from excessive noise.

Personnel workers deal with paper and data as much as with people. The paperwork entails the completion of forms in order to record or obtain necessary information. This information is collected and held in personnel files in the personnel office. Personnel workers also have to know other job-related information, such as how to credit vacation time to workers and how to figure sick leave credits. Personnel workers also deal with people, in that they interview and test applicants for jobs and advise employees of their benefits and rights at work. Personnel data are typically entered, stored, and retrieved using computers.

The success of personnel workers is dependent on their ability to perform these kinds of tasks. Their attitudes toward the work they do will probably, more than any other factor, determine their success or failure in the job. Personnel workers must be able to carry out their duties on a fairly continuous basis. Both the employees and the management of an organization depend on the workers to carry out their duties, whether they feel well, whether it is raining or shining, hot or cold. When a job-offer letter has to go out, it must go out, whether it is the seventh or seventieth letter of the day. Willingness to carry out assigned duties, even under adverse circumstances, will be necessary to succeed in human resource management.

The attitude of personnel workers must be cooperative and supportive toward fellow workers. Personnel workers labor for all employees of the organization, not just the boss of the personnel office. Successful personnel workers accept the obligation to perform for the benefit of all employees, because all employees depend upon the completeness and accuracy of the work of the personnel office.

Successful personnel workers respond to the needs and directives of management. They are cooperative and supportive of management's efforts to utilize human resources to the fullest while also ensuring the fairest treatment possible for all employees. Management has the responsibility for running the organization and keeping it in business; if a person cannot support management in this effort, he or she should not be in personnel work.

CHAPTER 4

REQUIREMENTS AND PREPARATION

In every occupation, there are certain qualifications for those who practice in it. These requirements come about, not arbitrarily, but as the result of years of experience and the principles of good management. These requirements and the measures necessary to obtain them are dealt with in this chapter.

REQUIRED QUALIFICATIONS

Because of the many varied and immediate demands upon HR personnel, the work is interesting, challenging, and satisfying. It is by no means, however, suited to everyone. The duties performed by personnel workers require that they possess certain individual, professional, and educational qualifications. The most important of these are included here.

Individual

The personnel worker must have these basic characteristics: horse sense, love for detail, ability to understand people, a good memory, power to persuade, integrity, courage, and spiritual values. If you hope to be successful in human resource management, you will need these characteristics to deal tactfully and patiently with others. You are expected to speak and write well. You will have to work and communicate effectively with people possessing various degrees of intelligence and experience. The successful HR worker will have a high tolerance for frustration.

Professional

The HR manager requires the ability to make decisions, solve problems, move toward goals effectively, and keep in perspective the factors bearing on specific matters.

At the executive level, you will need the ability to see the big picture and to translate the needs of the organization into policies, plans, programs, and actions. This includes not only the understanding of the organization internally but also the ability to catch the long-range implications of new legislation and changing public opinion.

At the managerial level, you will need the ability to develop and direct programs that will carry out organization policies. You will have to be supportive of both your superiors and your subordinates.

At the technical level, you, as an HR manager, must apply your detailed knowledge to personnel programs and problems. You will implement established programs.

At the specialist level, you need skills that enable you to keep several employees working smoothly. You must have thorough knowledge of personnel procedures and particular functions.

At the clerical level, you will apply skill, speed, and accuracy in completing personnel forms, maintaining personnel records, and performing general office duties. You will need to be alert and to understand directives in an environment you are just becoming accustomed to.

Educational

If you can't manage a college education, the field still is open to you. Many persons enter personnel at the clerical level and attend college part time. Some companies have in-service training programs to teach beginning personnel workers the operations and personnel procedures.

Specialized training or advanced degrees may be required for some jobs. This is understandable in light of the increasing complexity of employee benefit programs, government regulations, wage agreements, and employee selection procedures. The growing emphasis on professionalization in the field, resulting from increased specialization, has encouraged human resource management staff members to continue their educational growth throughout their working careers. Many personnel/human resource managers now hold master's degrees.

STANDARDS FOR EMPLOYMENT

Educational preparation is necessary to enable personnel to perform the duties required of them. Preparation needed for entry and service at the various levels is described below.

The Clerical Level

A high school diploma will usually be required for entry into the career field of personnel/human resources at the clerical level. In high school, your course work should include English, mathematics, and a general foundation in science, followed by courses to prepare you for office work, such as typing, shorthand, letter writing, office procedures, office machines, calculators, computers, and other related skill courses. To be a successful personnel worker at the clerical level, you will utilize all of these skills in the performance of your duties.

The Specialist Level

At the specialist level, you will be building on the skills acquired at the clerical level. The same skills will be used, but they will have to be developed to a much higher degree. Special schooling, such as short-hand or bookkeeping, may be required. At this level, you as a personnel worker may expand into payroll or payroll accounting or related duties. It is frequently convenient to have a specialist in the personnel office qualified as a notary public. Service at the specialist level requires highly polished office and secretarial skills, including computer operation.

The Technical Level

A college degree is almost universally required for entry into the career field of personnel/human resources at the technical level. This is the level of first-line management and at this level, technical HR functions are managed and supervised. As a manager at this level, you will be most valuable if you have a good, rounded education in the arts and sciences as well as a foundation in business and a broad understanding of HR management. Furthermore, you will need an in-depth appreciation of one or more of the technical functions of personnel. At this level of the organization, you will use your technical knowledge to develop programs in your areas of technical specialty and to supervise the performance of these particular functions. You will be most valuable when you have a detailed knowledge and practical understanding of your particular functional areas. You will have to manage the function and provide leadership for those under your jurisdiction.

The Managerial and Executive Levels

Persons serving at the managerial and executive levels of organizations will need a thorough knowledge of personnel/human resources in particular and a good understanding of business administration or public administration in general. Graduate education will usually provide the basis for an understanding of the processes that managers and executives must know to direct satisfactorily. Many managers and executives who do not have graduate degrees, master's and doctorates, have acquired the necessary knowledge through a vast amount of reading and experience. At these higher levels of management, there is a limit to the amount you as a manager will learn from formal education. After acquiring a particular knowledge of personnel/human resources, a general knowledge of business and public administration, and exposure to management development processes, it then is primarily up to you how you will perform. At this stage, formal preparation has done as much as it can do. Now success becomes a matter of experience and your own initiative.

EDUCATIONAL REQUIREMENTS

At all levels of work in the field of human resource management, there are requirements for knowledge and skill that are obtained through education. The paragraphs that follow address some of the most important aspects of this issue.

Many employees seek to fill beginning positions in personnel and labor relations with college graduates who have the potential to move into management jobs. Some employers look for graduates who have majored in personnel/human resource management while others prefer college graduates with a general business background. Still other employers feel that a well-rounded liberal arts education is the best preparation for personnel work. A college major in personnel administration, political science, or public administration can be an asset in looking for a job with a government agency.

At least 200 colleges and universities have programs leading to a degree in the field of human resource management. While personnel administration is widely taught, the number of programs that focus primarily on labor relations is quite small. In addition, many schools offer course work in closely related fields. An interdisciplinary background is appropriate for work in this area, and a combination of courses in the social sciences, behavioral sciences, business, and economics is useful.

Prospective personnel workers might utilize courses in personnel management, business administration, public administration, psychology, sociology, political science, economics, and statistics. Courses in labor law, collective bargaining, labor economics, labor history, and industrial psychology provide a valuable background for the prospective labor relations worker.

Graduate study in human resources, economics, business, or law provides sound preparation for work in labor relations. While a law degree seldom is required for jobs at the entry level, many of the people with responsibility for contract negotiations are lawyers, and the labor-relations-plus-law-degree combination is becoming highly desirable.

A college education is important, but it is not the only way to enter personnel work. Some people enter the field at the clerical level and advance to professional positions on the basis of experience. They often find it helpful to take college courses part-time, however.

New personnel workers usually enter formal or on-the-job training programs to learn how to classify jobs, interview applicants, or administer employee benefits. After the training period, new workers are assigned to specific areas in the company's department of human resources. After gaining experience, they usually can advance within their own company or transfer to another employer. At this point, some people move from personnel to labor relations work. Some people enter the labor relations field directly as trainees. They are usually graduates of master's degree programs in employee relations or law programs.

Workers in the middle ranks of a large organization often transfer to a top job in a smaller one. Employees with exceptional ability may be promoted to executive positions such as director of human resources or director of labor relations.

Personnel/human resources workers should speak and write effectively and be able to work with people of all levels of education and experience. They also must be able to see both the employee's and the employer's point of view. In addition, they should be able to work as part of a team. They need supervisory abilities and must be able to accept responsibility. Integrity and fair-mindedness are important qualities for people in personnel/human resources work. A persuasive, congenial personality can be a great asset.

According to the Bureau of Labor Statistics, a bachelor's degree is the minimum educational background for a beginning job in personnel work, a field that includes such assignments as recruiter, interviewer, job analyst, position classifier, wage administrator, training specialist, and employee counselor. Some employers look for college graduates who have majored in personnel administration, public administration, business, or economics while others prefer applicants with a liberal arts background and evident management potential. An analysis of the occupational field of personnel, training, and labor relations specialists and managers showed about 456,000 jobs in 1990. Significant growth is expected in the occupational field through the year 2005.[1] Those interested in jobs in human resource management must be prepared to compete with the increasing number of applicants for HR positions. Most openings will be occurring in smaller, newer firms in the private sector.

Cost of Education

An education is costly. Direct education costs might be considered to include tuition, fees, books, and supplies. Indirect costs include room and board, transportation, and personal expenses. Costs vary a great deal from one institution to another. However, the following table reflects recent average costs.[2]

---

[1]*Occupational Outlook Handbook, 1992–93*, 52.

[2]*The College Cost Book,* 13th Ed., New York: College Entrance Examination Board, 1993.

Transportation and personal expenses will vary widely and depend on individual circumstances.

Table 4.1. Education Costs

Item	Four-year Private University	Four-year Public University
Tuition and Fees	$10,017	$2,137
Room and board	4,386	3,351
Books and supplies	508	485
Totals	14,911	5,973

Educational Opportunities

If you plan to go to college, the following references may be helpful:

Barron's Profiles of American Colleges, Hauppage, NY: Barron's Educational Series, Inc., Directories of U.S. colleges, giving curricula, degrees

Lovejoy's College Guide, 22d ed., Prentice-Hall Press, 15 Columbus Circle, New York, NY 10023

Professional Certification

Almost all professional fields are progressing toward required certification of their members. This serves two purposes: first, it ensures that members of the profession who hold the certification have met minimum professional standards of performance and meet the ethical standards of the profession. Second, it assures the public that those professionals who hold the appropriate designations are, in fact, qualified to perform the duties required of the profession.

For many years, accountants have had to pass stringent examinations to acquire the designation *certified public accountant* (CPA). Medical doctors, after passing thorough examinations, are designated *doctor of medicine* (MD). Professionals in the field of personnel/human resources are now earning certification in the field through the Human Resource Certification Institute (HRCI), which is an independent, nonprofit, educational organization whose purpose is to raise and maintain standards in the personnel and human resource management field by

- providing and updating periodically the outlines of the body of knowledge to accommodate growth and change in the field
- promoting self-development of human resource professionals, and
- recognizing individual professionals who have mastered the defined body of knowledge

Certification is open to all professionals in the field—practitioners, educators, researchers, and consultants. It is awarded to specialists and generalists based on their demonstrated mastery of the appropriate body of knowledge. Certification may be awarded at either the basic level or the senior level.

The institute defines the body of knowledge, prepares study guides, and develops test questions. If you are interested in more information concerning certification, contact:

The Human Resource Certification Institute
606 North Washington Street
Alexandria, VA 22314
703/548-3440

STARTING YOUR CAREER

In any field, getting started is a tough proposition. There are many decisions to be made, and there are many unknowns that have to be investigated. Decisions are made at many points in a person's life, but those made from the age of about 15 to 25 may be the most important. During these years, directions are taken that will have long-range effects on people's careers. An individual's chances for success in a chosen career are enhance if she or he will devote the time and effort necessary to analyze her or his position in life and consider the many things that must be done. The paragraphs that follow discuss the major aspects that a person must consider in preparing and planning a career path. These things require time and mature contemplation.

SELF-EVALUATION

The first thing a person must decide is where he or she wants to be in life. Whatever the field or whatever the level, the person must decide where he or she wants to be in the distant future and express this desire in the broadest terms possible. "President of the XYZ Company" is too specific. "A top-level executive position in manufacturing" is more general and better for a start.

Next, a person must analyze where he or she is. This should result in as complete a description as possible. For example, an adolescent might describe himself or herself as a seventeen-year-old high school junior in Los Angeles, California.

After a person has decided where he or she wants to be and has analyzed where he or she is, he or she can take the next step and plan how to narrow the gap between the two. The route from being a high school junior to being a top executive includes a college degree, years of hard work, graduate study, and a wide variety of experiences. A person who recognizes this route early in life can facilitate planning a career path as he or she goes along. It is essential that a person keep in mind life objectives and career objectives so that he or she always knows the proper course to steer. With these things in mind, a person can make judgments whether certain activities will contribute to the attainment of those objectives.

This whole process, of course, is not simple. It involves many questions, and some of these will be discussed below.

Objectives

Let's get down to the nuts and bolts of where you want to be. You must define as carefully as possible your life and career objectives. Life objectives might include such things as being extremely wealthy, working out of doors, or making a contribution to society. Career objectives might include such things as being a top-level accountant, being a research chemist, being a minister, or driving a bus. The immediate follow-up activity is to analyze where you are and then decide or plan how to get from where you are to where you want to be.

Resources

A careful analysis of your resources will help provide a realistic look at the range of possibilities for developing a career. Lack of resources should not deter you from striving for your stated objectives. A realistic appraisal of your resources will permit an honest understanding of the tools you can use to reach your objectives.

POSSIBLE RESOURCES

There are several kinds of resources you should consider using in the pursuit of your career. These resources may not be balanced nor adequate. But they are what you have to work with, so you will have to make the most of them.

Finances

It takes money to pay for an education. It takes money to pay for food and lodging. If your family is very hard pressed for money, then an overriding consideration regarding your future may be the necessity for you to get a job and support yourself or possibly even contribute to the support of the family group. If your family is in the middle income bracket, possibly there is enough to support you through your college education without the necessity for your getting a job. This could be complicated, however, if there are five students to be put through college one after another. Serious illness in the family can have an impact on the financial resources available to you in support of your efforts to get started in your education or your career.

Self-appraisal

Successful career planning demands an honest self-appraisal. This evaluation includes an estimate of your own intellectual capacity and motivation. Without motivation, all the intelligence in the world won't get you where you want to go. Without the intellectual capacity to meet the requirements of the career field, motivation is not enough. In borderline cases, the will and drive to succeed will help immensely, but it can overcome just so much. If you got D's and F's in school, there is little likelihood that you have the capacity to be a nuclear physicist. We have to face the fact that half of us have below average intelligence. This statement is a little severe, for most of us are very near the average. Some people are smarter than the average. Some are not as smart as the average. Most people are at or near the average. But those of us who are near the average must acknowledge that we are not far above the average and therefore do not have the capacity to meet some extremely high and difficult requirements. There is a suitable job somewhere for each of us. Aiming for the impossible is only going to frustrate those of us who do not have the required intelligence and drive.

Education

After you have achieved a realistic understanding of your objectives and the resources available, you can consider educational requirements and their attainment. Some career objectives will obviously require a college education, and some will require study at the graduate level. A business manager, for example, will have to have a bachelor's degree, and it is advisable for him or her to have a master of business administration (MBA) as well. This study generally takes about six years—four years for the bachelor's and another two for the master's.

Will your resources stretch to meet this requirement? If not, then you will have to consider the alternatives. One is to take the lightest full-time study load possible and work during summers and vacation breaks. In other words, you might go to school full-time and work part-time. Another alternative might be to go to school part-time and work full-time. You can get a better job this way, but it takes a much longer time to get the education required to reach your objectives. These are the realities of life, and the wise person will acknowledge that these problems exist and will face up to them and figure how to cope with them. Wishing will not make them go away. They must be faced and overcome.

CHOICES: JOB OR SCHOOL?

One of the decisions most of us have to face at some time is the choice between taking a job and going to school. If your financial resources are limited, there may not actually be the opportunity to make a choice—it may be made for you. Without money it may be necessary to get a full-time job to support yourself. In that case, the education takes second place, but it need not be set aside entirely. Many people work full-time and go to school part-time. This makes the process of getting an education longer, but it is possible, and this path is chosen by many energetic, career-seeking people.

There are many advantages to going to school full-time. The most evident one is that the years spent in the educational process are reduced to the minimum. Another is that the job seeker has the best possible foundation before going out into the job market to find employment. Many students work part-time while going to school full-time.

There are, of course, many choices between studying full-time and working full-time. From one extreme to the other, they could be considered as full-time study with no work, full-time study with part-time work, half-time study with half-time work, part-time study with full-time work, and no study and full-time work. We all can learn more about our work, our environment, and our society. We should all strive to improve ourselves.

COUNSELING

We all need counseling occasionally. We need counseling in our work and in our choice of educational paths. No one should ever feel embarrassed to ask for assistance and counseling.

Counseling is the process of helping others evaluate things that concern them. Through the technique of discussion, a counselor can assist people to clarify their goals in life. A counselor can help people make an honest appraisal of their own financial and family resources and needs. The most effective counselor doesn't advise anyone what to do. Rather, the effective counselor assists people to think things through for themselves. Good counselors are experienced in asking the right questions and probing for key information. When counselors probe people's private lives, they are not hunting for gossip. They are doing their job thoroughly by helping people take into consideration those aspects of their lives that they may have taken for granted. Matters such as the number of years a supporting parent has yet to work may have an effect on the financial resources available to put a young person through college. If the parent is 65 and facing retirement, this is an important factor. Yet most of us think that our parents will go on forever.

The counselor will assist you to keep things in perspective. A high school or community college counselor is well equipped to outline the requirements and opportunities in a wide variety of careers. The counselor can explain in some detail the length of time required to complete the training or college required for career preparation, what the costs are likely to be, what the opportunities for landing a job might be, and how these things all relate to your resources, needs, and objectives.

No competent counselor will tell you what to do. No one should do that. You must make your own decisions. But the counselor can furnish information that will help you make decisions based on the most reliable data available. You have to live with the decisions you make, but the counselor can assist in relating requirements to resources.

Counseling is most effective when the student has done some homework first. For example, the counselor may ask the student, "What do you want to do?" If the student replies, "I don't know—that's what I came here to find out," the student isn't prepared for an effective counseling session. The student has to have some idea of what kinds of things he or she likes to do and what her or his intellectual and financial resources are. The most effective counseling session results from the student's doing as much preparation as possible prior to the session. Then the counselor can take the student from that point and help him or her find the better ways among the vast number of selections available in both educational choices and career paths.

At the high school level, there are generally two kinds of counseling available: career counseling and college counseling. The first is intended to assist the student in finding a career field of interest. The second is intended to assist the student to find a college or university that offers the kinds of courses that will provide career preparation in a particular major field. College counseling can be in general terms, such as business administration, or more specific terms, such as human resource management.

At junior colleges and community colleges, excellent counseling is usually available. Golden West College in Huntington Beach, California, for example, is typical and offers extensive counseling in career information and college guidance services.

Career information services include educational and career information on job descriptions, placements, labor markets, licensing and certification, federal and state employment, military service opportunities, guides to careers through college majors, occupations, delivery systems, college and university catalog microfilm libraries, professional publications, industry news, college planning, university departmental bulletins and brochures, community college career programs, and others. This service also includes vocational testing and planning, career counseling, cooperative education services, and vocational planning classes.

College guidance services include counseling in particular academic divisions of the college. They also include career information services such as career counseling, career information, guidance programs, and college and university catalogs.

The extent of the assistance available is illustrated by the outline of career planning services, which include the following:

- Career information services for feeder high school students
- Career planning information and assistance
- Labor market and current job information
- Part-time job experiences for students
- Job performance upgrading
- Full-time job placement service for graduates and others discontinuing education
- Educational planning for career preparation
- On-campus employer recruitment

A catalog of career training programs is available. This catalog includes a description of all the career programs offered and provides a description of job duties and working conditions, job preparation, and the employment outlook and advancement.

Counseling is also available at four-year colleges and universities. Educational counseling and testing is usually available in the counseling office. Career counseling is usually available in the office dealing with career planning and placement. The titles of these offices vary from institution to institution, but the services will usually be provided somewhere on the campus.

Some counseling assistance and career information are often available from labor unions, professional organizations, and public service agencies. For example, information on careers in human resource management is available from the Society for Human Resource Management, 606 North Washington Street, Alexandria, Virginia 22314. These all have to be contacted individually for the services needed.

APPLYING FOR A JOB

Eventually you must apply for work. With a high school diploma, you can expect to be considered for a position at the clerical or beginner's level. With a bachelor's degree, you might expect to be considered for a position at the lower levels of management, assuming the degree major is related in some way to the requirements of the job you are applying for. With a bachelor's degree and work experience, you might apply for a position at the middle management level. With a master's degree and experience, you could reasonably expect employment at the middle management level if your performance in previous assignments was generally excellent.

Whatever the level, there are certain procedures and mechanics you must go through to land a job. First, a job has to be located. This might result from scanning the want ads in the local newspaper, or a friend may advise you of an opportunity in her or his company. If you seem to have the qualifications to perform the job, then apply.

In order to apply for a position, you must file or complete an application form. This might be done by mail or in person in the personnel office or employment office of the company where the work is available. Each organization has its own particular application form. They are all a little different, but most of them will require the same kinds of information. The purpose of the application form is to inform the prospective employer of some of the basic information it must have concerning those who apply for work there.

Most application forms will contain spaces for the following information or questions:

- Name, address, phone number, Social Security number, and legality of residency status
- Position applied for: how did you learn of this opening?
- Age: are you over 18?
- Statement of physical condition to perform the required work
- Statement of veteran status
- Education: level and name of each school attended, number of years attended, grade completed, special courses, diploma, degree
- Extracurricular activities
- Honors
- Employment history for last three jobs or last ten years (employer; address; immediate supervisor; your position, title, and duties; starting salary; reason for leaving)

In addition to the application form, many organizations also utilize a confidential data sheet. They use this sheet to meet the requirements of the U.S. Department of Health and Human Services to compile summary data of the sex and ethnicity of applicants for positions. These sheets will typically contain information that may not appear on the application form and thus possibly constitute the basis for discrimination in hiring. The confidential data sheet is kept separate from the application form until after the successful applicant has been hired. After the person has won the job, the data sheet provides the statistical information that the employer is required to maintain and report.

A typical confidential data sheet contains the following items of information:

- Name, address, phone number, Social Security number, and citizenship status
- Position applied for
- Sex, birthdate, physical condition
- Ethnic identification:

American Indian	Other Nonwhite
African American	White
Mexican American	Filipino
Spanish surnamed	Do not choose to provide
Asian American	this information

- How the applicant learned of the vacancy

The Personnel/Human Resources Office

All personnel matters are administered in the personnel office of the organization. When you apply for work, you may be directed to file an application in the personnel office or sometimes, in very large firms, in the employment office established for this specific purpose. When you enter one of these offices, you will see an array of clerical and other office workers engaged in a variety of duties all related to personnel work.

There are several kinds of people you can expect to encounter in the personnel office.

Receptionist. This is the person who will greet you on entering the office and determine what assistance you need. You will, of course, need an application form and instructions necessary for completing it. The form might be filled out at a counter or in a room set aside for that purpose.

Interviewer. After completing the application form, you may expect to see an interviewer. The interviewer talks with you about the information on the application to make sure that it is clear to you and is able to explain many aspects of the position you are applying for. The interviewer may describe general work rules of the organization. One of the main purposes of the interview is to ensure that as an applicant you meet the requirements of the position and that you understand the requirements of the position and want the job.

Tester. After the interview is completed, it is possible that specified tests will be administered. For example, persons applying for secretarial jobs can expect to be given a typing test and possibly a shorthand test. Sometimes other tests are administered in the office or elsewhere in the place of work.

Others. There will be others in the personnel office who are engaged in various duties. Among those you might observe are the records clerks who maintain the personnel files. The benefits clerk or counselor may be advising employees concerning the benefits of the retirement program. And that person rushing through the office with a harried look is probably the director of human resources.

The Procedure

The usual hiring procedure will include those steps that have just been described—completing the application, the preliminary interview, and any required testing. When you pass all these hurdles, you will be referred to the prospective supervisor for the job interview. The supervisor is the person who will actually oversee the work of the new employee and thus is interested in the qualifications and experience of the applicant. The supervisor is also interested in those things that might be indicative of your success on the job. These would include your aptitudes, manner, sincerity, and response to the questions posed by the prospective supervisor. It is the supervisor who usually makes the decision to hire. The successful applicant will be informed and then will have to go through the hiring procedure, which entails getting more information and completing additional forms such as next of kin and beneficiary statements.

CHAPTER 5

LAUNCHING YOUR CAREER

Job hunting is a tough, competitive process. Few of us are handed a job on a silver platter. If the world hasn't beaten a path to your door by now, you may assume that you are going to have to go out and look for a job yourself. Most of us have to present ourselves to prospective employers and convince them that they should hire us. With this in mind, it might be wise to consider some questions that the employer could ask during an interview:

Why should I hire you?
What are your qualifications?
What experience have you had?
How have you prepared yourself for employment?
Why have you come to this particular organization for work?

One way or another, these questions will have to be answered. In the paragraphs that follow, approaches to the answers are discussed. Keep one thing in mind. You will have to do all the work in connection with landing a job. It is a full-time undertaking. It is your livelihood, and you should consider it worthwhile to give the process the care and attention necessary to land the best job you can get.

THE RESUME

People seeking employment at all levels of management and the top levels of white collar work should have a resume prepared. The resume is a brief outline of the applicant's qualifications and includes matters related to education, work experience, and other experiences that might point to the necessary qualifications to perform in the job.

There are many sources for information concerning the basic preparation of a resume, so these will not be discussed at length here. The nearest counseling office will have handouts concerning the preparation of resumes. They are useful and should be consulted.

Keep in mind that the resume is essentially a written communication from you to the prospective employer. It should tell important things about you clearly, and it should hold the interest of the reader. Just as a short story must hook the reader's interest and then hold it throughout the tale, the resume must do the same. Therefore, the resume should state your name, address, phone number, and then some statement of your objective. This tells the reader who you are and what you want. The arrangement of the remainder of the resume is up to you. In general, however, you will have to set forth your qualifications and experience in the sequence that will be most likely to hold the reader's interest. If your education is strong, put that next. If not, put it towards the end. If your work experience is strong, put that near the top.

How do you decide what is important? That really is up to you since you are trying to market yourself to a prospective employer. Specific items and their relative importance follow.

Most Important Items

Your name, address, telephone number, the date you are available for employment, your job objective, education and honors, foreign languages you speak, military service or veteran status, history of past employment, community activities, memberships, and offices in professional associations are the items that provide useful and important information to prospective employers.

Least Important Items

The years you got your degrees, overall grade averages, awards and scholarships, grades in your college minor, your class standing, honorary societies, student body offices, and hobbies can be omitted. Personal data such as marital status, height, weight, number of children, spouse's occupation or education, parental information, or religious preference must not appear in order to avoid charges of discrimination in hiring.

These comments should be taken as guides rather than absolute rules. Not everyone experienced in the field of employment will agree with all of these opinions. These rules do, however, provide a coordinated guide for preparing resumes.

Techniques

There are several ways of distributing your resume to those who might be interested in hiring you. One system is simply to broadcast it to any and all organizations that might hire people with your qualifications in your area of interest. Return from this technique is very small, but coverage is very wide. With enough hooks in the water, you ought to catch a fish.

Another technique is to send out a one-page resume covered with a one-page letter. This has the advantage of providing the most information in the smallest package for the employer to read. The letter should contain information that is not contained in the resume. For example, the reader will wonder why you are writing. Reasons might include that you are just getting your college degree and are looking for a job. It might be that you have a job but are looking for one with more challenge and greater potential for promotion. Maybe you are changing from one career field to another. There are many legitimate reasons for job hunting. The reader will want to know yours. When using this technique, it is worth the trouble to go to the nearest library and use the current edition of *Standard and Poor's* or *Dun and Bradstreet* or some other industrial index to find the name and title of the top person in the organization you plan to address. If you are applying for a job in personnel, then you will want the name and correct title of the top person in human resource management. Address your letter to that person by name.

LOCATING THE JOB OPPORTUNITIES

Job opportunities appear in a number of sources. The job seeker will have to pursue all the leads available in order to ensure the best coverage.

Although there are private agencies that help people find work for a fee, several free agencies are also available.

Public Services

All states have employment offices located in major cities and in central locations. Employment offices are interested in the qualifications of the job seeker and the kind of position he or she is looking for. The same offices also keep records of job opportunities listed by organizations. The employment offices try to match the job opportunities with the job applicants.

Advertising

Firms that have job openings also may advertise in the local newspapers or in professional publications and trade journals such as the *Wall Street Journal, HR Magazine,* and the *Personnel Journal.* These publications are available at the local public library in most cities. They may also be available in school libraries. When looking for jobs, check the headings, "Personnel," "Labor Relations," "Human Resource Management," or any of the occupational areas of your particular interest.

When seeking employment, comb through the want ads in the local newspaper. You should check these ads carefully to determine if you have the qualifications listed in the ad. If not, it may well be fruitless to respond. If you're close, it might be worth a try, but don't expect too much.

In responding to an ad, be sure to respond to each point made in it. This can be done in the letter covering the resume. This action simply serves to emphasize that you have the qualifications the company has deemed important enough to specify in the ad.

If the employer is named in the ad, you may want to consider whether you want to work for that company. If the employer is not identified— that is, you are asked to respond to a box number—you are responding blindly. Some firms place ads this way to avoid offending present employees or having to answer all applications. Responding to an ad should be done just as carefully as sending out resumes and cover letters.

Placement Offices

Most colleges and universities have placement offices that assist job-seeking students. They usually act as centers where students can arrange placement interviews with various company representatives.

Counseling Offices

Many high schools have career counseling offices in addition to college counseling offices. Young people interested in careers in professional fields, such as personnel/human resources, should check in both offices for information concerning job openings and career preparation.

Undecided

Maybe you are not sure that you would really enjoy a particular kind of career. Is it possible to get an idea during high school? Yes—volunteering to help in the counseling office during free period or after school will help you decide whether you like working with people. Volunteering to cover an information desk is also good experience. Visiting personnel departments in local businesses and industries and observing personnel workers on their jobs are perhaps the best ways to judge your interest in that field.

THE JOB INTERVIEW

The job interview provides an opportunity for the applicant and the management of the firm to become acquainted with each other. Even though the employer has already read your resume and your application, there are many more things he or she wants to know about you. If you and all other applicants are equally well qualified for the position you are applying for, the only differences among the candidates are those that will show up in the interview. It behooves the applicants to prepare for the interview and to present themselves at their best.

Preparation

Do your homework. Know something about the firm and the key people you may see. This can be done by looking up the company in the latest edition of *Dun and Bradstreet* or *Standard and Poor's* compilations of information on American businesses. This knowledge will strengthen your background for discussions in the job interview. An outline of information and points you wish to make or find out about is very helpful.

Groom yourself properly. This means clean clothes and a neat and fresh appearance. The company is less interested in the details of your dress and grooming, such as beard or length of hair, but it will expect you to be suitably dressed for a management position, wearing clothes of contemporary style but not so extreme as to be distracting. Dress and grooming should be appropriate for the place of employment, kind of work, and your age.

Techniques

The interview is a give-and-take procedure. When you are asked a question, answer it thoroughly but briefly. It takes practice and judgment to determine when a question has been answered completely. But it is important not to go too far. If a brief answer is not enough, the interviewer will ask for more details. You will make a good impression on the interviewer if you help by giving the information he or she seeks. Few managers know how to interview well. Help the interviewer get the information he or she wants.

You will have some control over the direction and depth of the interview. Tell the interviewer about yourself, but try to hold something back. If the interviewer wants to know more, he or she will say so.

Try for a win in each interview. Be enthusiastic and know what you are talking about. Don't carry a briefcase or resumes with you into the interview room. Take notes and paper in your pockets. It helps to be articulate and to use correct English.

What to Say

In your comments, mention your interest in that particular firm. Demonstrate that you already have some knowledge of the industry, its processes, and developments. Mention your qualifications in general terms. You might highlight interesting aspects of your studies, work experiences, or travel. There will be an opportunity for you to mention what you believe you can contribute to the firm. This might be youth, imagination, or vigor. You must believe that you have something going for you. Go ahead and mention it. Don't brag, but learn how to put yourself forward in a factual way. Mention specific accomplishments without boasting of what great things they were. You state the facts. Let others judge the degree or quality of the achievement.

You will usually be given the opportunity to ask questions or state particular interests. You should be able to do two things: first, be prepared to make a statement of personal objectives that will be consistent with the objectives of the firm. Second, don't ever let the opportunity go by without expressing an interest in more knowledge about the firm. For example, always be ready to say, "I'd like to know more about . . ."

What to Do

Do your best. Try hard to make a good impression. Put your best foot forward. Your manner should be pleasant, interested, and it should reflect relaxed self-control.

Try to get the interviewer to talk about the position, the company, the industry, how long he or she has been with the firm, and what the greatest current problem is. Find out why the position you are applying for is open. If it is a new position, that is one thing. If the last employee in the position got fired, watch out—someone may be waiting in the shadows to do the same to you. If, however, that employee got promoted, that is quite another thing. Listen closely for key facts and attitudes. Probe these matters very carefully. This phase of the interview gives you the opportunity to learn more about the firm and, particularly, about the position you have applied for. If the interviewer answers your questions in a straightforward manner, then you can learn much about what you may be facing. If the interviewer is evasive, be careful—it may be difficult to pinpoint what is wrong, but you can bet that something is awry if the interviewer will not answer questions candidly.

What Not to Do

Avoid telephone interviews. These put you at an unnecessary disadvantage. You will do better face to face. If a firm is really interested in you, it will extend you the courtesy of an interview in person.

Avoid jokes and strained pleasantries. They can easily fail you. Easy pleasantries are fine. Avoid arguments. Rather than argue, probe the bases of the opinions held by others. You will learn more from this and also exhibit an interest in the views of the other person.

Never give references without checking first to get their approval. Don't name your references until you and your prospective employer both seem to be favorably disposed toward your employment in that organization. Get the best references you can. Avoid any that you are not sure will be favorable.

Salary

Inquire about salary and fringe benefits only after all other major matters have been discussed. If the interviewer asks you what your salary requirements are, say that you cannot estimate your requirements until you have more information concerning the responsibilities and requirements of the position. You should go into the interview with a salary range in mind. A higher figure might be appropriate for greater responsibility and few fringes. A lower one might serve for less responsibility and many fringes. A pleasant work environment might serve to compensate for a somewhat smaller salary. Proximity to your home may be a factor.

Eventually, you will have to ask what is being offered, or the interviewer will have to know your requirements. This is the time for some plain talk and maybe some negotiations. You should be aware of the value of what you have to offer a prospective employer. You can find some information concerning current wages in the latest wage survey of your geographical area and occupational field published by the U.S. Department of Labor, Bureau of Labor Statistics.

Follow-up Contact

After the interview and within two days, write a letter to the person who interviewed you. Do not write a trite or flowery letter of thanks for the interview. Instead, review the highlights of the interview. Bring up any additional pertinent points, especially any that might help the interviewer solve problems raised in the interview. Add any strengths or experiences that may not have been covered in the interview for lack of time. Don't get petulant. Just inquire about the status of your application for the position and express your continued interest in it.

Self-development

Each interview should be used as a learning experience. You should analyze the interview in order to learn what to do and what not to do. Each interview presents the opportunity for self-development as a result of a careful analysis of its good and bad aspects.

Note the highlights of the interview. Make a record of names, addresses, titles, phone numbers, and relationships of those who interviewed you or those whose names came up during the interview. Critique the interview in terms of strengths and weaknesses. Be sure to take any follow-up action indicated, such as contacting someone or looking up some statistics or the provisions of a particular act of legislation.

If an interview doesn't result in a job offer, don't get discouraged. You will be fortunate if out of every 100 contacts you make you get five job interviews, and from those, one job offer.

If you had 99 unproductive interviews, don't let it get you down. You should approach that one hundredth interview with just as much enthusiasm as you approached the first and with a lot better preparation. You should do better—after all, think of all the experience you have had now. Hang in there and keep trying.

SUCCESS AND ADVANCEMENT

Many first jobs are part-time work which students use to pay part of their school or living expenses. If you can find a part-time job while still in school, you will be one step ahead.

Your first employment in a personnel career could very well be a job as a junior interviewer, personnel clerk, assistant job analyst, or labor relations assistant, depending on your education, experience, and the position available. After getting some work experience and, sometimes, in-service training, you may move up to become the head of a department and eventually go to a top personnel/human resources position. Some HR executives who reach the top of their department in a small company transfer to a larger firm with more sophisticated personnel programs and higher salaries. As the labor force expands and as the demand on personnel departments broadens, it becomes increasingly possible for personnel managers to become top-level managers of their companies.

Success on the Job

Success on the job will depend on three basic and essential aspects of all positions: knowledge of job content, performance on the job, and relationships on the job. *Job content* refers to knowing what is expected of you on the job and what things you are required to know. This includes not only facts (what), but also the processes involved (how). These things relate to the rules and regulations, including legislation, that place certain requirements on the office. The requirements of the job will usually be contained in the job description. There may also be a position description that will provide more specific details of the content of the assignment. The employee should be thoroughly familiar with the job description.

Performance on the job refers to the way you carry out your assignment. The speed and accuracy with which you do the tasks that constitute your job reflect on your total job performance. Managers usually look for thoroughness, accuracy, and speed in the duties of the assignment. This usually means that the person performing the job sets high standards of performance. To do your best in the job is to put forth a conscientious effort to give all that you are being paid for and more. If you are going to worry about doing more than you think you are getting paid for, you are hampering yourself. You will neither enjoy the assignment nor perform it well.

Few jobs are performed in isolation. Almost all assignments, and certainly all those in the field of personnel/human resources, require relationships with others at work. These others are your superiors, your colleagues, and those in other offices in the organization as well as those outside the organization who have business dealings with your office and your position. In these relationships you must be able to understand work assignments given you and then carry out the tasks necessary to complete the assignment. You will be working in conjunction with the other workers in the same office and many others in other offices in the organization. These relations usually involve exchanging information or processing papers in some sequential order so that the work one person does depends on the proper completion of the previous step. Relations external to the place of work will usually require getting or giving information. The successful worker will know how to communicate under these various circumstances.

Advancement

Advancement in an organization will depend first on the existence of a vacancy or a need in the organization. Assuming there is such a vacancy in the organization, what can a worker do to be advanced?

Advancement may depend on two factors related to the persons themselves. First is the matter of how well they have performed in previous work assignments. Superior performance in a current or previous assignment usually is indicative of a worker's competence, and the inference is that the person will probably work equally well in a higher position.

Another key factor of consideration is preparation for the advanced assignment. Keep in mind that within any occupation, the differences at various levels within the field are degrees of skill and responsibility. At higher levels, the skills and responsibility are greater. The person seeking advancement to a higher level should be prepared to perform at a higher level of skill as well as to accept a higher level of responsibility.

It is not out of line to inform your superior that you seek work at a higher level in the organization. The supervisor will ask if you are prepared to perform at a higher level of skill and accept the greater responsibility. You could then demonstrate your higher-level skills and assure the supervisor that you seek more responsibility. If you are not qualified, then you should ask the supervisor what preparation you need to quality yourself for advancement. This shows the supervisor that you are interested and that you want to know what you must do to better prepare yourself for advancement. A good supervisor will always help subordinates prepare themselves for higher-level assignments, even though it means that eventually they will be leaving for another assignment and a replacement will have to be trained. In notifying your boss that you seek advancement, don't give her or him the impression that you are looking for a way out. Tell your supervisor how much you have learned from her or him, that you want to learn more, and also that you hope to qualify yourself for advancement.

In a profession such as personnel/human resources, it is usually assumed that beginners in the field will continue their education and development both on and off the job. Advancement depends on competent performance and development.

THE OCCUPATIONAL OUTLOOK[1]

The anticipated increase in the nation's labor force is expected to create a need for more personnel workers to carry on existing activities

---

[1]This section derived from *Occupational Outlook Handbook, 1992–93*, 50–53.

and to handle new personnel problems as they arise. The outlook for personnel work is excellent, according to both industrial and government sources. Figure 5.1 shows the expanding work force and also the rapidly increasing number of workers employed in the field of personnel/human resources. The number of personnel workers is expected to

Figure 5.1. Work Force and Human Resource Workers

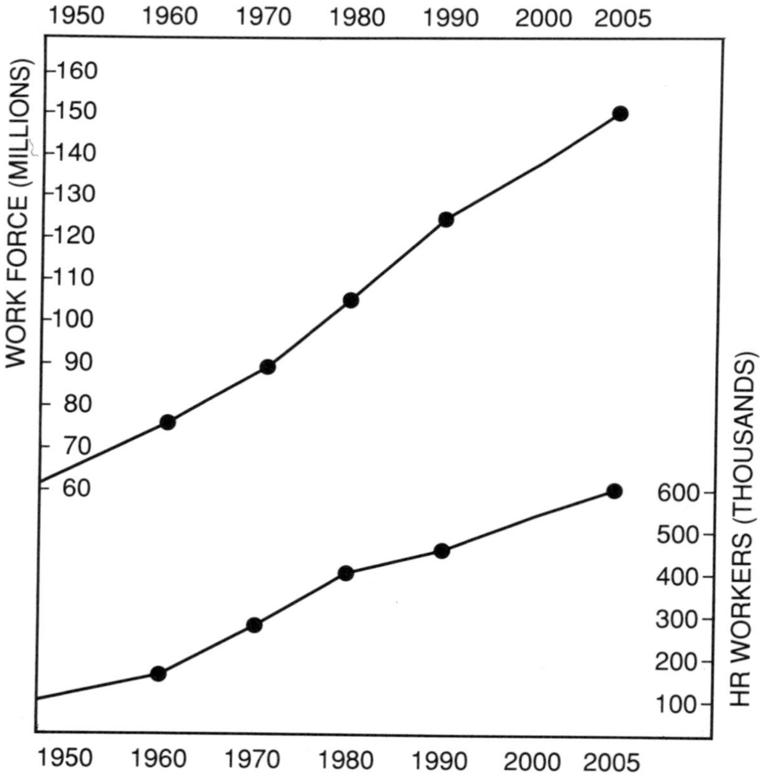

Source: U.S. Department of Labor, Bureau of Labor Statistics, *Outlook 1990–2005*, BLS Bulletin 2402, May 1992.

increase through the 1990s as employers recognize the need to maintain good employee relations.

Although the competition is increasing, there are numerous openings for young people willing to start in subprofessional or junior-level positions. A growing number of industrial and government employers are setting up in-service training programs for this purpose. Employment prospects will probably be best for college graduates who have specialized training in personnel/human resource management.

Employment

Personnel, training, and labor relations specialists and managers held about 465,000 jobs in 1990. They were employed in virtually every industry. Specialists accounted for 278,000 positions; managers, 178,000. About 12,000—mostly specialists—were self-employed, working as consultants to public and private employers.

The private sector accounted for 85 percent of salaried jobs. Service industries—including business, health, social, management, and educational services—accounted for nearly 4 out of 10 jobs; labor organizations—a service industry and the largest employer among specific industries—accounted for more than 1 out of 10 jobs, while finance, insurance, and real estate firms also accounted for 1 out of 10.

Federal, state, and local governments employed about 15 percent of salaried personnel, training, and labor relations specialists and managers. They handled recruitment, interviewing, job classification, training, salary administration, benefits, employee relations, mediation, and related matters for the nation's public employees.

Training

Entry-level workers often enter formal or on-the-job training programs, where they learn how to classify jobs, interview applicants, or administer employee benefits. Next, they are assigned to specific areas in the personnel/human resource department to gain experience. Later, they may advance to a managerial position overseeing a major element of the personnel program—compensation or training, for example.

Exceptional personnel, training, and labor relations workers may be promoted to director of personnel/human resources or industrial/labor relations, which can eventually lead to a top managerial or executive position. Others may join a consulting firm or open their own business. A Ph.D. is an asset for teaching, writing, or consulting work,

Certification by a professional society is an indication of competence and can enhance one's advancement opportunities. The Society for Human Resource Management offers certification at the professional (PHR) and senior professional (SPHR) levels in human resources.

Job Outlook

The number of personnel, training, and labor relations specialists and managers is expected to grow faster than the average for all occupations through the year 2005. In addition, many job openings will result from the need to replace workers who leave this relatively large occupation. However, the job market is likely to remain competitive in view of the abundant supply of college graduates and experienced workers with suitable qualifications.

Most growth will occur in the private sector as employers, concerned about productivity and quality of work, devote greater resources to job-specific training programs in response to the increasing complexity of many jobs, the aging of the work force, and technological advances that can leave employees with obsolete skills. Demand for human resource specialists and managers should also increase as legislation and court rulings setting standards in occupational safety and health, equal employment opportunity, benefits, and other related areas has substantially increased the amount of record keeping, analysis, and report writing in these areas. In addition, data gathering and analytical activities will increase as employers continue to review and evaluate their personnel policies and programs, but few additional jobs are likely to be created because of offsetting productivity gains associated with the automation of personnel and payroll information.

Employment demand could be particularly strong in management and consulting firms as well as personnel supply firms as businesses increasingly contract out personnel functions or hire personnel specialists on a contractual basis to meet the increasing cost and complexity of training and development programs. Demand should also increase in firms that develop and administer the increasingly complex employee benefits and compensation packages for other organizations.

Demand for HR personnel, both specialists and managers, is also governed by the staffing needs of the firms where they work. A rapidly expanding business is likely to hire additional personnel workers— either as permanent employees or consultants—while a business that has experienced a merger or a reduction in its work force will require fewer personnel workers. In any particular firm, the size and the job duties of the human resources staff are determined by a variety of factors, including the firm's organizational philosophy and goals, the labor intensity and skill profile of the industry, the pace of technological change, government regulations, collective bargaining agreements, standards of professional practice, and labor market conditions.

Table 5.1. Civilian Labor Force, 1990 and Projected to 2005

Labor force	1990	124,786,000
Entrants	1990–2005	55,798,000
Leavers	1990–2005	29,851,000
Labor force	2005	150,732,000

Source: U.S. Department of Labor, Bureau of Labor Statistics, BLS Bulletin 2402, May 1992, 39.

Table 5.2. Median Ages of the Labor Force 1990–2005

1990	36.6
1995	38.0
2000	39.4
2005	40.6

Source: U.S. Department of Labor, Bureau of Labor Statistics, BLS Bulletin 2402, May 1992, 41.

Future Assignments[2]

Future personnel departments are expected to provide staff services, but their director will be a full-fledged manager in the executive group. Several current developments point to this conclusion. Among the most important are these:

1. The new generation of executives is convinced that the first responsibility of management—the responsibility for planning—has to include special attention to human resources. As the speed of technological change accelerates, skill requirements must be predicted far in advance. Lead times for many new skills are long. Selection and training require far-sighted planning.
2. Similarly, organizational planning means planning for people. The pace of organizational change is accelerating. New patterns of organization are emerging, and more radical innovations are widely predicted. A major problem is that of preparing employees for rapid change and reducing their resistance to it.
3. Investments in people are expanding. A firm cannot afford to regard these investments lightly; they must be conserved and protected. Planning and organizing must build on these investments, using modern training and development programs. The executive group must recognize the economics of investments in people, the costs and benefits of training/development programs, and the contributions of new learning theory and related programs.
4. Problems of employee commitment and motivation become increasingly difficult as citizens become more sophisticated, mobile, and economically secure. New reward systems must be developed. Top management cannot assume labor costs as fixed for the future. Executive decisions must take advantage of new work theory and a new package approach to rewards.
5. Increasing employment of professional workers, including scientists and engineers, requires new patterns of day-to-day admini-

[2]Yoder and Staudohar, *Personnel Management*, 25–27.

stration. Top management cannot expect line managers to change without guidance and assistance. Transitional, updating refresher programs must be provided, prescribed, and supported by executive action.

6. Multinational operations also create a new demand for management development. Selecting and preparing managers to work in foreign cultures and having them ready when needed requires informed planning and decisions at the top executive level.

7. For successful competition, an enterprise must innovate and experiment in its management of human resources. Labor costs can be reduced as productivity increases. Alert top managements will authorize and encourage such experiments.

8. Changing public policy on the employment of human resources adds to the complexity of personnel management. Rising minimum wages affect rates at higher levels in wage and salary structures. Rising public benefits create new problems for financial reward systems. Improved public employment services increase labor mobility and the range of available job choices. Campaigns against poverty, dropouts, and discrimination propose that individual firms accept increasing responsibilities.

Educational Implications

Personnel directors and departments are expected to provide the traditional personnel services for management, and the head of the division is being drafted for service in management—top management—at the executive level. Personnel executives must not only be specialists in the many functions they perform, but they now require a broader knowledge of general management in action. This trend has created problems for personnel managers; not all of them are confident about their capabilities in handling the newer, added responsibilities.

Much of the current popular impression of human resource managers and jobs shows little knowledge of these developments. Movie and television characters in the personnel role still act as staff to management. They are concerned with the technical services to management that have been traditional. Personnel managers are characterized as specialists in services rather than as managers first and then specialists in the management of human resources. All managers must have a thorough grounding in the theory, policy, and practice of managing people. At the same time, the personnel manager must qualify as a manager and be prepared to accept line responsibilities and to contribute to the planning and decision making of line executives. The personnel manager must have the capability to move to various management positions in order to be promoted to top management. Those who plan careers with an emphasis on the management of people must make sure they are educationally prepared for careers in management.

CAREER EXPECTATIONS

People entering the field of human resource management have every right to expect a successful and satisfying career in the field. Those qualified, such as people with college degrees, may enter the field at the lower levels of management or the level of first-line supervision. Those with lesser qualifications can still enter the field at the clerical or technical level and expect to find satisfying employment.

Since the field is growing, there is every reason to believe that there will be promotion opportunities for those who apply themselves and learn the substance and processes of human resource management. At both the managerial and the white collar level, workers in personnel who apply themselves and learn more about the field will have opportunities for more responsibility and broader application of their knowledge and experience.

Some people will prefer to specialize in particular areas such as wage and salary administration. Others will prefer to remain generalists dealing with all the technical aspects of the field. There are opportunities for advancement for both of these types of personnel workers.

Figure 5.2. Rate of Growth of the Population

Chart 1.   **Labor force will slow in the future due to
slowing population growth.**

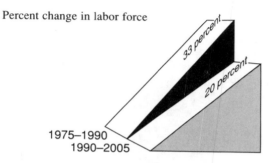

Percent change in labor force

33 percent

20 percent

1975–1990
1990–2005

Source: U.S. Department of Labor, Bureau of Labor Statistics, *Occupational Outlook Handbook, 1992–93*, BLS
Bulletin 2400, May 1992.

Figure 5.3. Distribution of the Labor Force by Race

Chart 2.   **Distribution of the labor force by race and Hispanic origin.**

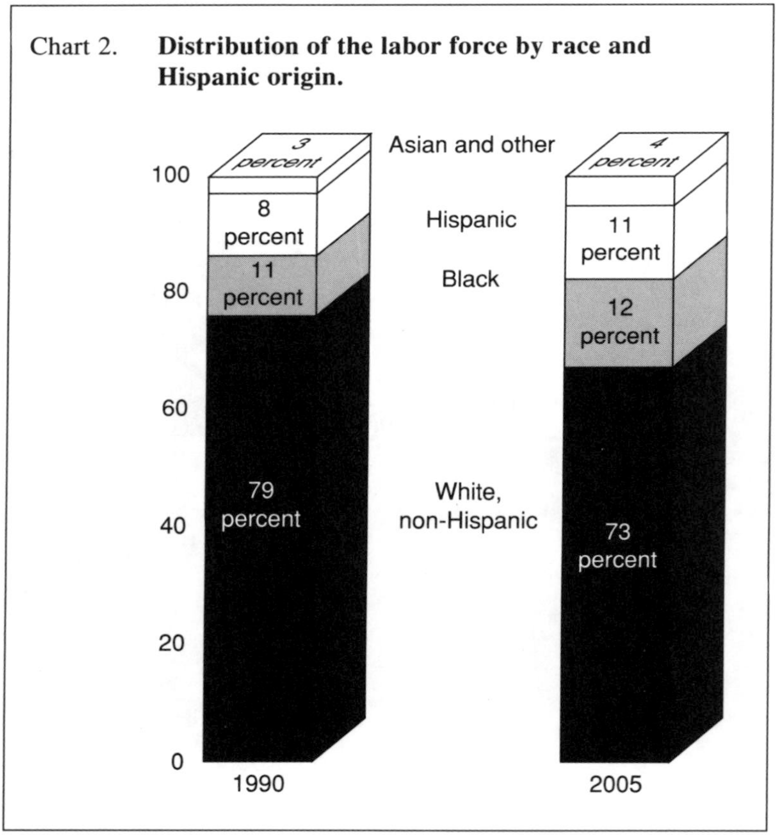

Source: U.S. Department of Labor, Bureau of Labor Statistics, *Occupational Outlook Handbook, 1992–93,* BLS Bulletin 2400, May 1992.

Figure 5.4. Age Distribution of the Labor Force

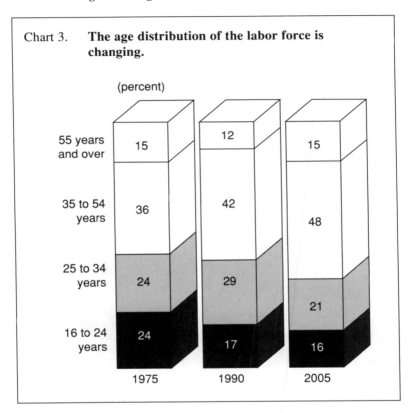

Chart 3.   **The age distribution of the labor force is changing.**

(percent)

	1975	1990	2005
55 years and over	15	12	15
35 to 54 years	36	42	48
25 to 34 years	24	29	21
16 to 24 years	24	17	16

Source: U.S. Department of Labor, Bureau of Labor Statistics, *Occupational Outlook Handbook, 1992–93,* BLS Bulletin 2400, May 1992.

Figure 5.5. Distribution of Jobs by Industries

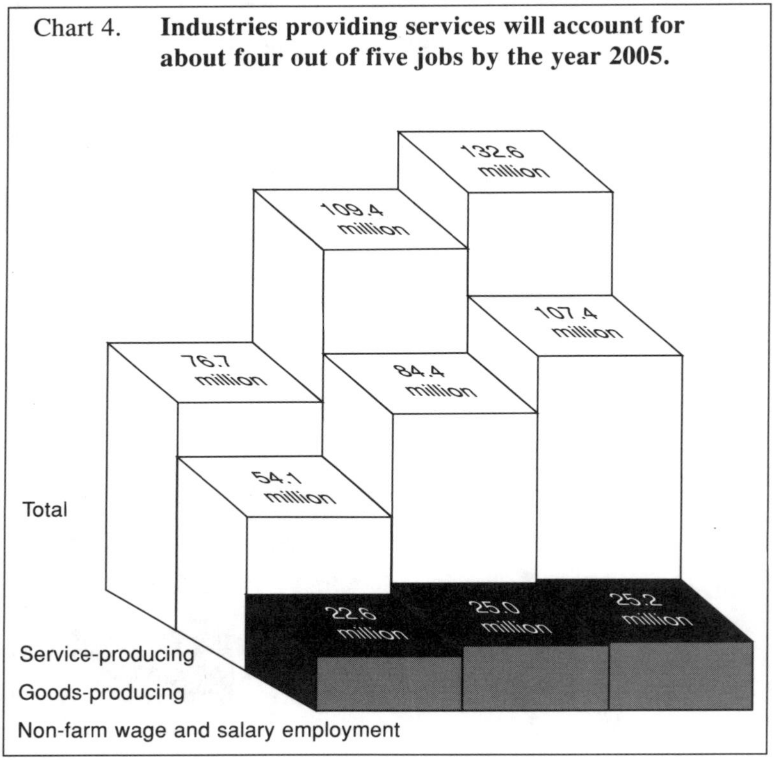

Chart 4.   **Industries providing services will account for about four out of five jobs by the year 2005.**

Total

Service-producing
Goods-producing
Non-farm wage and salary employment

132.8 million
109.4 million
107.4 million
76.7 million
84.4 million
54.1 million
22.6 million
25.0 million
25.2 million

Source: U.S. Department of Labor, Bureau of Labor Statistics, *Occupational Outlook Handbook, 1992–93*, BLS Bulletin 2400, May 1992.

Figure 5.6. Percent of Changes in Employment of Various Industries, 1990–2005

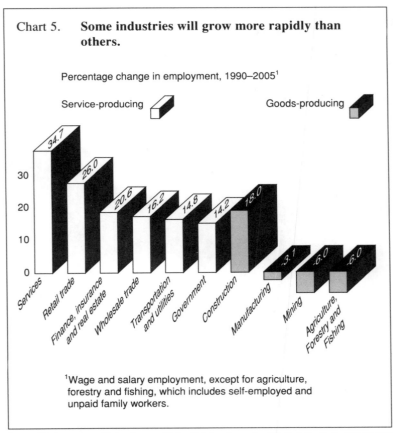

Chart 5.   **Some industries will grow more rapidly than others.**

Percentage change in employment, 1990–2005[1]

Service-producing   Goods-producing

- Services 34.7
- Retail trade 26.0
- Finance, insurance and real estate 20.6
- Wholesale trade 16.2
- Transportation and utilities 14.8
- Government 14.2
- Construction 18.0
- Manufacturing -3.1
- Mining -6.0
- Agriculture, Forestry and Fishing -6.0

[1]Wage and salary employment, except for agriculture, forestry and fishing, which includes self-employed and unpaid family workers.

Source: U.S. Department of Labor, Bureau of Labor Statistics, *Occupational Outlook Handbook, 1992–93*, BLS Bulletin 2400, May 1992.

**Figure 5.7. Job Opportunities Resulting from Growth and from
Replacement**

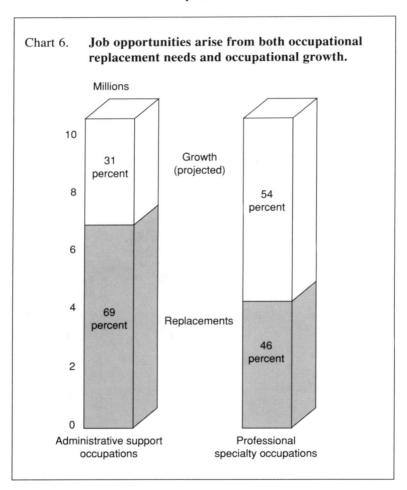

Chart 6.   **Job opportunities arise from both occupational
replacement needs and occupational growth.**

Millions

10

31 percent   Growth (projected)

8   54 percent

6

4   69 percent   Replacements

46 percent

2

0

Administrative support
occupations   Professional
specialty occupations

Source: U.S. Department of Labor, Bureau of Labor Statistics, *Occupational Outlook Handbook, 1992–93*, BLS
Bulletin 2400, May 1992.

CHAPTER 6

TODAY'S ISSUES IN HUMAN RESOURCE MANAGEMENT

There are many issues currently affecting human resource management. These issues may take years to resolve, but presently they are having a major impact on the management of human resources. Some of these issues are not new, but, nonetheless, they are current social and business concerns. Most human resource departments do not have separate issues management departments. Instead, HR department staff members struggle to keep up with these developing issues and frequently spend much of their time managing them.

WORK/FAMILY BENEFITS

The Family and Medical Leave Act (FMLA) was signed into law by President Clinton in February 1993. The act required employers with 50 or more employees in a 75-mile radius to grant up to 12 weeks of unpaid leave for "the birth, adoption or placement into foster care of a child; the care of a spouse, child or parent of the employee if the person has a serious health condition; or an employee illness that requires time off to convalesce or recuperate."

Many companies were concerned that they would see their cost of doing business rise since many employees would take a leave of absence, making the company shorthanded. The cost of doing business also would increase because other employees would have to work overtime to get the job done or the company would hire temporary workers, who would produce at a lower rate. As of this writing, a major cost increase has not materialized. Since the leave is unpaid, very few employees are actually taking the time off. Those who can afford to take time off (the higher levels of employees) may have alternative arrangements available to them since they are in a higher income bracket, thus reducing their need for the leave.

Time will tell if the major cost increase materializes. A future possibility with this act is that Congress will see that very few employees take the unpaid leave and will propose and pass legislation to require employers to provide paid family and medical leave.

MINIMUM WAGE

Five years ago, in the last edition of this book, minimum wage was an issue and it still is. The Clinton administration recently proposed that minimum wage be raised from its current level of $4.25 per hour to $4.75 per hour beginning January 1994 and indexed to inflation. There are two other pieces of legislation to increase minimum wage. One bill proposes to increase the minimum wage to $6.75 per hour beginning September 1996 and also to index it to inflation as Social Security is indexed. Another bill that includes indexing would raise the minimum wage to $5.50 per hour beginning in 1994.

Arguments for increasing the minimum wage include moving more people out of the poverty ranks and into higher income brackets. Arguments against increasing it center around the impact of increased cost on the profitability of each company. Based upon the interest in increasing the minimum wage, it appears to be a safe bet that the minimum wage will be going up in the near future.

AIDS

AIDS, or Acquired Immune Deficiency Syndrome, has been an issue for quite some time. It is an issue now as it relates to the Americans with Disabilities Act (ADA). Under the ADA of 1990, AIDS is a protected disability. This issue involves health care for disabled employees. A few employers have lowered their health care coverage for AIDS. They do so to cut their risk and lower their health care expenses.

The courts have held that it is legal to lower health care coverage for catastrophic illnesses. One court said it was legal under the Employee Retirement Income Security Act (ERISA) to lower the coverage as long as it was done for business reasons. As further legal decisions are reached, the framework for future business decisions on this matter will be formed.

HEALTH CARE

President Clinton has made Americans aware of the double-digit increases each year for the cost of health care, and there are differing opinions on how best to resolve the issue. It will take time to finalize the debate and come up with one good plan for the United States.

It appears that the plan proposed by the President will provide health insurance for all Americans. The cost for this health care will be picked up by employers not currently providing health care and by taxes. Small businesses are concerned that the additional burden of health care expenses will force them to reduce their staffing levels or possibly go out of business.

Obviously, HR managers have to get involved in this issue since most human resource departments administer employee benefits, including health care. Many managers are already involved in trying to reduce, or at least control the amount of increase in, their company's health care expenses.

Many employers have implemented flexible benefits plans as a way to reduce their health care spending. By doing this, they can shift part of the company's cost to the employees. Other companies have tried setting budgets for their health care dollars. Any money spent over the budget is spread to all employees, and they each pick up a portion of the cost. Any money saved is shared with all employees. The sharing of savings is done on a pro-rata basis, so that those who use fewer health care dollars get more from the company. Another approach to reducing health care costs is the use of managed care. Managed care is used to reduce or eliminate unnecessary procedures and expenses. Managed care can include the following:

- Health maintenance organizations (HMOs), which are groups of physicians who hold costs down by taking preventive action instead of waiting until a person is very ill and has to be hospitalized. The idea is to eliminate hospital stays.
- Preferred provider organizations (PPOs), which include doctors and other providers who agree to provide certain services at special rates. This type of network encourages users to utilize these preferred providers by offering a discount. The employees can go outside of this network but will pay a higher price.
- Point-of-service program (POS), which is a combination of an HMO and a PPO. Like an HMO, each person chooses one doctor to be his or her primary care giver, and like a PPO, the employee can use someone else but will pay a higher price to do so.
- Utilization review (UR) is used with any type of plan to examine medical treatments and hospital stays and review hospital bills. UR usually involves a case management worker who monitors a person's case to make sure he or she does not stay in the hospital longer than necessary and works with the employee to assure the needed care is provided at the lowest cost. Hospital bills are reviewed to make sure that there are no unnecessary charges. Some employers even award a percentage of savings if employees review their own bills for false or incorrect charges.

There are many innovative ways to try to drive down the cost of health care or to keep it from increasing. The main thing most companies try to do is make their employees aware of the cost of health care and try to get them to be good consumers and shop prices when a medical need exists.

As of this writing, the debate has just begun on this issue. Because of its high visibility and bipartisan support, it appears that some package will pass. It will take many months to resolve this issue, and it may be several months after that before the effects are felt.

OSHA REFORM

The Occupational Safety and Health Act (OSHA) was enacted in 1970. For some time Congress has considered reforming it. There are several bills filed that propose changes in the way employers do business that will affect human resource management.

The main changes as currently proposed require employee safety committees for companies with 11 or more employees in a location. These committees must meet on a regular basis and evaluate whether there are safety issues and how they can be eliminated. These meetings require paid time that many consider unproductive. An alternative view is that employees will have a say in the safety of their work environment and will ensure that unsafe practices do not occur.

Another result of the reform could be increased criminal penalties under the law. The purpose of this provision would be to encourage businesses to clean up their acts, as managers would go to jail if found to have willfully violated safety requirements. OSHA reform will have an effect on businesses in general and HR managers in particular.

LABOR LAW REFORM

There are several issues involving labor law reform. The main issue calls for a total rewrite of the labor laws crafted in the 1930s, 1940s, and 1950s. The President has formed a commission to study the effects of the current laws on business today and determine if they need to be rewritten.

There appears to be a hidden agenda of sorts, though it really isn't hidden. The committee represents the labor position very well but does not have any representation from the union-free side of the business community. The hidden agenda is to change labor law, giving labor unions a decided advantage in trying to organize companies and in negotiating contracts that are favorable to union membership. One of the things that is recommended is to eliminate the need for a secret ballot election to vote a union in. The plan is to allow the union to be certified if 50 percent plus one employee sign union cards. As the law currently stands, signing cards may ensure an election, but it will not ensure that the union will be the sole bargaining representative of the employees. This change will make it easier for unions to organize businesses.

Another change would make it illegal to hire permanent replacement workers in the event of an economic strike. While this sounds good on the surface, it is important to note that replacement workers are seldom used. There are two kinds of strikes: unfair labor practice and economic strikes. Permanent replacements can be hired in economic strikes but not in unfair labor practice strikes. Unfair labor practices occur when either a business or a union refuses to bargain in good faith or a business refuses to acknowledge a union that was legally voted in. There are other forms of unfair labor practices that are beyond the scope of this discussion. An unfair labor practice strike occurs when the union goes on strike because an unfair labor practice was committed. Economic strikes occur when the union and company cannot agree on wages, benefits, or other terms and conditions of employment. A union strikes to try to get management to agree with the union position.

Under current laws, both sides—management and the union—have something to risk and something to gain. The union risks having its members permanently replaced under an economic strike. The company risks a loss of business or bankruptcy if the union goes on strike. In the past, both sides have taken that risk. By removing the permanent replacement of economic strikers, the balance of power is disrupted, and unions can go on strike but risk losing nothing because the union membership cannot be replaced. As soon as the strike is settled, the strikers are brought back to work. In most labor markets, there isn't a large availability of temporary workers (especially temporary workers who will cross a picket line) who are skilled. Management would have a tough time finding temporary replacements and would have to settle with the union or give in to the union's demands or face bankruptcy.

ELECTRONIC MONITORING

Electronic monitoring is the "collection, storage, analysis or reporting of information of an employee's activities by means of technology that is conducted by any method other than direct observation."[1]

Many employers use various types of electronic monitoring to keep track of daily production without intending to use it to discipline employees. Some firms use access cards to monitor entrance to secured areas. Other companies use computers to calculate the productivity of their employees, or they use them to handle the daily work flow in an on-line system such as a cash register or a mobile data terminal in a company service truck. Some companies use video cameras or tape recorders to monitor access to facilities. Companies that have customer service telephone systems may have a computerized method of monitoring the number of calls handled per customer service clerk. These are some examples of the different types of electronic monitoring that various companies may use.

Legislation pending in the U.S. House of Representatives and Senate would severely restrict the use of this type of monitoring on all employees with less than five years' seniority and would ban most of it for all employees with more than five years of seniority. The human resources manager would have to get involved if electronic monitoring is banned or restricted in order to determine other ways to collect similar data to accomplish business objectives. The HR aspect of this naturally involves the performance appraisal process.

DRUG/ALCOHOL TESTING

Drug testing has been an issue for many years. The Drug Free Workplace Act requires federal contractors to take certain steps to ensure that the work environment is drug free. Other federal agencies

---

[1]Washington Scoreboard, *HR News,* Society for Human Resource Management, September 1993.

require certain industries to implement drug testing programs. These programs usually include pre-employment testing, post-accident testing, and for-cause testing. For-cause testing would occur when an employee appeared disoriented or was acting erratically. Most random testing requires that 50 percent of the total number of employees be tested on an annual basis.

Alcohol testing is used in the transportation industries. Certain other industries may be required to implement alcohol testing programs under the mandate by the Department of Transportation (DOT). Alcohol testing will have similar guidelines to drug testing. The one difference is in determining "for cause." Under the proposed rules, a supervisor has to suspect that an employee may have been drinking, and he or she can have the employee tested. Under the drug testing rules, the supervisor has to have more than a suspicion.

Human resource managers get involved with the training of supervisors, development and administration of programs, and reviewing and storing the results. The HR manager is also part of the review committee if an employee tests positive.

Drug and alcohol testing is not cheap. Large companies spend several hundred thousand dollars a year on them. If one major accident is averted because a person tested positive, the cost is well worth it.

DIVERSITY MANAGEMENT

There are many different definitions of diversity. In the first chapter, the nineties were described as the decade of diversity. Diversity is more than male and female or black and white. Diversity is all of the differences, large or small, that make people who they are.

Some examples of the different types of diversity include:

- race
- sex
- age
- disabilities
- language

- sexual orientation
- religious preference
- hair color
- weight
- height

In order to manage diversity, the corporate culture must change to value the diversities among all employees, not just certain differences. In order to make this culture change happen, management must take responsibility to make sure it has a diverse work force. Managers and supervisors must be held accountable through the performance appraisal process and the financial plan.

By not managing diversity, a company could end up in EEO quicksand. Charges of discrimination could come forth from any group within the company. Not valuing or respecting the differences among all employees could lead to lower productivity and low morale, and it could result in having the wrong person in the wrong job.

CONTROLLING WORKER'S COMPENSATION COSTS

Just as the cost of health care, worker's compensation costs have been rising rapidly. U.S. employers spent an estimated $72 billion dollars in 1991 on job-related injuries and sickness. In 1992, insurers paid out $40 billion dollars for low-back injuries.[2] Employers and HR managers, in particular, are trying various ways to stem the rising cost of worker's compensation. Many companies provide light or limited duty to keep the employee at work so that the incidence rating and the resulting insurance premium do not increase. Other companies are using a case management approach, which involves working with the employee and maintaining contact while trying to return the employee

---

[2]*Human Resource Management: Current Issues and Trends,* Bureau of Business Practice, 1993, p. 9-1.

to work as soon as possible. Other companies are providing proper training and safety equipment so that the possibility of an accident's occurring diminishes. The bottom line with worker's compensation is that employers have to manage it, or it will truly get out of hand.

COMPENSATION

The top three current issues in compensation are:

1) pay for performance
2) broadbanding, and
3) executive compensation

Pay for Performance

Pay for performance traditionally meant merit pay for white collar employees and some type of incentive, such as a piece rate, for manufacturing employees. Today, pay for performance includes the following types of plans:

- All-employee incentive or bonus plan, paid annually. These plans can make payouts on an individual or group basis. The payouts on a group basis may include factors such as company, division, or department success. A recent survey conducted by the Wyatt Company, a Washington, D.C., consulting firm, "found that 63 percent of business had these types of plans in place for their executive staff, 39 percent for exempt employees, and 15 percent for nonexempt/hourly workers."[3]
- Small group incentive plans. These types of plans usually are paid to small work teams or project teams. The payouts occur when goals are met or objectives are accomplished.

---

[3]Ibid., p. 6-2.

- Gainsharing plans. There are several types of gainsharing plans. The Scanlon plan allows employees to offer suggestions and share in the rewards. The Rucker plan normally covers production workers who again share in the savings from their ideas and provides a one-to-one sharing-to-savings ratio. For every 1 percent increase in the value of production, the employees get a bonus of 1 percent in their pay. Improshare is a productivity plan that bases bonuses on the productivity of the work group. Bonuses are based upon the productivity gains the group makes in producing more in less time.
- Spot award programs. These programs award people for their effort or accomplishments "on the spot," or as soon as is practical after the fact. They can be cash or gift certificates or some other form of payment such as tokens redeemable for merchandise.
- Skill-based pay. These types of plans award employees for learning more skills. The more employees know, the more they are valuable to the company since they can perform more tasks. Companies that use these types of plans usually require the employee to learn a job and be able to perform it for a short period of time before the additional compensation is granted.

As you can see, there are a variety of ways to encourage employees to produce more at work. These types of plans have been successful for companies implementing them properly. Some companies have had successes of 10 dollars saved for every dollar invested in the plan. Others have a return approaching 200 percent.

Broadbanding

Broadbanding is the newest twist in compensation. This is a very new approach with not much background to determine if the results will be successful. It does look promising. Broadbanding is the process of combining several salary grades into one salary grade. Many companies have numerous salary grades, which are complex and can confuse their employees. The typical approach is to combine two or more grades into one wider grade, or band. The purpose of broadbanding is to make transfers easier initially and deemphasize promotions. By providing more room to grow within a salary band versus an old salary range, the company gains flexibility and time in not having to perform so many job evaluations.

Executive Compensation

Executive compensation has become an issue lately due to the large salaries paid to executives. Congress recently passed a law that eliminates the tax deductibility of executive compensation over one million dollars. A compounding effect is the increase in the tax rate to people making over $200,000.

It has become imperative that companies now tie executive compensation to performance. The performance issues need to include the overall performance of the company, which could be reflected in the price of stock. Many companies base their incentive plans on stock options or restricted stock. By tying a plan to the performance of the company stock, the management team will work for the betterment of the company.

RIGHT TO KNOW

The right-to-know laws have been in effect for several years, requiring employers to keep their employees informed about chemicals and other hazards that they come in contact with on a daily basis. It appears that right to know may now also apply to other aspects of business. In 1992, an attorney sued her former firm for misrepresenting the type of work she would be performing. The attorney argued that she was hired under fraudulent terms, and her career was harmed in the process. The Second Circuit Court of Appeals allowed the lawsuit to go forward, acknowledging that employees have a right to know about a company's plans.

Another example of the expanding right-to-know doctrine is from Colorado. In 1991, an employee sued her employer when her project was canceled, eliminating her job. A Colorado court ruled that the employee had a right to know that her prospective employer wasn't very stable, possibly resulting in her project's cancellation.[4]

These two court rulings are the tip of the iceberg of what may be forthcoming for business about right to know. Historically, businesses do not share much information with their employees about their business plans. Companies who may be more enlightened than others are now starting to share this type of information. As more companies empower their employees and involve them in day-to-day decisions, the next logical step is to involve them in business plans so that the employees will own the plan as well and become important partners in making it work. If companies do not start sharing this information voluntarily, the government, through legislation, will require employers to share business plan information with their employees. How much better the situation would be if employers voluntarily shared the business information instead of being forced to do so.

TECHNOLOGY

Technology is changing. Current technology is sufficient to take the average HR department to the next plane. Computer specialists can develop software using the Windows format on many types of personal computers. The Windows format allows users to click on a picture or icon with a mouse. This creates a user-friendly format.

Some of the larger companies are starting to provide voice computer technology for employees to sign up for benefits or complete employee surveys. The technology allows the employer to have a message, including instructions, followed by voice or telephone pulse data entry.

---

[4]Keen, Christine D., "Right to Know: Informed Consent in the Workplace," *HR News,* Society for Human Resource Management, August 1993, p. A 15.

Once the data is entered, it can be tabulated or manipulated as under normal circumstances.

Some companies are starting to use video teleconferencing instead of spending a lot of money on travel expenses to send employees to a meeting. In larger cities, video teleconferencing centers that can be rented have begun to open. Video teleconferencing works like a normal teleconference, except that there are video cameras placed throughout the meeting room to transmit pictures of the meeting room and the participants. The initial cost is quite high, but it should come down as the technology improves.

OLDER WORKER RECRUITMENT/RETENTION

As the number of young, qualified new job market entrants declines, older workers are becoming even more important. The companies that seem to be making strides in recruiting and retaining older workers are either fast food or retail related.

Older workers constitute a valuable resource that should be utilized, but frequently is not. In the fall of 1992, the American Association of Retired Persons (AARP) and the Society for Human Resource Management (SHRM) conducted a joint survey on companies' practices in the recruitment and retention of older workers. The majority of the companies participating in the survey (72 percent) do not have a policy encouraging their older workers to stay on the job. Of those that do have a policy and realize benefits from it, 87 percent recognize that older workers still have skills to contribute to the job.

Some of the benefits of hiring older workers include their stability, good attendance records, good examples, good work ethic, and previously acquired skills. As the work force grays and the number of qualified new entrants declines, it will be increasingly more important for employers to develop policies to retain their competent older workers as well as recruit others to work for them.

CHAPTER 7

ADDITIONAL INFORMATION ABOUT HRM

Professional organizations and many labor unions have a vested interest in the dissemination of information about human resource management. There are a number of organizations that will provide help to those who seek career information about work in the human resource administration and industrial relations field. To obtain this assistance, you should write the organization and request information concerning what helpful data and assistance are available to those seeking careers in human resource management and industrial relations. Most organizations have printed pamphlets and brochures that explain their roles and information concerning the services they provide.

ORGANIZATIONS

Organizations that might interest you include the following:

AFL-CIO
  815 16th Street, NW
  Washington, D.C. 20006

American Management Association (AMA)
  135 West 50th Street
  New York, N.Y. 10020

American Society for Training and Development (ASTD)
  1630 Duke Street
  Alexandria, Va. 22313

Bureau of Labor Statistics
U.S. Department of Labor
3d Street & Constitution Avenue, NW
Washington, D.C. 20210

Bureau of National Affairs (BNA)
1231 25th Street, NW
Washington, D.C. 20037

Equal Employment Opportunity Commission (EEOC)
2401 E Street, NW
Washington, D.C. 20506

Federal Mediation and Conciliation Service
2100 K Street, NW
Washington, D.C. 20427

Internal Revenue Service (IRS)
111 Constitution Avenue, NW
Washington, D.C. 20224

International Personnel Management Association (IPMA)
1313 E. 60th Street
Chicago, Ill. 60637

National Association for the Advancement of Colored People (NAACP)
1790 Broadway
New York, N.Y. 10019

National Association of Manufacturers (NAM)
1776 F Street
Washington, D.C. 20006

Occupational Safety and Health Administration (OSHA)
200 Constitution Avenue, NW
Washington, D.C. 20210

Office of Federal Contract Compliance (OFCC)
200 Constitution Avenue, NW
Washington, D.C. 20210

Pension Benefit Guaranty Corporation
P.O. Box 7119
Washington, D.C. 20044

Society for Human Resource Management (SHRM)
606 N. Washington Street
Alexandria, Va. 22314

Don't overlook the possibility of obtaining career information from local organizations and agencies such as the Chamber of Commerce and the state employment agency. Additionally, information and assistance may be available from the local offices of various individual labor unions. Some of those that have been active in this regard, in addition to the AFL-CIO, are the Teamsters (IBT) and the Machinists (IAM).

The brochure from the Society for Human Resource Management is entitled, "Careers in Human Resource Management" and includes information on the following topics:

Personnel function
Personnel office
Personnel specialists
    Employment and placement
    Training
    Labor relations
    Wage and salary administration
    Benefits and services
    Preparation
Personal requirements
Salaries
Outlook for the future

There is also the possibility of finding information through student organizations. Many colleges and universities have student chapters of the Society for Human Resource Management.

ADDITIONAL SOURCES OF INFORMATION

"Careers in Human Resource Management," Society for Human Resource Management, 606 North Washington Street, Alexandria, Va. 22314. Six pages. Ask for current revision as well as other available pamphlets and booklets relating to careers in human resource management and labor relations.

"Personnel Training and Labor Relations Specialists and Managers," a section of the *Occupational Outlook Handbook,* issued biannually by the U.S. Department of Labor, Bureau of Labor Statistics.

"Hospital Personnel Director," American Hospital Association, 840 North Lake Shore Drive, Chicago, Ill. 60611. Four pages, free.

Information about personnel careers in government may be obtained through free pamphlets available from the International Personnel Management Association, 1313 East 60th Street, Chicago, Ill. 60637.

"Personnel, a Challenging Career in Management," International Association of Personnel Women, 358 Fifth Avenue, New York, N.Y. 10001. Single copy, free.

"The Human Equation—Working in Personnel for the Federal Government," U.S. Office of Personnel Management, Washington, D.C. 20415. Free.

"Occupational Briefs," Chronicle Guidance Publishing Company, Inc., Moravia, N.Y. 13118.

"SRA Occupational Briefs," Science Research Associates, Inc., 155 North Wacker Drive, Chicago, Ill. 60606.

"Career Information: A Directory of Free Materials for Counselors and Teachers," Sextant Systems, Inc., Western Station, Box 4283, Milwaukee, Wis. 53210.

A Career in Business Administration, a filmstrip from Pathescope Educational Films, Inc., The Associated Press, 71 Weyman Avenue, New Rochelle, N.Y. 10802.

The Occupational Thesaurus, Lehigh University, Bethlehem, Pa.

The Dictionary of Occupational Titles. See your local school library.

VGM Career Books (see the last page of this book for a listing).

Don't forget the following additional sources of information:

- The high school career counseling office
- The high school college counseling office
- State employment security agencies
- Private employment agencies
- Newspaper advertising
- National Career Information Center, local office
- U.S. Office of Personnel Management
- Local offices of AFL-CIO unions
- Local offices of independent unions
- Local chapters of professional societies

BIBLIOGRAPHY

Bennett-Alexander, Dawn. "Sexual Harassment in the Office." *Personnel Administrator.* American Society for Personnel Administration, June, 1988.

Bolles, Richard Nelson. *What Color Is Your Parachute?* Berkeley: Ten Speed Press, annual.

Burack, Elmer H. and Nicholas J. Mathys. *Career Management in Organizations.* Lake Forest, Ill.: Brace-Park Press, 1980.

College Cost Book: College Board Annual Survey of Colleges, 1988. New York: College Entrance Examination Board.

Davis, Keith. *Human Behavior at Work.* 8th ed. New York: McGraw-Hill Book Company, 1989.

Faze, James. "Parental Leave Measure Reintroduced in Senate." *Resource.* Alexandria, Va.: American Society for Personnel Management, July 1988.

Franklin, Geralyn McClure and Robert K. Robinson. "AIDS and the Law." *Personnel Administrator.* American Society for Personnel Administration, April 1988.

Glueck, William F. *Personnel: A Diagnostic Approach.* 3d ed. Plano, Tex.: Business Publications, Inc., 1982.

Ling, Cyril Curtis. *The Management of Personnel Relations.* Homewood, Ill.: Richard D. Irwin, Inc., 1965.

Mathis, Robert L. and John H. Jackson. *Personnel/Human Resource Management.* 7th ed. St. Paul, Minn.: West Publishing Company, 1994.

McGregor, Douglas. *The Human Side of Enterprise.* New York: McGraw-Hill Book Company, Inc., 1985.

Place, Irene. *Opportunities in Business Management Careers.* Lincolnwood, Ill.: VGM Career Horizons, 1986.

Ropp, Kirland. "HR Management for All It's Worth." *Personnel Administrator.* ASPA/Hansen 1987 Human Resource Management Compensation Survey. American Society for Personnel Administration.

Sherman, Arthur W., Jr. and George W. Bohlander. *Managing Human Resources*. 9th ed. Cincinnati: Southwestern Publishing Co., 1992.

Steade, Richard D. and James R. Lowry. *Business: An Introduction*. 11th ed. Cincinnati: Southwestern Publishing Co., 1987.

U.S. Department of Labor. Bureau of Labor Statistics. *National Survey of Professional, Administrative, Technical, and Clerical Pay: Private Service Industries*. Bulletin 2290. Washington, D.C.: Government Printing Office, 1987.

U.S. Department of Labor. Bureau of Labor Statistics. *Occupational Outlook Handbook, 1992–93*. Lincolnwood, Ill.: VGM Career Horizons.

The World Almanac and Book of Facts. New York: Newspaper Enterprise Association, Inc., 1988.

Yoder, Dale and Herbert G. Heneman, Jr., eds. *ASPA Handbook of Personnel and Industrial Relations*. Washington: The Bureau of National Affairs, Inc., 1979.

Yoder, Dale and Paul D. Staudohar. *Personnel Management and Industrial Relations*. 7th ed. Englewood Cliffs, N.J.: Prentice-Hall, Inc., 1982.